D0486138

S.L. JENNINGS

Ink & Lies

Cover: Hang Le
Artwork: Ashley Sparks
Editor: Tracey Buckalew
Proofreader: Kara Hildebrand
Formatting by Champagne Formats

ISBN-13: 978-1523840083
ISBN-10: 1523840080

For Grandpa Ed and Grandma Dtim
I am because you were.

Winter

YOU KNOW THAT PIVOTAL MOMENT in every love story, when the hero or heroine makes an imperative move that leaves the other with a life-altering choice? Whether it be a pronouncement of love (I've been in love with you my entire life, and I don't care that you're my stepbrother) or a salacious secret (I'm pregnant and the baby isn't yours) or a shocking decision (I've decided to embrace what I am. I'm transitioning into a unicorn, and I'm pregnant…by my stepbrother), we can always count on this familiar occurrence.

I've always deemed them cliché yet necessary in the romance genre. A good plot twist is as vital to a story as its characters. Without it, the hero and heroine would have no reason to change, to evolve. They'd have no reason to step out on faith and madness and take hold of their destiny. Take hold of their story.

I once lived for the perfect plot twist.

I just never expected to actually *live* it.

I look down at my boarding pass for the eightieth time in the last fifteen minutes. Gate 3B, Seat 2A. GEG to LAX. Final boarding in…now.

Sixteen hours ago, I succumbed to the insanity of feeling, and made my crucial confession. I began that almighty trek up a story's climactic mountain. And every hour, every minute since, I've waited for her to make her choice.

To make *me* her choice.

The attendant glares at me from over her intercom receiver and announces that the gate for flight D5611 will be closing in sixty seconds. She's saying it for only me, because I'm the only one here. Waiting. Crumbling.

I take one last look down the corridor that leads to security. I just knew that she'd show up, racing through the airport, screaming for someone to stop the plane. That was how I'd imagined my story…our story. The greatest cliché of all, and I still couldn't breathe it into fruition. I still couldn't get her to read between the lines scrawled on my heart.

I guess the most epic romances are still tucked away within the pages of her favorite novels, safely swathed in inked lies and faded paper promises. Forever fictional. Just like love.

Fall

YOU WANT TO KNOW THE secret to writing the most epic shit of my career?

Simple. Don't *try* to write the most epic shit of my career.

Trying is nothing but an endless murky abyss of self-doubt and loathing, where I choke on every flowery fucking word and puke up purple prose like it's last night's whiskey. Then I bang my head on the desk and pour another shot to keep my fingers from gouging my eyes out.

Drink, delete, repeat.

I used to try. Now I just lie.

Yup. Lying is much easier. Lying landed me on every best

seller's list I had ever dreamed about. I wrote shit that women wanted to read and pretty much lived off their fantasies and unsatisfied sex lives.

Ah yes. Life was sweet in the land of liars.

Then the bubble burst.

They thought it was Hope Hughes bringing their book boyfriends to life. Certainly not August Rhys Calloway (That's me, by the way.) And once upon a time, I had this insane idea to become a writer. Not much I could do about it either. Once the words choose you, you're doomed. So that's what I set out to be—the next great American literary.

Just so you know, I tanked. Like Titanic tanked. My ass still has frostbite from that damn iceberg.

Biting it in such a big way really discouraged me for some time, but somewhere between delirium and desperation, I decided to turn my epic fail into an epic win.

I wrote a romance novel.

Now, I know what you're thinking… how can a straight, cynical, slightly arrogant guy capture the all-consuming romance that each woman craves? Easy. He listens.

He listens to all the complaints from past failed relationships. He conjures up terrifying memories of three-hour-long phone calls and eight-page letters. And he enlists the help of his hopeless romantic best friend and her train wreck of a love life. After that, he slaps a very feminine pen name on the cover—along with some busty dame enraptured in the boulder-like arms of Fabio Jr.—And *voila!* You've got yourself a romance novel.

Of course, there's much more to it. But to be honest, I BS'd my way through 85% of that book. Ok, 90%…93%. But

I'd like to think it was that 7% of pure August gold that helped it climb the charts of every bestseller's list that matters. Not the hot monkey sex I had properly regurgitated throughout.

Being Hope Hughes, romance novelist, was much more profitable and ego-indulging than being August Rhys Calloway, struggling writer. So I ran with it—all the way to a sweet book deal with a top publishing house and a massive following.

Who knew?

Three novels later, Hope is still here, but so is August. Less than a year ago, it was revealed that Hope was, in fact, male. Somehow, it only made the Hope brand more popular, both professionally and personally. A man was capturing these poetic words of passion and longing? A man finally got it? Hope was hotter than ever. But creatively? August was dunzo.

The mojo has left the building. The words—the very same that had so incessantly pursued me—have now abandoned me. So yes, I'm still here, but the words are gone.

My favorite waitress at my favorite bistro approaches my favorite table, asking me if I'd like to order a drink while I wait. I set down my worn Moleskine and look up at her to answer, just in time to catch my best friend bustling in, a tiny tornado of chestnut hair and smeared mascara.

"Few more minutes," I tell her while giving Fiona the stink eye. She flops into the seat across from me, apologizing profusely.

"Sorry, I'm late, Rhys," she huffs, picking up her menu. She doesn't call me August. She hasn't since the day we met back in college, nearly ten years ago. She said August was an uptight, pretentious tool that took himself way too seriously. Rhys was her cool, casual friend that would suffer through every chick flick on Netflix and split Hawaiian pizza with her because no one else would dare sully a pie with pineapple. He was the guy who would recite famed love stories from her most beloved writers, and dry her tears with the pads of his ink-stained thumbs. He was the one that was there to smother broken promises and shattered hearts with sarcasm and whiskey weekends followed by innocent spooning underneath her favorite old quilt.

She doesn't meet my gaze. I slowly pull down the vinyl binder with the tip of my finger. "Um, nice of you to join me, dear. Rough night?"

She diverts her smoky raccoon eyes and tries to casually smooth her rooster-like locks into something less telling. That's when I take in the rest of her. Wrinkled, white, silk blouse. Tight, black mini that's more suitable for the queens over at Irv's drag show, and platform pumps that'll have her limping with blisters for a week.

I raise a knowing brow. "Why, Miss Fiona Shaw, did you just walk-of-shame your ass in here smelling like stale sex and some random's cheap cologne?"

"Shhh!" She waves me away and retreats behind this week's Fresh Sheet. "Keep your voice down. And not some random's cheap cologne. It happens to be Joshua's, and it's definitely not cheap."

"Ah. The elusive Joshua." I sit back in my seat and steeple my fingers in front of me with all the flair of an evil genius plotting world domination. "And when am I going to meet this mystery man? It's been what…three months now? I'm nearly convinced that Joshua might very well be a six-foot tall Sinthetic doll you've got stashed under your bed."

"Sinthetic doll? What the what?" She sets down the menu just as our server approaches. We order the first of many libations that will be consumed this morning. I order a much-needed Bloody Mary, while she prefers OJ and bubbly. In her words, it makes her feel extra fancy.

"Sinthetics. Super realistic sex dolls with customizable features. You can choose everything from nipple size to cock wrinkles. Supposed to be like the real thing." Before her expression morphs into one of shock and horror, I tack on, "Book research."

"Oh, really? So does that mean you have pages for me?"

That takes the wind out of my puffed-up sails. I shake my head, earning looks of both concern and longing from across the table. Fiona's been my only beta reader for years, and is one of only four people who actually know that I'm Hope. So seeing the disappointment on her face is just a reflection of what's been eating away at me.

I haven't written anything worth reading in weeks. Months, if I'm being completely honest. It's like, the very second it was revealed that Hope was a dude, the words went *poof.* Which doesn't bode well for me and my approaching deadline. My publisher thought it best to continue with the Hope Hughes pen name, considering that it's already an established brand, and no one really knows that *I'm* the man behind the pen. But as time dwindles away, so does my confidence that I'll actually produce something good. Hell, I'd settle for readable at this point.

Fiona picks up her menu and peruses the selections—the

same selections she could probably recite verbatim without missing a beat. We've been coming to this bistro for Sunday brunch every week since we discovered it, which was pretty much the minute it opened for business. It shares a building and a bathroom with our favorite bookstore—a mom and pop op that features indie and local authors, as well as the acclaimed greats. I remember dreaming of the day my name would grace the worn oak shelves of Auntie's Bookstore. I'd drag Fiona along as we'd scour the place for hidden gems and time-honored treasures. We'd sit side-by-side cross-legged in back aisles, while I'd recite my favorite passages from tales that moved me, inspired me, created the man I am today. Each story was engrained in my DNA, and the ink was my immortal lifeblood. The words were my flesh and the pages my bones. I was birthed within those dusty aisles on the walk-worn carpet, the bright-eyed offspring of Dickens, Fitzgerald, Wilde, Hemingway, Faulkner, Lee and Márquez. I was born to be extraordinary. Born to be a writer.

Fiona preferred the stories of Jane Austen and the Brontë sisters, along with the more recent contemporary romance offerings. She's always been hopelessly romantic, which is probably why I've had better luck with questionable leftover sushi than she's had with relationships in the past few years. So when I say *hopelessly*, I kinda mean unfortunately...pathetically. Romance, love, marriage...it's all fine and dandy between the whimsy pages of beloved novels. But that's the only place it makes sense. In the *real* world with *real* interpersonal relationships, love is a grand, elaborate lie, manipulated by retailers to sell cards, flowers, albums, movies, and of course, books. I should know.

"I think I'll have the kale hash today," she muses.

I roll my eyes. "No you won't. You'll have the brioche French toast with extra syrup and a side of bacon, like you do every week. You may think you want something new and different…the quiche, the crepe, the croque monsieur…but you'll always go with what you know."

"Nope. Kale hash for me. Joshua says that kale is a superfood, and I should be both drinking and eating it daily."

"Oh, God. Here we go again with *Joshua*." I roll my eyes at the displeasure of having his name on my tongue. Fuck Joshua. And fuck kale. "So I guess it's safe to assume he is responsible for you traipsing down Main in last night's thong like a hooker on furlough."

She tries to hide her sly smile, but coupled with the rosy apples of her cheeks, the jig is up. She can't play coy when the evidence is snagged in her bush of bed head.

"Fine. If you must know, last night was the first time I stayed over at Joshua's apartment."

"Oh? First time? You've been hitting that for months, Fi."

"Well, you know how he doesn't like to have overnight guests just in case he gets called in the middle of the night…"

"Called in the middle night?"

"Yes. He is a doctor after all."

"He's a plastic surgeon. What? Will he get called in for an emergency vaginal rejuvenation?"

She huffs out an aggravated breath. "He's a doctor, August." Her voice takes on that Mom tone that tells me to chill out, and she even calls me by my first name. I've struck a nerve.

I snort and let the subject drop. It's a cop out. Pure, potent horseshit. But I don't tell her that. I never try to hurt her feelings. Fiona, or Fi as I've called her since college, is my best friend, my safe haven from all the unwanted Hope press and self-inflicted chaos. I love her in the way that a boy loves the dog he grew up with. Not that she's a dog in any sense of the word. Fi is delicate and undeniably feminine, which means her heart is too soft and fragile for this world. It's also probably why we became fast friends. She fulfilled my innate male urge to protect a weaker being—not that she was weak. But when it came to frat boy bros drunk off ego and beer piss, she didn't stand a chance. So I started looking out for the mousey girl in oversized sweaters and Doc Martens. Plus she always had a different book in her hands, which instantly intrigued me.

"What you reading this week, Fi?"

"Pride and Prejudice."

"Again?"

"Again."

Anyone that loyal and dedicated to her literary love was pretty fucking perfect in my book. And to me, Fiona was every heroine in every book that I ever cherished.

"I'm sorry. Tell me about last night, Fi. Please. I want to hear it." I couldn't stand when she was mad at me. The rest of the world could compose sonnets about beating me to death with my own books and critics could wipe their ass with my pages, but the only person whose opinion really matters is and always has been Fiona Shaw.

Warmth and exuberance restored, she excitedly recounts the night before. Our terse words are instantly forgotten without a smidge of grudge. "He invited me over for dinner, said he wanted to cook for me. But since he didn't get home until late, dinner wouldn't be ready until 10."

Ten? Ok, that's approaching booty call hours. But I didn't dare mention it. "Dinner, eh? And what did he prepare for you?"

"Well…actually. He didn't have everything he needed, so he asked me to pick up something on my way over."

So the bastard couldn't even provide her with a decent meal. *She* fed *him*. I take a swig of my Bloody Mary to avoid saying something and signal for another. "Go on."

"After dinner, he suggested we watch a movie—some thriller about these guys who have a penthouse that they use as an eff pad, and someone gets murdered."

I chuckle inwardly. Fi still can't even say the word "fuck." It's adorable. And I have to admit that I love that she isn't sullied by the harshness of slick-tongued millennials and obscenity-soaked media.

Her face flames with warm remembrance. "You really want me to keep going?"

I take a beat to consider her words before sliding my notebook in front of me and flipping to the first available blank page. If she's sharing, I might as well take notes. All in the name of research. And since I have an uncanny ability to see the story—*live* the story as if it's being played out right in front of me—this could very well be some prime inspiration. With Fi's blessing, of course.

"Sure. Let's hear it."

"Ok… here goes…

"My eyelids are heavy, but I'm trying to fight the enemy of sleep. I rest my head on his shoulder and exhale softly when I

feel his arm wrap around me, swathing me in his heat. His fingers trace little patterns against my skin, first coasting up and down, then small spirals. The calming movements lull me into a shallow dreamland. My eyes are closed, my breath heavy, yet I can hear the muffled sounds of the television. There's talking, shouting. Then moaning. Raspy, tortured moaning. It's distant at first, but then it becomes louder, more frenzied. They're so close, I can hear the lust behind every mewl and whimper. I can taste the sweetness of pleasure on my own lips. I can feel the passion pooling in my own panties as phantom friction elicits an inferno of burning desire..."

"Burning desire?"

Fiona looks up from the champagne flute she's been staring into since she began recounting her salacious story. She grips the stem so tight that I'm afraid it'll be ground to sand between her fingertips.

"Do you want to hear about last night or not?"

I tap my notebook with the top of my pen. "Proceed."

"*...an inferno of* burning, hot, sweltering *desire between my thighs. I gasp as I realize what's happening. Something—someone—is touching me. And it's not the TV that has me panting in my sleep. It's me. It's Joshua. Joshua is caressing me as I am cradled in the crook of his arm. And I'm carrying on so loudly, so unabashedly, that I'm almost embarrassed at the explicit sounds escaping my lips. Still, I don't open my eyes. He has to know that I'm awake, but this game is just too enticing to give up now.*

"*He lays me flat on my back, carefully placing my head on a pillow. I stay completely still, my eyes still closed, my lips parted in anticipation. I feel the sofa dip at my feet, and the soft scratch of pressed wool at my knees. His fingers rake over my stockings, like needles over silk. I'm internally begging him to rip them off me—shred them in his palms—but he's so controlled and patient. He takes his time with me...*"

"Patience. That's a sexy trait." I roll my eyes, but keep my head down as I continue to scribble down anything that I can use. My heroes are never patient. They're hungry, ravenous, and mad with passion. They can't stop touching their heroines, yet every touch is not nearly enough. The feel of their skin pressed together is the only thing they live for within those moments of savage lust.

"It *is* a sexy trait. Patience is vital for long-lasting, meaningful lovemaking. So what? You're going to get the poor girl all worked up only to last thirty seconds? Do you know how insanely frustrating that is?"

I shake my head. "Nope. I don't. And the hero always lasts longer than thirty seconds in romance. He goes hours without breaking a sweat or needing to stop to stretch or get a drink of water. Patience has no purpose in love stories. When you want someone so badly—so completely—there's nothing on God's green earth that will keep you from having them. To touch them, to feel them, smell them, taste them, pleasure them...it's their only purpose for being. It's madness so raw that it transcends biology and logic."

Fiona stares at me with wide, unblinking eyes and swallows. We must've absentmindedly placed our orders some time before the *inferno of lust* because there's food in front of us: Tasso omelet for me and brioche French toast for her. Fucking right.

"My, August Rhys Calloway," she breathes, taking on her

feathery southern belle accent circa Scarlett O'Hara. "Such mighty passionate words for a gentleman who rejects all forms of honest-to-goodness, soul-crushing, all-consuming love. Maybe you believe more than you care to let on."

I shoot her a narrowed look and cut into my omelet. "Not a chance. I believe in words. And in this case, the words are purely fictional. Continue."

"I gasp aloud when I feel this fingertips at the tops of my stockings. He slowly eases them down my legs, careful not to snag them. When they reach the very tips of my toes, he brings each foot up and kisses the arch."

I gag. Literally gag.

"My panties are the next to go, and after he frees me from them, he brings them up to his nose and takes a deep whiff. Then he stuffs them into his pocket."

"Wait. Time out. The fuck? He did *what* with your panties?" The sound of my Mont Blanc dropping mid-scrawl onto the paper serves as the figurative *screech* on this conversation.

"It's no big deal, Rhys," Fiona whispers furiously, as if my disdain is offensive, not Joshua's sick fixation with dirty underwear. "Why are you even surprised? Didn't you write about the same thing in *House of Noire?* I'm pretty sure Antonio did the same thing to Gisele during their first love scene."

"First of all, Antonio and Gisele never made love. They fucked like wild, dirty animals. Come on, it was a book about a young, naïve, virginal girl trying to make it in the porn industry. And second, that's fiction! Do people actually do shit like that? Yeah, probably. But then you'd have to take into account what other undies he's got stashed away. You don't know their hygiene situations. And what does he do with them later? Frame them? Rub them all over his body, crotch side up? And just how many other pairs of panties has he collected? A drawer-full? A trunk-full? Come on, Fi. You're better than a pair of worn panties in some corny guy's trophy room."

I don't know why I'm getting so worked up about the subject; hell, I may have snagged a pair of panties in my day. But Fiona just isn't the type of girl that should be attached to a memory like that. She's so much classier, so much smarter, than a size 2 scrap of silk and lace applique.

I just wish she could see what I see. Someone genuinely *better.*

She shakes her head. "It's not like that, Rhys. *Joshua* isn't like that. He just thought it'd be sexy, you know. And it was. I've never experienced something so hot before in my life. And aren't you the one that's always telling me to put myself out there and live beyond the pages of my favorite books? I don't want to keep reading about romance and love, and yes, sex. I want to have it for myself."

I take another bite, forcing myself to carefully consider my next words. This is Fiona's sex life, not mine. I can't dictate whom she dates and what she does with them. But I don't have to like it either. However, I do have to support it, just as she's supported me through all my flavors of the month. Even the ones that were two fries short of a Happy Meal, and had me sleeping with one eye open after we had parted ways. She endured every cringe-worthy moment without judgment or complaint. She sat through dozens of awkward introductions and uncomfortable dinners because she cared about me and my happiness. And I owe her the same.

"You're right, Fi. Please. Continue your story. I won't make a peep, I swear." I nod my encouragement, and pick up my pen. *It's just a panty sniff*, I tell myself. No big deal. Certainly that pales in comparison to all the raunchy stuff I've divulged over this very table.

"Fine. So…" She takes a deep breath. Untouched Brioche French toast stares up at her in anticipation.

"There I am, bare for him. Open for him. So ready for him. He's hard in his slacks, scarily so. He looks like he would burst right through the fabric if relief does not come soon. He hurriedly rips off his belt and tears through the buttons of his pants. My hips are cradled in his hands, his fingers digging into my backside, and then we… do it."

"You do it?"

"You know… we do it. We make love."

"Wait a minute. That's it? All that build up, movie molesting and crotch sniffing and…that's it? You *do* it?"

She finally turns her attention to her food, which coincidentally, looks a bit cold and limp. "What else can I say? It was nice."

"Nice? Did you just say sex with him was nice? Oh, come *on,* Fi. You're holding out. Something went down and you're totally trying to hide it."

"It's nothing. Really."

"Bullshit. Smelly, steaming bullshit. What happened?" I push my plate away in disgust of said bullshit and put my notebook in front of me, giving her my undivided attention.

She shakes her head. "I don't know. It's just… things were going great, or so I thought. I was into it. But then he says he wants to… try something."

"Ok... try something like what?"

"I really don't want to talk about this, Rhys." If she hovers any closer to her plate, she'll give herself a vanilla bean maple syrup facial.

My voice drops an octave, but my words echo loud and clear. "Did he do something to you that you didn't want? Did that son of a bitch hurt you?"

"What? No! Nothing like that. It was just...I don't know. Weird."

"How so?"

"Do I have to relive it? Seriously. I'm still kinda skeeved by it."

"Spill it, Fiona. I'm listening."

She collects her bearings, and proceeds with every detail of the dirty.

"He moves inside me slowly, going in as deep as he possibly can before pulling out to the tip. His fingers trail down my belly and to the mound over my pelvic bone. "You're so beautiful," he whispers haughtily. "But you would be perfect, if it weren't for this." He tugs at my short patch of hair down there, pinching enough between his fingers to give me a sharp, stinging jolt. I know what he means, but I ask him anyway. He tells me that he likes his women completely bare and smooth. He says it makes me...cleaner for him. Younger for him."

"What the hell, Fi! He said that to you? Some balls on that one."

"Shhhh, there's more."

"He tells me he can make me perfect for him, and it will take our lovemaking to new heights. He asks if he can shave me. He says it is incredibly erotic and will please him to touch

me like that. I don't know what to say, but I don't want to disappoint him. So I nod my head Yes.

"He quickly leads me to the bathroom where he turns on the shower. We shed our shirts in silence, then I watch him open a drawer where he keeps razors and shaving cream. Girly stuff too. As if he had premeditated and planned this for us. It's adorable too. He has so many different types and brands for me to choose from, every scent and color. He asks me which one I'd prefer he use on me."

I so badly wanted to tell her that he hadn't planned it at all. That he probably kept the drawer stocked for all the women he demeaned and shaved for his pleasure. Shit yeah, it could be sexy to shave a woman. I wasn't knocking it. But it was something that both parties were comfortable with. Joshua was using it as a form of control.

"He leads me under the hot spray and tells me to lean against the wall. With his eyes pinned on me, on my sex, he slowly drops to his knees and hoists my foot onto his shoulder. He's right there…staring…aligned with my love biscuit…"

I nearly spew vodka and tomato juice all over Fiona and her neglected breakfast.

She's been calling her vagina her *love biscuit* for as long as I've known her, and I still can't get used to it. She can let some douche rocket shave her, but she can't even say the word *pussy*. Insane.

"He shaves me with careful, slow strokes, ensuring he doesn't miss a spot. He even has me turn around and spread—"

"Ok, ok. I get it. We don't need the gory details. Keep going."

"When he's done, he touches me. Every bit of the skin he's

meticulously shaved. He says I feel as smooth as a teenage girl, and he can't wait to be inside me, sliding his flesh against mine. We make love right there in the shower, then again in his bed. He says it's so much better now. He says he can feel every soft inch of me. And now I can feel all of him too. I'd never seen him so hot for me. It's like he's another person entirely.

"We fall asleep in each other's arms, him softening inside me. And as I float off to dreamland, I realize that I am in love. Irrevocably and undeniably in love with him."

A long time passes before either one of us look at the other. So long that our server has already cleared the table and brought the check.

"So?"

I look at Fiona, and pray that my expression doesn't give me away. "So."

"What do you think?"

What do I think? I look down at my notebook. I'd stopped scribbling notes somewhere between *"smooth as a teenage girl"* and *"I am in love."*

"You honestly want to know what I think, Fi?"

"Yes. I do. I wouldn't have told you all that if I didn't."

"Ok. Where should I start?" I lean forward and rest my chin on my rigid fingers. "Should we begin with how he took your underwear as a trophy? Or how he blatantly insulted you by suggesting you needed "sprucing up" down there to be "perfect for him?" Or how about how he compared your bare-naked vagina to one of a teenage girl? As if he knows firsthand what a teenage girl would look like down there? Or maybe we should just dive into the fact that you just said you're in love with Captain Creeptastic. After all that, you actually think you're in love with him!"

"I don't think, August. I know. Joshua is a good man and I can really see a future with him, whether you realize it or not. So please save your cynical spiel and try to be happy for me. Because *I'm* happy. For the first time in a long time, I can truly say that I'm happy."

"You think you're happy, Fiona, but you don't even know this guy."

"And you know any of the dozens of girls you sleep with?"

Her words give me pause, and I take a moment to realize that all eyes are on us. Even through our fervent whispers, people can feel the tension coiling like a viper between us.

"Look, Fi," I sigh aloud, slapping a few bills with the check. "I want to see you happy, but most importantly, I want to see you secure. So if you think this guy can provide both, then I'll keep my opinions to myself and support you no matter what."

Her petite hand landed on top of mine, on top of the notebook that contained her secrets. And mine too. "No, Rhys. I don't want you to lie for my benefit. I want you to genuinely like him."

"I can't promise you that." I look away.

"No? You love me, right?" She gives my hand a squeeze, forcing me to meet her eyes. "Right?"

"Right."

"So don't you think that you could possibly like Joshua, considering that you love me and I love him? Don't you think he may have at least one redeemable trait that would be…I don't know…likable to you? At least tolerable? Just give him a chance, please. For me. If you care about me, at least try to care about him too."

I take her in—big, doe eyes pleading, delicate lips pressed into a hopeful smile. I've never been able to say no to her. Even with a tumbleweed attached to her head, I am a victim of her unsuspecting charm.

"One tolerable trait."

She nods enthusiastically. "One tolerable trait. That's all I ask."

"Fine," I huff out.

"Great!" she squeals, nearly jumping from her seat and tucking her clutch under her arm. "Because we're having dinner Friday night."

"Wait…what? How do you go from begging me to tolerate him to having dinner with him?" She shuffles out of the restaurant, and like a lost, dumbstruck puppy, I follow her, wondering how the hell I got suckered into breaking bread with Dr. Dickhead.

"You said you'd try to get along with him, yet you've never met him. Joshua is off Friday night, so it'll be perfect. You two make up exactly two-thirds of the men in my life, so bringing you together is important to me. And speaking of my men…how is your grandfather?"

"Doing well. I'm actually going to see him today."

My grandfather is the greatest, wisest man I've ever known, and the only reason why I didn't totally turn out to be a hollow, self-centered prick. Benjamin Orson Calloway is a living legend in my eyes, and not just because he was a decorated officer who served in two wars. He was the one who put the first classic book in my hands—*A Tale of Two*

Cities—when I was eight. At that age, I didn't know what the hell I was reading, and I deemed it a poor choice of gift from the old Colonel. But with passing time and maturity, I found myself fishing the old hardback from the drawer where I had crammed it, hoping to grasp the magic bound in Dickens' words. And I read and reread that book until that magic floated off those yellowing pages and embedded itself inside my soul.

Now, the Colonel, plagued with age, lives out his golden years in a senior citizen community where he's been since the love of his life passed away six years ago. Taciturn, stubborn and hardened by his military days, he refused to pack up and move down to Boca with my parents. He'd rather battle out torrential winters and unbearably dry summers than be away from his Lee, the commander of his heart and soul for over half a century.

"Give the Colonel a kiss from me," Fiona says before pecking me on the cheek. "I'll drop by to see him this week. And tell him I'll bring him treats if he's nice."

I smiled. The Colonel was never nice. But he did love baked goods. It was the only thing sweet about him. "Will do. You want to do the bookstore today?"

"Can't. Need to get home and shower. It's bad enough that I just sat through an awkward brunch without underwear."

I ruffle her unkempt hair the way a big brother would his little sister. "By the way, don't ever do that again." Then I bend down to kiss her forehead.

She makes a tsking sound and lifts her chin defiantly. "And why not? Those other women you hang out with probably have never even seen a pair of panties. At least not a pair with an actual crotch attached to them."

I open my mouth to answer but she rolls her eyes and waves it off, walking backwards towards her car. "Let me guess… *Fi, you're not those other women*," she shouts, doing a downright disgraceful impression of me.

I shake my head and grin. "No, Fi. Those other women aren't you."

Aunties Bookstore is like the attic of bookstores. It's drafty in the winter, kinda dusty, old and filled with treasures. None of the armchairs or lamps match, and even the shelves aren't quite uniform. But it is— indisputably—my favorite place on earth.

"Hey, August!" the weekend cashier says from behind the counter, straightening a tree of bookmarks.

"Hey, Delores. How's it going?"

"Pretty calm today. Hey! Looks like you sold a book!"

Delores points to the section designated for local authors, and the small space reserved for *Tears of Glass* by August R. Calloway is indeed short by one book. I'm genuinely surprised. Since self-publishing *ToG* right after college, Aunties has displayed it proudly and has even included it in various promos. However, in six years, it has sold less than what a Hope Hughes book has done in a week. And that's including friends and family pity buys.

"Way to go! Any news on your next book? You know we've been waiting on it." The sheer pride and admiration on Delores's round face is genuine, and it almost makes me feel bad for deceiving her. For deceiving all of them.

Like most bookstores, the bestsellers display sits right in the front. And amongst the sea of literary elite sits Hope's newest title, *Heat Wave*, a steamy romance involving muscle-bound, tattooed firemen. According to my agent, copies have been flying off the shelves at an alarming rate since Hope's gender was revealed by an unknown source. Secretly, I think she was the one to leak the info in an attempt to build hype before release. I hate to admit it, but it worked. Still, it doesn't make me feel any better about my failure at writing something I'm truly passionate about. Between those pages of *Heat Wave* are over-exaggerated sex scenes mixed with watered-down writing. And the kicker is, most of those scenes are birthed from truth. I pulled from my catalog of wild experiences with women around town, even adding a few of Fiona's more unique stories. I definitely borrowed the lovey dovey crap from her. There's no way I've ever said anything remotely as corny as, "I'd walk through hellfire to kiss you just one last time." No fucking way.

I take a few minutes to scan the New Release table and grab the new Dan Brown for the Colonel. He's a fan of the popular stuff, as well as military dramas and memoirs. I offered to write his story, but he insisted that his life wasn't nearly interesting enough to document. Growing up listening to his stories, I knew he was being modest.

"Next month, we're hosting a local authors signing." Delores smiles as she rings up my purchase. "You know we'd love to have you here."

"Why? I've already sold my one book for the year. Let's not get greedy, Delores."

She laughs, causing her full cheeks to nearly eclipse her small brown eyes. "Oh, August. You'll get there one day, dear. You just wait and see."

I arrive at the senior village, hardback and two maple bars in hand, and find the Colonel in the entertainment den, situated in front of a football game. The Seahawks are up by fifteen, so I know he's in good spirits.

"No beer?" he grumbles in greeting, not even bothering to glance in my direction. It's a mystery how he knows when I'm near. I always swore he had eyes in the back of his head. The man was impossible to sneak up on.

"Sorry, Colonel. Not today. How about donuts?" He's been asking for beer for longer than I can remember, knowing he can't drink. Pancreatitis and mild dementia sealed that deal.

He grunts out a response and scoots over so I can sit down, his eyes still glued to the screen. "These *Whiners* are getting spanked today. I didn't realize it was possible for *Colon* Kaepernick to get any shittier."

I take a seat beside him and open the bag of fried, frosted deliciousness. "Good one, sir. Hey, why can't Kaepernick use the telephone?"

"Why?" he replies before tearing into a maple bar.

"Because he can't find the receiver."

"Hey, son, want to hear a joke?"

"Sure," I nod.

"Colin Kaepernick!" He barks out a husky laugh before devouring his donut. I slide him a to-go cup of coffee that he eagerly gulps down. A passing nurse shoots a look in our direction and shakes her head.

"Colonel, didn't I tell you to ease up on the coffee? Water. You need to be drinking more water. And that junk food isn't doing you any favors either."

Eyes still on the television screen, Grandfather grumbles a retort and grudgingly slides the rest of the contraband over to me.

"Mr. Calloway," the nurse begins, pointing her attention to me. "Please don't let your grandfather trick you into bringing him snacks. He's supposed to be watching his intake, doctor's orders."

"Sorry, Nurse Tabatha. It won't happen again. I'll even make sure he drinks a few cups of water and takes a walk before I leave."

At that, the Colonel mutters a curse and Nurse Tabatha gives us a *"Mmmm Hmmm"* before strutting off. I chuckle under my breath.

"Well, looks like I better tell Fi to bring carrot sticks instead of baked goods."

At that, the Colonel perks up. "Fiona? Ah, how's my girl?"

"Doing well, sir. We just had brunch a little earlier. She sends her love and promises to come by soon."

"Good. That sounds…good." While his eyes are trained on the game, the hard line of his jaw visibly relaxes. "She still seeing that doctor?"

"Yes, sir."

"Shame. I don't like him."

Ha! So it's not just me. "You met him?"

"No. I don't need to. Just don't like him."

Before I can even fix my mouth to question the Colonel, we're interrupted by a familiar voice. And considering the way my grandfather grunts out his distaste, it's not a happy interruption.

"Benny? Benny is that you? I thought I heard voices. Oh! It's that handsome, movie star grandson of yours. How are you, honey?"

"I'm fine, ma'am," I say, rising to my feet as Helen Ashford enters the common room. Helen is a 70-something spinster who has been after my grandfather since the day he moved in. Although he's made it clear that he is anything but interested, she still insists on hounding him, calling him Benny and going out of her way to intrude on his space and sanity.

"Why, yes you certainly are," Helen replies, molesting me with her eyes. I hurriedly sit down to escape her ogling. "I've been telling Benny that my granddaughter just moved into town, and I'm sure she'd love to meet some new friends. Did you tell August about my April, Benny? I'm sure they'd hit it off."

The Colonel mutters under his breath, and I'm only able to catch the words "crazy" and "old." Although he's the one who instilled in me the value of respect and manners, especially towards women and my elders, apparently he's forgotten those lessons.

"Oh, Benny, wouldn't they be adorable together?" Helen

continues, oblivious to my grandfather's aggravation. "How about you take my April on a date, August? Show her around."

"Oh…um…well…" I'm stammering, completely at a loss for words. Seems like the words really have abandoned me in every aspect of my life.

"Oh? Is there something wrong, dear? Do you have a girlfriend?"

"Um, no, but—"

"Are you a gay? Because if that's the case, it's ok with me. It would make sense. The pretty ones are usually fruits."

"Helen!" the Colonel barks. "Knock it off, you old bat!"

"What, Benny? There's nothing wrong with it. We all suspected, just as well. Didn't you say he was a writer? And his pants are quite snug. Not to mention those pouty, girl lips…"

"That's enough, Helen!"

The white-haired vixen waves him off, again completely undeterred by the Colonel's terseness. I, on the other hand, am delightfully amused by their exchange, even with my sexuality in question. I'm tempted to whip out my notebook and take notes.

"August, if you're looking, I do have a grandson. I've always suspected he was a little funny…"

"I'm flattered, ma'am, but no, thank you," I say through a chuckle. "I'm not gay. I like women."

"Oh?" At that, her interest peaks, and I'm not sure if it's solely for her granddaughter's benefit. She turns around to a group of tables where some women are playing a hand of Gin Rummy, eavesdropping, no doubt. "Did ya hear, Caroline? He's not a fruit! I told you so," she calls out. Then she looks back to me, mischief gleaming in her eyes. "So… my granddaughter?"

I look to the Colonel for help, and find him wound tighter than a knot. We both know Helen won't let up until she gets what she wants. That's why she's so hell bent on gaining my grandfather's attention.

"Ok. I guess I could show her around…"

"Great!" Helen trills, clasping her tiny, wrinkled hands together. "She'll be thrilled. Maybe the four of us can double date…"

"Not a chance in hell, Helen," the Colonel grumbles. "You got what you came for. Now let me enjoy the game in peace."

The snow-capped cougar struts away, round hips swaying in her pink and purple jogging suit. I stare after her, wondering what the hell I've gotten myself into, and try to concoct a way to get out of it.

It's halftime when the Colonel finally turns to look at me. "She's pretty," he says.

I look around. "Who? Helen?"

"No. Her granddaughter. She's pretty, and you'd probably have a good time. And if she's anything like her grandmother, you won't be disappointed."

I nearly choke on my next breath as I stare at my grandfather in disbelief. "Colonel…you didn't."

"Don't be ridiculous, boy. Of course I didn't. I'm a married man." According to the Colonel, *"Til death do us part"* did not apply to his devotion to my grandmother, Lee. Their love was the definition of a true romance. A young airman traveled across oceans, risked his life day in and day out in the belly of battle, only to be completely disarmed by a wide-eyed, beautiful girl during a week of R&R in Thailand. Her name was Sumalee, but the Colonel called her Lee for short. He found her serving drinks in the Red Light District of Phuket. She was barely seventeen, and under normal circumstances, would have been paraded as merchandise available to tourists and horny soldiers for rent by the hour. But, her mother was a madam and, up to that point, she'd refused to sell her daughter. Unless…it was the right price.

Apparently, one hundred American dollars was the right price back in 1965.

He didn't buy her to sleep with her or take advantage of her. He wanted to save her. He saw her—living in filth and ruin within the confines of paradise—and he couldn't imagine a light so bright, so beautiful, being dimmed by circumstance.

He married her without ever even touching her, and brought her back to the states. In time, she learned to love him just as madly, deeply as he'd loved her the very moment he laid eyes on her. It was pure, undiluted by pride and pretense, and it was real.

That was love. Not the agonizingly self-serving shit people claim to feel these days through Instagram pics and corny Twitter hashtags. #OhEmGeee #SoEffinInLoveWithMyBae (heart-eyed emoji, kissy face, heart)

#PleaseChokeOnADick (side eye emoji)

"I never doubted you, sir, but you said…"

"I know what I said. People talk. I listen. They think I don't, but I do."

The older man looks back at the television, his jaw tense. I know it bothers him that I've insinuated that he's been with another woman. We've discussed it before—him moving on after my grandmother died. I knew he was lonely and I couldn't bear the thought of him wallowing in grief until it killed him…until I lost him too. But he was more than adamant that he would remain faithful to Grandma Lee's memory, and did not appreciate me challenging the sanctity of his vows.

"So…she's pretty?" I ask, trying to smooth things over. The Colonel isn't sensitive, but he has no patience for foolishness.

"She is. Blonde, blue eyes, tall…your type. Says she's an aspiring beautician or something like that. She's pretty. But not like Fiona."

Ah. Of course she's not like Fiona. No one is, in the Colonel's eyes. And this girl sounded like the exact opposite of her.

Fi is just a pixie of a woman with wispy brunette waves and small, delicate features. Her frame is slight, yet soft, and she's modest with her subtle curves. She moves as if she's made of water—fluid and weightless. And her voice is merely a whisper of autumn wind on a brisk day. She smiles at complete strangers and laughs at nothing. Animals and babies make her teary-eyed, and she is fiercely in love with all things love. She isn't just sunshine on a rainy day; she is refuge in a hurricane. And she's my best friend. Yet, somehow, the Colonel can't seem to remember that.

"She's dating the doctor, remember, Colonel?" Insisting that Fi and I were just friends would be beating a very dead horse.

"Humph. He's no good for her. I don't like him," he

grumbles, reiterating his disgust.

"Well, apparently, we're having dinner on Friday."

"You and Fiona?" There's a hint of hope in his voice.

"Me, Fiona and the Doctor."

He grimaces as if a nasty taste has just invaded his mouth. *Yeah, Colonel. I feel the same damn way.* Still, I find myself saying, "She's happy. Fi is happy with him."

"And are *you* happy with that?" he asks, turning to me. Age and wisdom shine in eyes painted with the same shade of deep brown that he passed down to me.

"I guess I have to be."

He grunts, saying all there is to be said, and we go back to looking at the television. He wants Fi to be happy, just like I do. But he wants her to be happy with me, and that's just not possible. What she's searching for…I can't provide. I can't give something that I don't believe even exists. And I won't ruin ten years of real friendship to step out on a fairytale. *Her* fairytale, not mine. The idea of commitment is more along the lines of Stephen King's *It* to me.

"Hey, want to hear a joke?" the Colonel says, as the second half begins. I expect another dig at Kaepernick. Next week, Michael Stafford will be the butt of our jokes when the Seahawks play the Detroit Lions.

"Sure, Colonel."

"What do you call a man that says he doesn't believe in love?"

I turn to my grandfather, complexity resting on my brow. "What?"

"A goddamn liar."

SHE STOOD BEFORE THE FULL-LENGTH mirror, ice blue eyes sweeping over every naked inch of her 5-foot 7-inch frame. Long strands of spun gold cascaded down her back and over her bare shoulders, causing the curled ends to tickle the tops of her full, heavy breasts. Her fingertips traced the curve of her collarbone before sneaking downward, grazing her erect nipples—

Erect? Like two mini hard cocks? No. Definitely no.

...grazing her pebbled nipples. She could still feel his mouth on them—licking, sucking...biting. If she closed her eyes and pinched them hard, it was like feeling him again. The memory was so fresh in her mind that warmth and wetness began to pool between her still trembling thighs. She throbbed for him, ached for him. She needed him to fill the hollowness

within her with his…

~~Massive rod?~~

~~Hardened flesh~~

~~Glorious shaft?~~

Fuck. Me.

…to fill the hollowness within her with his pulsing length. Every second without him inside her made the void that much deeper, and every minute sent her spiraling into an endless pit of yearning.

The throbbing between her legs intensified to the point of pain, and she groaned in her impassioned misery. She needed relief. She needed to feel that fullness. She needed to feel his heart beating inside her again, giving her life…giving her sweet death.

With tentative fingers, she parted silken folds and stroked the burning—

Burning? Is it Gonorrhea? Shit…

…touched the sensitive, sizzling skin that quivered under her touch. She moaned loudly and caressed herself again. And again. And again. Until the need for more became too severe to ignore any longer. She slid her fingers to the empty place that wept with craving. Slick with her own desire, she inserted one finger into her hot sex until her palm rested atop her trembling mound. She stroked herself fiercely, hungrily. Desperately. Another finger and she was crying with the need for release. The need for him. *She squeezed her eyes shut and imagined her fingers were his. And when she added a third, she fantasized that it was his hard cock impaling her and making her scream for more.*

She was right on the cusp of crumbling, panting out her

surrender through lips smudged with red when the sound of footsteps startled her from behind. But it was too late to stop now. She catapulted through fear and shame and allowed herself to break apart. And as she stood there, staring at her flushed face and shaking in the wake of the storm, she watched as strong arms wrapped around her body.

She collapsed into him, too exhausted to even hide or explain. He touched her jaw gently, angling her face up to his so he could taste the deceit on her crimson lips. She moaned in his mouth and he sucked her tongue. They kissed like it was the very first time… and the last.

Then in an act so seductive, so erotic, he reached down and slowly guided her fingers from her body and brought it up to his own mouth. With dark eyes trained on her reflection in the mirror, he licked the arousal from her hand, lapping up every sticky, sweet droplet.

When he was sated by the taste of her sin, he brought his lips to her ear and whispered, "You taste like sex. And lies."

She turned to him, pressing her bare breasts against his rumpled linen shirt. The very same shirt she'd had pressed and starched that morning.

And with her voice flat, devoid of any and all emotion, she said, "So do you."

I sip my third cup of coffee and reread the words I've just typed. Four hours. Four hours I've sat here, and this is all I have to show for it. Still, something is better than nothing. Even if it's not a great something.

Fuck it.

I look up at the wall clock fashioned like a cat that Fiona

gave me years ago. I hated cats. Loathed them with a fiery passion. But, as fate would have it, I inherited a stray that the Colonel had taken in but couldn't keep at the senior village. And what do you know…I'm a cat person. Probably because I realized cats are much like writers—moody, withdrawn and prone to fall asleep at any given moment.

Just as the small hand points at eleven, my own little furry asshole, Bartleby, slides his body between my feet, his purrs a plea for attention. It's eleven o'clock at night, and I haven't moved from this spot all day. Hell, I haven't really moved from this spot since Sunday night—three days ago. My dingy, faded *Where the Wild Things Are* t-shirt reeks of stale whiskey and sweat, and may actually sprout arms and legs and peel itself from my body. My golden brown hair is a greasy, matted mess, and I can't remember the last thing I ingested that wasn't Cocoa Puffs or coffee. Or the main food group in a writer's diet—alcohol.

How did I get here? And what the hell have I missed?

Bartleby jumps onto my desk, strolls across the surface littered with multi-colored sticky notes, coffee stains and tattered notebook pages, and sits his fat ass right on my keyboard. He looks at me, challenging me to shoo him away. *Don't even think about it, asshole.*

"Alright, alright, Bart. I'm done for tonight."

Bartleby yawns, blasting me with his rank cat breath. I scoot him over enough to ensure my progress is saved, earning a satisfied look from him.

After a much-needed shave and shower, I grab my silenced phone and go through the dozen or so text messages I've ignored within the past 72 hours.

-Hey, Rhys. Just making sure you're still alive. Call me when you come up for air. (kiss emoji, wink emoji, fist bump emoji)

That's from Fiona, of course. Just like I put up with her, and her alone, calling me Rhys because it reminds me not to take myself so seriously, I put up with the emojis because they remind me of her—childlike, ridiculous and so cute it's aggravating.

She's used to me falling off the grid and bunkering down in the writing cave. Too bad any words I've produced are about as stinky as Bartleby's overflowing litterbox.

-August, I need an answer and a status update asap. Call me.

That's my agent, Kerrigan. She's been sending the same text message every week for a month. But until I see some shouty caps and an over-abundance of exclamation marks, she's just another name in my social slush pile. I'll get back to her tomorrow. Maybe.

I scroll through the rest of the texts, all whispering the same provocative message. You see, even though I don't desire an actual committed relationship, that doesn't mean I don't want and need companionship—of the physical variety, of course. I just don't believe I need the same companion for life. So I date. If you want to call greasy takeout followed by raunchy sex, dating.

The writer life is a lonely one, and when I feel like doing the social thing, flexibility and availability is key. So I tend to keep a few ladies on the roster that can handle my erratic hours.

Maureen is a magenta-haired bartender that works from late evening until early morning. She's into tattoos, classic rock and art. Her favorite canvas is my body, and her skilled, studded tongue is the perfect paintbrush. We'll call her Breakfast.

Sunny is a barista at one of those lingerie coffee stands. I met her three months ago after an intense writing binge, and quickly abandoned my nearby coffee shop for the a.m. eye candy. She scribbled her number on my coffee cup, and within the next eight hours, I was peeling off her espresso-scented negligee. Her hours range from ass crack of dawn to noon. We'll call her Lunch.

Louisa works at the city library from 9 to 5 Monday through Friday. Ever have a naughty librarian fantasy? She's it. And yes, we've fucked in the stacks. After hours, of course. Sometimes we grab dinner. Most times, she is Dinner.

That leaves Denae, also known as Dessert. She's a law student and regularly stays up into the wee hours studying. She's into role-playing, and I've starred as the perverted professor while she's donned a plaid skirt and braids, playing the role of naïve schoolgirl. When she's feeling extra frisky, she recites law text while I bang her from behind, wearing a judge's robe. Definitely wins every case.

So tonight, Denae gets the call back. She, like all the ladies I see, understands that my time is limited, along with my level of commitment. We're still in the fun stages, and the moment that seeing each other becomes more obligation than pleasure, we've agreed to part ways. Well, that's my game plan anyway.

"I thought you had forgotten about me," she purrs through the receiver.

"How could I ever do that? What are you doing?"

"Pouring over Civ Pro notes. Want some company?"

Concise and to the point. I like that. No empty promise of *Netflix and Chill* needed. "You know I do. Hungry?"

"Always. Want me to pick something up?"

"Yeah. I'll give you what I owe you when you get here."

"I know you will."

Half an hour later, we're chowing down on chicken quesadillas from a late night taco truck. Twenty minutes after that, I'm dressed in a floor length black robe and nothing else. Denae is naked, kneeling before me, begging for leniency. She's both counsel and criminal tonight, and I plan on punishing her to the full extent of the law.

"What do you say to these allegations, Miss?" I ask, looming over her. I'm trying not to laugh, but it's getting hard to keep a straight face. Seriously, old, crusty ass judges get her hot?

"Please, your honor. Don't drop your big, heavy gavel on me too hard."

"You're out of order!" I bite the inside of my cheek to keep from snickering. The first time we played one of her little games—over 6 months ago when we started hanging out—I'd barely held it together. This shit never gets old, which is probably why I like her so much.

I let Denae play out her little fantasy, which ends with me sentencing her to my bedroom. She's just as creatively kooky in the sack, and begs me to handcuff her to the headboard and "make her my bitch." Her words, not mine.

"I wish I could see you more," she sighs as we lay in the afterglow. She stretches her limbs like a cat, and I reach over to grab a notebook and pen. I keep a stack there just in case. Sex inspires me. And I still have on the judge's robe. It actually feels pretty good against my skin. Don't judge me.

"Yeah. Sorry. Been busy."

"Yeah, yeah. I know. You're writing. You're always writing. What are you working on now, August?"

I scribble some of tonight's highlights and shrug, my eyes trained on my messy scrawl. "Nothing important."

The only thing Denae knows about my body of work is *Tears of Glass*, along with some editorials I've done for a few magazines. And other than brick-thick law texts, she doesn't read, which is sad for humanity, yet great for me. If she ever picked up one of my books, specifically my latest one, she'd be surprised to find that she inspired a few of my more... creative scenes. The fire chief's daughter, who also has a salacious affair with a hunky firefighter, was a law student with a penchant for role playing.

You know the bit... *Hey baby, read any good books lately?* It's not just a cheesy line for me. It's a test. If a girl reads, especially the romance genre, it's an automatic stop sign. Because chances are, she'll pick up a Hope Hughes book. And if she's memorable, she'll be *in* a Hope Hughes book. My sexy librarian, Louisa, is the only exception. She thinks modern romance is drivel and would rather blow her nose with the pages of anything remotely smutty than read them. Sometimes I recite Shakespeare while she goes down on me. Best. Blowjob. Ever.

Denae reaches over to rummage through her purse,

pulls out a pack of Marlboro Lights and sparks one up. She takes a deep draw and exhales with a sated sigh. "Hey, you mind if I smoke this in here?"

I roll my eyes. She knows good and damn well that I can't stand the smell of smoke. Not since I quit three years ago. But that's just because I hate myself for still craving it. "It's fine. You've already lit it."

I read over the words I've just written before tossing the Moleskine on my nightstand with the rest of them. It's shit. It's all shit. I'm so uninspired. I thought sex would break me out of this funk, but it only seemed to make me…restless. Unfocused. The heroine is all wrong, from her long, blonde hair to her perfect fucking tits. The hero is a cold-hearted, narcissistic prick, yet somehow changes entirely for the heroine. It's too cliché. Too predictable. And while this formula has worked well for me in the past, my heart is just not into it now. I don't get it.

I reach over and grab my phone to scroll through the messages again. Maybe Denae isn't what I need. Maybe a taste of Maureen's creative juices is what I crave. Or maybe Sunny's youth and carefree disposition are what I'm missing.

My thumb hovers over the text message from Fiona, sent yesterday afternoon. I touch my finger to the screen and type out a quick response. She answers within seconds.

-I'm alive. What are you doing? Playing doctor?

I don't expect her to answer—it's nearly two a.m.—but to my surprise, she does.

-LOL. You wish. No. Joshua has an early surgery. I can't sleep so I'm rereading my favorite passages from *Mansfield Park*. How goes the writing?

-Slow. Hard. Torturous. But chicks dig it like that, right?

-Haha. You would know, Mr. Romance.

-(rolling my eyes) Don't call me that.

-Just own it, Rhys. No one can write words as heartfelt as yours and not believe in love.

-Lies. All lies.

-You can't evoke that type of soul-crushing emotion without actually feeling it. You can't fake beauty so bold and so complete that it brings complete strangers to tears. No one is that good of a liar.

I am.

I stare at the screen, musing over Fi's last statement. Denae has been prattling on about something she saw on *How to Get Away with Murder*, and how she thought it was insanely hot and disturbing and provocative. I make sure to nod and throw in a few *uh huh's* to make her believe I'm still listening.

I wish Fi were here instead of her. I wish we were sitting cross-legged on the floor of my living room, surrounded by crumpled Post-Its scribbled with notes and cartons of Thai food. She'd force me to play Train and The Fray, but only the earlier albums, and I'd pretend to hate it while quietly humming every word from memory because I have all their CDs from when CDs were actually popular. I'd talk her through the story as I see it in my head, and she'd listen intently, telling me how each imagined scene gives her all the feels. My fragile ego stroked, I'd find the confidence to keep writing, to keep dreaming… for her.

Not for Denae or Sunny or Louisa or Maureen. Not for any of the countless women I've slept with in a quest for inspiration. I keep writing for Fiona. Because she is the only person on earth that can decipher my empty words and reveal my soul.

My cell vibrates in my hand and I look down to see another text.

-Will I see you before Friday?

-Friday?

-Dinner with Joshua. You promised.

-Oh. Yeah. That.

I remember. You don't forget the social equivalent of a scheduled colonoscopy.

-You are coming, right?

-Yeah. Sure.

She reminds me of the details—7pm at some new hipster place that serves miniscule portions for astronomical prices. Which means I'll be forced to sit through twelve courses of awkwardness. Awesome. And, yeah, I'm not strapped for cash or anything, after signing a publishing deal with a seven-figure advance, but the ruse of a starving artist only works if I'm not squandering a compact car payment on a single meal. People believe I'm a trust fund baby, and that's fine when it comes to the ladies. But for some reason, I'm not cool with letting the Pantysniffer think I'm just some spoiled rich kid without any real marketable skills or accomplishments to show for.

-You're overthinking this, aren't you?

The words appear on my cell phone screen, and I smile.

-Only when I'm awake.

-Dinner tomorrow?

-Can't. Meatballs. The Colonel has been looking forward to Thursday night football since I missed Monday.

-Ah, that's right. I saw him yesterday. He looks good.

-He does.

-So lunch? I can take a long one. It's supposed to be nice out.

I want to say yes, but I need to write. I need to feel the words again. I need to hear the voices. Yet, it's gone. It's all gone.

I look over at Denae, her back turned to me, and her cigarette stubbed out in an empty soda can. I've already forgotten what it felt like to be inside her. I can no longer feel the warmth of her breath or the smoothness of her skin. She used to be my inspiration. They all were.

My fingertips trace the sensual curve of her back all the way down to the top of her ass. She sighs melodically, arching for me, and for one brief moment, I hear the whispered voices again. The whispers are always the prelude for the words.

I tap out the message in lightening speed.

-Yeah. The park?

-It's a date.

I smile. Talking didn't work. Days locked away in the writing cave didn't work. Even sex wasn't doing the trick. Maybe some fresh air with Fi is exactly what I need to get my head on straight. But first...dessert.

"WHAT ABOUT THAT GUY?"

Fiona and I are strolling along one of the several trails at Riverfront Park, as we share a Bahn Mi sandwich from a food stand. I look over at the homeless guy leaning against an old, massive oak. His eyes are closed, and he's smiling. Covered in filth and dejection, while complete strangers walk through his sod-floored living room, he begins to nod his head from side to side.

"He was a famed composer for many years, and had captivated audiences at Carnegie Hall in his heyday. His music was breathtaking…groundbreaking…and he owed it all to his wife. She had been by his side since they were children, and had always loved to hear him create magic. She'd stay up all night with him as he composed the most magnificent pieces about her eyes, her hands …the sound of her voice when she whispered his name. She was his muse, and he was her life.

"They lived in careless bliss until the day she couldn't get out of bed. He carried her to the doctor, only to find that she would leave him soon. The cancer was terribly aggressive, and treatment wouldn't save her. At her bedside, he composed his last and most beautiful piece. She died to the sound of him humming it to her, his head swaying side to side, his hand clutching hers. To this day, not another soul has heard it, because the moment she stopped breathing was the moment he stopped hearing the music.

"However, just now, in a whispered gust of wind, he heard her laughter. Smelled her sweet scent of fresh-picked cherries from their tree and Chanel No.5. He felt her warmth and goodness radiate all around him. He heard the music again. Just for one second, he remembered what it felt like to be alive."

I feel Fi's gaze on me, but I don't look at her.

"August Rhys Calloway, how do you do it? How do create such beauty and heartbreak?" There are tears in her throat.

I shrug and look down at the ground. "That's all life is—beauty and heartbreak. I just narrate it. Besides, it's not like I'm changing lives here. My books are fluff and fucking, at best."

"Are you kidding me? You're burning up bedrooms all over America! Vibrator manufacturers should make you their official mascot."

"They could put my head on the head," I chuckle.

"Maybe they'll even make a mold of your manhood." She blushes and covers her face. "Oh, the horror!"

I laugh and shake my head. "Like I said, Fi… fluff and fucking. My stories are like *The Wedding Singer* of Lit. They won't impact your life in any significant way, but they're great for the time being. No one ever names *The Wedding Singer* when they're asked about their favorite film. But if that fucker pops up on Netflix, you better believe you're gonna watch it!"

She looks affronted. "I happen to like *The Wedding Singer*."

I sling an arm around her slight shoulders and pull her into my chest. "I know, Fi. I know."

We continue to stroll down a path leading towards the picturesque Spokane Falls, creating make believe backstories for unsuspecting passersby. Our little game first started years ago as a creativity exercise to keep us both inspired. Like me, Fiona was an English major, although she now works at a temporary staffing and recruiting agency. Real good use of that shiny degree, huh?

I take a bite of the sandwich and pass it to Fiona. "Ok," I mutter, swallowing down the last bit of shaved BBQ pork and pickled daikon. "How about them?"

Fiona follows my gaze to an elderly couple sitting on a park bench. The frail, gray pair is huddled together over a scoop of ice cream, and the husband slowly feeds his wife a bite with a shaky hand, concentrating not to drop the creamy confection in her lap. She smiles as it hits her lips then reciprocates, her grip on the plastic spoon much steadier.

"They've been in love since they were children. Since junior high school," she begins, picking at a julienne carrot.

"He was a big, strapping athlete, and she was a quiet, bookish girl. He needed help with his Algebra, and she would tutor him after school. He thought she was lovely, yet she was much too shy to pick up on his subtle flirtations. Then one warm evening after tutoring, he bought her an ice cream. She insisted they share it. They fell madly, deeply in love over that scoop of vanilla, and they've been sharing ice cream ever since."

Fiona turns to me and smiles, and I swear I hear a dreamy sigh leave her lips. "Isn't it wonderful? To be in love for a lifetime?"

I cut my eyes at her. Must be all the pot in the air. The park is breeding ground for stoners.

I visibly shiver. "Love for a lifetime? Sounds more like a judge just brought the gavel down on my balls and gave me a life sentence."

"Aw, come on, Rhys," she says, skipping ahead only to turn around to face me as she walks backwards. "Could you imagine, waking up every morning to the woman of your dreams, and getting to go to sleep with her in your arms every night? Just think about it—no matter if you get old, or fat, or sick, that person will always love you. They'll always want you. And they'll always, always choose *you* over everyone and everything else. You can't tell me that's not romantic."

I shrug. "Romantic, sure. Realistic, *hell* no. I can't imagine it, because it doesn't exist. No one values that in a relationship. No one sticks it out for the grand scheme of true love. You get old? Time to get someone younger. You get fat? Find someone thinner. You get sick?" I look back at the elderly couple, still sharing the last of their scoop of vanilla.

The man is trying furiously to still the shaking in his hand, and his wife waits patiently, nothing but love and admiration shining in her eyes. Not a single drop of judgment clouds her gaze. "That…that's not real, Fi. No one is that genuine and loyal. Not anymore."

"I am." I turn back to my best friend, who's stopped walking altogether. "I am, Rhys. If you get old, I'll feed you Jell-O. If you get fat, hell, I'll get fat with you. If you get sick, I'll hold your hand and tell you it will be ok."

"That's different, Fi."

"How so?"

"You haven't committed your life to me, and I wouldn't expect you to. I wouldn't *want* you to."

Pain paints her wind-whipped cheeks. "Why not?"

I close the distance between us in three strides and take hold of her shoulders, pulling her so close that our chests nearly collide. She's barely 5'3 and I'm over 6 feet tall. It's like holding a delicate, porcelain rose in the palm of my hands. "Because I wouldn't want you to devote your life to a lie."

She looks up at me, her big brown eyes searching for more than what my lips can offer. "You don't believe that," she whispers.

"Oh, but I do. Because it's true, Fi." I turn her around and grasp her hand, gently pulling her forward. "I see love and relationships the way most people look at ghosts."

"Ghosts?"

"Ghosts. You know what they say: if you don't believe in them, they won't exist for you. But if you engage in the paranormal stuff and leave just a little room for curiosity to blossom, expect Casper and his homies to come creeping out your closet door. I don't believe in love. So it will never happen for me."

"Oh, bullcrap, Rhys."

"It's true! I've dated my fair share of women, and not one has made me see forever in her eyes. Some have come close, but there's always something to fuck it up."

Fiona heaves out an exasperated sound and rolls her eyes. "Here we go again. There's always something *wrong* with them. Too clingy, too talkative, eats too much garlic, doesn't like Thai food, a mouth breather, chews with her mouth open. I swear, you make this stuff up just to force yourself not to fall in love."

"Nuh *uh*," I insist with all the gusto of a five-year-old. "Those are real deal breakers for me. I can't seriously date a girl that can't close her fucking trap when we go to a nice restaurant."

"Nice restaurant? When have you ever taken a girl to a place that doesn't sit on four wheels?"

"Well, don't blame me for trying to support small businesses." I take what's left of our shared sandwich and toss it in a nearby bin. No less than two seconds later, a homeless woman fishes it out. "Look around you, Fi. We're not exactly in the mecca of culture and opportunity."

She does as requested, and looks around, taking in the lush green grass, towering trees and tweaked out potheads littered about like leaves. "Maybe not, but it's home. And so what if Spokane is like a poor man's Seattle. There's nothing they've got that we don't. *Hello?* We just got a Panera Bread!"

"Are you shittin' me? Alert the presses! This is big city livin' right here, y'all! What's next? A Chick-fil-A?" I mock, earning a smack on the arm.

"Oh, knock it off. You know you were the first in line for a bread bowl of cheddar and broccoli soup. And if we did get a Chick-fil-A, you'd be first in line for that too."

"Damn skippy."

We circle around toward the pride of Spokane, a grandiose carousel, boasting whimsical, hand-carved pieces dating back to the early 1900s. Fi's office is just a block away, so I walk her back, contemplating how to broach the next subject.

"I talked to my agent today."

"Oh? And how is Kerrigan doing these days?"

"She's well. Had an offer for me." I try not to sound too interested, but honestly, the words have been kicking up a waterspout in my gut all morning.

"Another publishing deal?"

"Not exactly. She was contacted by a major network, offering me a writing gig. Well, basically creating a show loosely based on my life."

"That's amazing!" She jumps me like I've just told her I'm stashing cupid's arrows in my back pocket. "Oh my God, Rhys! You'll be like the male Carrie Bradshaw! And I can be Charlotte!"

"Well… not exactly, but yeah. Doesn't matter. I'm not taking it."

She unravels her limbs from mine and looks up at me, those big brown eyes winced in confusion. "Why not? It's the offer of a lifetime."

"Eh," I shrug. "Not what I want to do."

"Huh? What could be better than your own show? Honestly, what *do* you want to do?"

I gaze back at her with absolute clarity. "Write epic shit."

"Excuse me?"

"I want to write epic shit. I want to touch the world with my words, as cliché as it sounds. I want to be bad ass in my own right."

Fi stops up short, like she can't believe what she's hearing. "Um, hello? You already do, and you already are."

"No," I insist, shaking my head. "I want to write for me, not because it's popular or profitable. I want someone to be forever changed by something I wrote."

"And you don't think you're changing people now?" she asks with a raised brow. "Nine months after your book releases, there's a baby boom! I'd say pregnancy is pretty life-changing."

We continue walking toward her building, a historical looking fourteen-story giant that houses dozens of businesses, from an accounting firm to a bank.

"You're exaggerating. And even if you weren't, that's not the type of change I want to inspire."

"Then what do you want to inspire?"

Now it's time for me to pause. Because I honestly don't know what I want to invoke in the hearts and minds of my readers. But when I look at Fiona, I know one thing for sure: I want to make her fall in love. Not that superficial shit she goes gaga for in chick flicks and paperback porn. Not even the hollow attachment she thinks she has for Joshua,, or Harrison from two summers ago or Colby from undergrad. I want to make her feel love like she's never felt before. Not love for me, of course. But for my words, and the meaning behind them. Other than my grandfather, I really don't give a damn about impressing anyone else but her. And if I can somehow impact her life, then I'd know I did something right.

"You know that feeling after you've just read the words *The End* of something so incredible, all you can do is sit there and stare at nothing, clutching that book to your chest like it shares your heartbeat, unable to talk or move or even think of anything other than the words that have ignited magic inside your soul? You just sit there and feel it moving inside you, wicked tendrils of emotion that touch parts of you that you never even knew existed. I want to make readers feel so much that just for a moment in time, they become numb to the outside world, too consumed by the gravity of my words to feel any more sensation. I want to captivate readers in a way that feels like falling in love. The deepest, realest, most infectious type of love. One that never, ever dies."

I don't notice that we're already at her building until I look up from Fiona's wide, teddy bear brown eyes. "I better go," I say, bending over to kiss her cheek. We stand in silence for a minute, maybe even five. I can't tell when she looks at me like that, wonder and reverence in her gaze.

"Tomorrow night, Rhys," she manages to rasp before turning towards the entranceway.

I stand there for a good thirty seconds, watching as wisps of brown hair disappear from sight, and wondering how the hell I'm going to get through dinner with doubt eating a hole through my stomach.

Meatball Thursdays are an event at the senior village, and while I don't make them every week, I try to be a good sport for the Colonel. Plus…football. My dad was never into it, so the Colonel made sure I followed the game, even if I was too scrawny and awkward to play as a kid. It wasn't about football for me anyway. It was about bonding and feeling like I was just one of the guys. He'd cheer and yell at the television, and I'd do the same, without really even knowing what the hell I was screaming about. I felt like I belonged, like I knew my place in the world. With the Colonel, I always felt like I could do and be anything, just because he believed it too.

"These SOBs get bigger every week," the Colonel grumbles, stabbing a marinara topped meatball that looks to be the size of a baseball on his plate. He's right. They do get bigger every week. But when half the cooks are battling arthritis, you can't expect them to be uniform.

I nod my agreement. He's extra prickly today. Probably has something to do with his doctor's appointment earlier. He hates to be poked and prodded. "How was your check-up?"

"Eh," he shrugs. "Nothing I didn't know already. I'm old."

"You're not old, Colonel. You still have a lot of years ahead of you. Isn't there anything you still want to do? Or see?"

"Like what?" he replies, his bushy, gray brows shading his eyes in a frown. "I've survived two wars, experienced countless recessions, and watched an Olympic hero became a woman. I've seen enough."

"Well… how about Los Angeles?"

"Los Angeles?"

"Yeah. I have to go there for a meeting in a couple weeks. Something my agent wants me to follow up on. This TV network wants to develop a show around a male writer who moonlights as a romance novelist, and while I have no intention of signing on, the trip is on their dime. Plus, the beach is concentrated inspiration. Might be just what I need."

He raises a bushy brow. "Still having writer's block?"

"Yeah." I look down at my plate of ground meat spheres and pasta, almost ashamed of admitting it. "I've got *something*, but it's not what I want. And every word is like pulling teeth."

"Hmmm," the Colonel muses. "Well, son, maybe the reason you're struggling with this story is because it's not the story you're supposed to be writing."

I look up to find that the Colonel's gaze is softer than it was just a moment ago. "What do you mean? It's the story I pitched to the publisher."

"You can't force these things, son. You can't make your head recite what your heart can't tell." He looks down at his plate and resumes stabbing at his food as if he's just remembered himself. "Or something like that. What do I know? I'm just an old man."

"You're not old, Colonel. That's why I want you to come to LA with me. We'll go sightseeing, go to the beach… it'll be fun."

He shakes his head. "Nah. I'm not too keen on the noise and heat. You go. And don't discount what they have to say. Hear them out. Might be a chance of a lifetime."

"Now you sound like Fiona," I mumble.

The smile on his face is undeniable. "So she agrees with me about LA?"

I shake my head. "I haven't told her about actually going there. And I don't think I need to. Taking the job means I'd have to relocate, and I'm not willing to do that."

The Colonel is quiet for a beat, pushing food around his plate. "Ok. What's stopping you?"

I jerk as if he's just smacked me across the back of the head, like he used to do when I was a young rascal. "I'm not moving. I'm not leaving you here alone."

"Bullshit. Why not? Your parents moved away. Why can't you? I'll be fine!"

"No, Colonel," I reply with finality. "I'm not going. You're here, and Fiona…"

"Yes?" There's that damn smile again. People used to say a young Benjamin Calloway was as tempting as the devil himself, especially when he smiled.

"Nothing."

"You don't think she'll approve?"

"No. I *know* she'll approve. I know she'll tell me to go conquer my dreams, all while choking on tears. She'll tell me she's proud of me, yet she'll hate herself for saying it. It's easier if I stay."

The Colonel shakes his head and grunts. "No one ever achieved greatness by doing what's easy. But if you want to stay for her, I can understand."

I open my mouth to object, but before the words can leave my lips, we're struck by the cackling of Helen Ashford, followed by a much younger, blonder, taller version of herself.

"Good evening, Benny. Fancy seeing you here, August," she grins, clasping her hands in front of her. "The fates must be aligned. I'd like you to meet my granddaughter, April. Isn't she a beauty?"

Using the manners my grandfather had instilled in me, I jump to my feet to greet them both, allowing my eyes to take in the nearly six foot tall, ice blonde vixen before me. April is definitely a beauty with her porcelain skin and blue, bedroom eyes. Her lips are thin, as is her nose, and her body looks like it was made for the runway, even under black jeans and a gray turtleneck.

"Pleased to meet you," I say, slipping my hand around her slender fingers.

"Likewise," she smiles. White teeth. Mauve-painted lips. "My grandmother has told me so much about you."

"I told her you weren't gay, even though you look it," Helen tacks on, rather proudly.

"Oh, well… thank you?" I stammer, not sure if I should laugh or attempt to prove my hetero status. How tight *are* my jeans today? Hell, I'd never had any complaints before. Quite the opposite, actually.

"I'm glad to hear that," April replies, her hand still resting in mine. I pull away. I'm always the first to pull away in every situation.

"Leave the boy alone, Helen," the Colonel barks, although with a bit of humor in his tone. I think he enjoys me being the center of Helen's attention for a change.

"Oh hush, Benny. Don't they look absolutely adorable together? April and August… isn't it funny that they're both named after months? It was meant to be! And I was just telling April that August is a big-time writer. What was that book you wrote, dear?"

"Um, uh, *Tears of Glass*, ma'am," I answer, flashing a sheepish grin. "And I'm hardly famous." At least, that's mostly true. August Calloway isn't famous, and probably never will be.

"Yes, that's the one. And what's that about?"

"Um…it's, uh, fiction, and it's a story of…" What is it about talking about your art that reduces you into bashful, blubbering fool? It's as if someone has just asked you to tell the story of your life in one hundred words or less, which is pretty damn impossible. Writers are wordy fuckers.

The four of us finish what I had initially begun to be an awkward dinner. Even the Colonel seemed to grumble and grunt less when Helen engaged him. I know I wasn't complaining. April is pretty interesting actually, and I find myself actually *listening* to her, in hopes of getting to *know* her. And not just horizontally.

"So, six months into grad school, I realized that botany just wasn't where my heart was. So I quit, went to cosmetology school, and moved here for a job as a makeup artist at Nordstrom. I work for NARS."

I spoon out a portion of Isabella Mancini's homemade tiramisu. She's been a resident at the village for two years, and the woman is like the Italian grandmother you've always wanted. Warm, boisterous, and always ready to fatten you up with decadent foods. She even prepares a small dish of tiramisu and cannoli for me to take home.

"Wow. That's pretty ballsy. So I'm assuming you've found your calling," I say before sliding the bite of lady fingers and mascarpone between my lips.

"I think so. As corny as it sounds, I want to make the world beautiful," she smiles. She's pretty when she does that… beautiful even. Her teeth are bright yet not completely straight, and she has a slight overbite. Her lips are on the thin side, so she over-lines them with makeup to make them appear larger. But after eating, it's smudged off, revealing who she truly is. What she deems as flaws is exactly what attracts me—the tiny details that tell a story. Was she teased about her teeth? Did she spend hours on YouTube, trying to perfect the Kylie Jenner lip? These are the things that create the character.

She catches me staring at her mouth, and nervously covers her lips with her hand. Before I can stop myself, I'm pulling it down, daring her to object.

"Don't do that. Don't hide what makes you… remarkable."

"Remarkable?" she whispers.

"You're insecure about your teeth…your lips."

Her cheeks flame bright red and her wide, blue eyes glaze over with embarrassment. She tries to cover her face again, but I grasp both her hands in mine, refusing to let her retreat from my touch.

"Don't be. Don't be ashamed of the very traits that make you extraordinary. I see a smile that could brighten the darkest night. I see lips that long to be devoured. I see unblemished beauty and rarity. But what I don't see is anything about you that needs to be hidden. Not from me."

A smile slowly creeps onto her face, and her cheeks flush in coy desire. Out of all that, she'd heard exactly what I wanted her to hear. "You really think I'm beautiful?"

Got her.

"YOU SAID *WHAT* TO HER?"

I take a sip of fresh coffee and ease back into the cushion of my worn desk chair. "I told her about her insecurities, and how I found them unbelievably sexy."

Fiona clucks through the receiver, and I can imagine her shaking her head. "I can't believe that crap works for you. What kind of woman wants you to pick out her biggest flaws, only so you can feed her some BS about how her vulnerability turns you on? Where do you find these girls, Rhys? Are you trolling support group meetings again?"

Laughing, I fire up the mean machine. I need to write, even if it is late. "Not today. She's Helen Ashford's granddaughter."

"Hell-on-Wheels Helen? From the senior center?"

"One and the same."

"Holy crap! So let me get this straight... Helen Ashford has a granddaughter."

"Yes."

"Which means she also had a child once upon a time."

"That's usually how it works."

"So that also means Helen could have been married."

"Not really necessary to get knocked up, but, yeah, it's possible."

"Don't you see, Rhys? Someone had a child with Helen. And if that old battleax can nab a man, then there's got to be hope for me!"

"Really, Fi? You're comparing yourself to an old woman? Helen Ashford is one of the OG Golden Girls."

"Whatever. She still gets more action than I do."

Can't argue with her there. I'd heard the stories, and she wasn't exactly shy about her intentions with me. Shit, come to think of it, Helen is probably getting more action than *me*, which is saying something.

"So what happened?"

"Well, Fi. When two people are attracted to each other, they sometimes like to show it by stripping naked and getting into bed, and—"

"Oh my God! Spare me the disgusting details! I meant, what happened? How did you go from noshing on meatballs to making bacon within mere hours of meeting at an old folk's home?"

I shrug. "We connected. She's cool."

"She's cool? *Cool?*"

"Yeah. Smart. Funny. Easy on the eyes."

"And that tells me nothing of how she ended up in your bed." I can just imagine her shaking her head at me in disappointment. "Seriously, Rhys. If you sleep with every woman you're attracted to, how will you ever really get to know them?"

"Uh, I thought I was. I got to know April pretty well earlier tonight. Inside out, if you will. So well, she just limped out of my apartment in search of cranberry juice."

Fiona makes a retching sound. "Not in the biblical sense. I mean, *really* get to know her. We both know that once you do the deed, all hopes of an interpersonal connection are dashed."

"Not true," I scoff with mock indignity. Bartleby slinks under my chair and rubs his side against my legs, prompting me to pick him up. He's been in hiding ever since April came over. He, too, is not amused by the women I bring home.

"August, it totally is. You might not love them or leave them, but you definitely have no interest in creating a meaningful relationship."

"Oh, so I'm August now?"

"You know what I mean. I'm being serious. It's like sex somehow friend-zones them. You keep them at arm's length, placating them with late night hookups and pretty words in afterglow. You're purposely sabotaging yourself by having sex with them."

I blink once. Twice. "Um, you do realize that sex isn't an act of sabotage, but is actually my main objective, right?"

"But is that your *only* objective?"

"Abso-fucking-lutely. I'm not looking for anything more

than what I have with these ladies. I'm not in need of a permanent fixture. Besides, I have you." On that note, Bartleby cosigns with a meow.

"Really? You really don't want anything more permanent?" There's a sense of loss in her voice.

"Really."

"Not even when you're old and gray?"

"Fi, I plan on being the second coming of Clooney."

"But he eventually got married!"

"Well…sometimes the sequel is even better than the first."

Two thousand words and five hours later, I finally climb into bed. I'm so exhausted that I don't even bother to change the sheets. Just as well. The scent of April's perspiration is my inspiration, and I fall asleep dreaming of long legs wrapped around me, blonde hair tickling my bare chest and echoed whispers of a voice I don't know.

When I wake up from my mini coma, I know it's well after noon. After a workout, I shower, trim the scruff from sasquatch to vagrant chic and do what I swore I wouldn't do. I call my agent.

"Holy fuck. You actually got your head outta your ass and called."

"Kerrigan, you sound shocked."

"Shit yeah, I am," she rasps, her voice harsh and gravely from years of smoking two packs a day. "You must be intrigued."

"I wouldn't say that."

I hear her exhale, and I can imagine putrid, glorious

smoke billowing around the phone, sending phantom wisps through the receiver. Talking to her makes me miss smoking. I'm a weak bastard. "So you're just calling to waste my time?"

"No. I want to know what they're willing to do to protect my anonymity *if* I decide to hear them out."

Kerrigan inhales, causing her voice to sound strained. "I'm glad you asked." Exhale. "I've already had Legal draft an iron-clad NDA, and arranged for you to meet with one studio exec at a private location. And honestly, leaking your identity isn't conducive to what they hope to achieve with the show. It's a sitcom about a group of writers, the star being a romance writer. He's handsome, cynical, self-indulgent, slightly whorish… he's you."

"Self-indulgent?" *That* stings.

"August, you're a star, and they'll know that as soon as they meet you. They won't want to ruin their chances at making a shitload of money off your story. Without that element of mystery, you're just like any other writer."

Any other writer.

Any. Other. Writer.

As Hope Hughes, I'm special. I'm exotic, in a sense. People want to covet that. As August Rhys Calloway, I'm just like everyone else.

"Set it up. I'll meet with their exec."

"Great! I'll get back to you soon."

We hang up without formalities. I've learned to expect and appreciate Kerrigan's brashness. She's a helluva agent, and has brokered some incredible deals for me. I just don't know if this is one of them. Books are one thing; there's a sense of protection…a sense of obscurity. But television and movies is a different beast entirely. And I still haven't even mentioned LA to Fiona.

Fiona.

I look up at my kitschy cat clock and realize that I need to get off my hide and get dressed. I could blow off dinner with some lame excuse about needing to write while I'm feeling the words again, but I'd played that card too many times already.

Honestly, any time a writer tells you they can't make it to a social engagement because they have to write, 9 times out of 10, it's bullshit. They just don't want to be bothered with you. Or people in general. It's nothing personal. See the thing is, when you spend sixteen-hour days conversing with fictional characters in your head, you tend to lose touch with reality. You almost forget what it's like to actually connect with another human being. And a part of you learns not to miss it. At least that's what you tell yourself at 3 am when you're lying in bed alone, trying to fill the cold space beside you with imaginary warmth. Trying to convince yourself that loneliness is just part of the job description, and that you've fashioned your life exactly how you want it.

Table 15 is an intimately lit hot spot tucked away inside the even hipper Grand Hotel, which means it caters to an abundance of New Money, wanna-be New Money, the young-and-sexy, the pseudo young-and-sexy (but really the aging-and-ok), and people that generally like to pay top dollar for small portions of mediocre food. This also means that I try my damnedest to avoid it.

The moment I step into the dim space, I know that I'm not in Kansas anymore. Look, I'm no stranger to fine dining, and I can clean up pretty nicely when I want to. But considering the attire of the hostess, wait staff and most of the diners, I know that I am grossly underdressed. I feel like Katniss Everdeen on her first day in the Capital before Cina got ahold of her. Any minute now, Xzibit is going to jump out from behind the crushed velvet curtain and try to Pimp My Style. I may leave with an Xbox in my back pocket.

Apparently, I'm late (well, duh) and the hostess, eloquently named Misha, tells me that my party is expecting me. Shit. No chance of running now.

The first thing I notice on approach is a petite brunette in a tight black, one-shouldered dress that hugs every inch of her slight curves. She sits beside a proud-faced blonde man with the type of strong jaw that I've written entire chapters about, and blue eyes that are actually the color of ocean water. He's tall, but not so tall that it's skeevy of him to date short women, and he's built, but not so built that he can't reach around to wipe his own ass. His hair is model-ish long, not hippie-ish long, and his suit is obviously expensive without being ostentatious. He's regally handsome.

He's Darcy.

He's Cullen.

He's Grey.

He's Fiona's ideal Book Boyfriend.

"Rhys!" she smiles when Misha leads me to a chair across from where the beautiful couple is seated. They are. A beautiful couple, I mean. That's new.

"Good evening," I say dipping my head. Dipping my head? That's new too. But being in the presence of these seemingly ethereal creatures is making me feel more out of place than usual. I mean, this girl sounds like my Fiona. And when I squint real hard and look past the smoky eye and precisely styled hair, she kinda looks like my Fiona. But beside this guy that appears more cover model than surgeon, the truth is made crystal fucking clear. She's not my Fiona. She's his. And that fact has made her happier than I've ever seen her. Happier than she's ever been.

Fiona smiles like she's a spokesperson for Crest White Strips. "Rhys—I mean, August—this is Joshua. The man I've been telling you about."

We shake. He smiles. I nod again. Fuck.

"August, great to finally meet you. FiFi has told me so much about you."

Pause right here.

Ok, the first revelation that slaps me across the fucking face is the accent. Joshua is Aussie. So, it's not enough that he has the golden blonde hair with no signs of thinning, the stature, the broad shoulders, the goddamn dazzling smile. Oh no. He has an accent to boot! Just wait. I'm sure he'll have some crazy ass stories about riding into the sunset on kangaroos or wrestling crocodiles with his bare hands.

The second thing that downright jolts me into a state of WTF-dom is the fact that he just called Fiona, FiFi. *FiFi.*

Fi is cool. Short, sweet and to the point without being obnoxious. FiFi makes me want to blow chunks. The fuck? Are we doing this? Are we really calling my best friend a nickname reserved for a prize-winning poodle?

I very literally bite my tongue to keep from saying something that'll have Fi pissed at me for a week, and take my seat. "Has she now? Funny. I don't recall her mentioning you."

Taken aback, Joshua's baby blues grow wide with embarrassment, and he looks to Fiona for explanation.

"He's kidding," she smiles to him encouragingly, before turning her gaze on me. "August, tell him you're kidding."

"I'm kidding." I resist the urge to roll my eyes.

Joshua laughs heartily as if I've just said something Kevin Hart worthy. "You're good, mate! You had me going."

I shrug a shoulder. "I try. Fi doesn't let me out much, so I get my kicks where I can."

"Oh stop. August has no problem stirring up trouble around town. You know, with him being brilliant and all. I've been telling Joshua all about *Tears of Glass* and how he needs to read it like yesterday."

"Ah yeah. FiFi's been raving about your book. Trouble is, I'm not much of a reader aside from the occasional magazine or newspaper." Joshua smiles like he's proud of that fact. As if the disclosure of his ignorance makes him all the more charming. And Fiona bathes in the glory of that smile like his mere presence is a blessing to mankind.

Barf.

"That's unfortunate," I mumble, reaching over to grab a glass of water to busy my mouth. What kind of self-respecting man doesn't read? That's like saying he doesn't feel the need to eat or bathe either. Reading is nurturing of the mind…a cleansing of the soul. It opens our eyes to unseen beauty, and our hearts to the untouched pieces of ourselves that we've hidden away from the world. A man without words is a man who has no real awareness of anything or anyone outside of himself. And that worries me, especially when it comes to Fiona.

"A writer's a respectable trade. I've always thought about writing a book one day, but I don't think I could ever do it, so kudos to you. Hey, maybe you should write my life story. I certainly have some interesting tales to share," he grins, completely serious. It's taking everything in me not to laugh in his pretty face.

What is it about telling people you're a writer that makes them think it's an invitation to regurgitate their shit as if I really give two fucks? And what makes them think that their narcissism and delusion would be oh-so intriguing to the masses that it's even worth the ink to write about? Seriously. Unless you've cured cancer, are deemed a war hero, or are a wrinkly old dude in a smoking jacket with a bunch of naked chicks wearing bunny ears living in your crib, I don't give a fuck. That's why there are diaries and shrinks. Use them.

"Joshua is on the shortlist of plastic surgeons nominated for an AAPS award," Fiona boasts, seeing the perturbed look on my face. She knows more than anyone how much that pisses me off.

"Oh, darling. Don't start that again," Joshua retorts with mock modesty.

"No, really. He's a brilliant surgeon. He may even guest star on that show *Botched*."

"*Botched?*" I ask, as a server brings over the scotch neat I managed to order between awkward introductions. Managed is an understatement. I practically growled it out before I even made it to the table.

"You know that show, buddy? Those two Real Housewives doctors correct the surgical catastrophes caused by lesser professionals?" Joshua explains. "It's a real winner of that entertainment channel. Apparently, they want to bring in a few guest doctors with certain specialties."

I know I shouldn't, but I can't resist. "Oh? And what is your specialty?"

I expect him to say lopsided boobs, or crooked snouts, or even Kim K. ba-donka-donks. But what I don't anticipate is him proudly answering with, "Buttholes."

Say *whaaaa?*

The look of horrified confusion as I look from Fiona to Joshua then back to Fiona motivates him to clarify.

"Of course, we do your run-of-the-mill implants and Brazilian butt lifts. But what I'm really passionate about is Anal Rejuvenation. Bleaching, tightening, re-strengthening, as well as more dire anal needs such as reconstruction due to hemorrhoids and sexual trauma."

Oh, this is good. This is just too damn good.

"Anal Rejuvenation? So you're a butthole specialist? A master of assholes?"

"You could say that."

"So let me get this straight—you're pretty much elbow-deep in poop chutes all day?"

"More or less," he nods, completely unaware that he is making my fucking life right now.

"And that's a thing—anal rejuvenation? Like people pay you to spruce up their bungholes."

"Oh, you'd be surprised. Of course, here in Spokane it's still an underrated procedure. Huge in places like Beverly Hills, Manhattan and Las Vegas. But it's beginning to catch on."

"And how does one decide that they are in need of anal

rejuvenation? And as a master at your craft, how do you determine what is a good looking chocolate starfish?"

Joshua leans forward, fitting his hands together in a way that makes me think that he's letting me in on a secret joke. But the guy is dead serious about his mud shafts. He is not playing around when it comes to beautifying the world's fart funnels, not even a little bit. "Oh, my friend. The rectum is a delicate flower that must be pruned, so to speak. It may grow in feces, but it is still a flower, just the same. With many years of training and experience, I've perfected the art of creating the ideal anus."

I catch our server approaching out the corner of my eye, along with her stunned expression. She's just about to make a run for it when Joshua looks up to flag her down.

"Ah yes, waitress. We'd like to order." He doesn't wait for response, just starts prattling off a bunch of random dishes without any say from the other two people at the table. "And a kale salad for the lady, dressing on the side, no seeds, light on the shaved parmesan. That'll be all."

I look down at the menu sitting before me. I haven't been able to go over it yet, but I'm pretty sure kale salad would not be Fiona's first choice. "Fi, they have those Korean Kalbi short ribs you love. You should get them."

Fiona looks at me with apology in her eyes and opens her mouth to answer when Joshua leans over to kiss the side of her face. "Ah, Fiona and her meat. I've told her about the long lasting effects of fatty red meat on the colon, and ultimately the anus. She'll have the kale salad tonight. Fiber is your friend, right, love?"

Fiona clears her throat and looks down, defeated, yet she

smiles out of embarrassment. I mean we're talking about her bowel movements, for fuck's sake! Not to mention, Dr. Down Under just 1950'd her into submission like a petulant child. Shit, I'm embarrassed for her. And two seconds away from kicking Joshua's perfectly bleached and tightened ass.

"No worries, Auggie. This place is known for their exquisite tapas. I've taken the liberty of ordering all their tastiest dishes so we could have a taste of everything. I hope you don't mind. And of course, it's my treat."

I'm amazed I can even speak through the tightness in my jaw. "It's August."

"What?"

"My name. It's August."

"Oh. Sure it is, champ. Or would Rhys suit you better?"

"No, it would not. She calls me Rhys," I say, tipping my head toward a red-faced Fiona. "Her and only her. You can call me August."

We've somehow made it unscathed through half a dozen small plates when Fi excuses herself to the ladies room. That's when I really get a good look at her. Her tight attire is unlike anything I've ever seen her wear, considering she prefers loose layers, long cardigans and boots. Her hair has been professionally styled, and I think she's added a few golden blonde streaks to her brown mane. She's different, yes, but she's also absolutely stunning. And something within me has to tell her so.

"You look…lovely, Fiona," I say on a breath of undefined emotion.

"That she is," Joshua chimes in. "Love, turn around so I can get a better look at you."

Her cheeks red, Fiona slowly pirouettes, careful not to stumble on her heels. I've never seen her dressed up like this. I've never really looked at her like this. And I damn sure have never been so aware of her body like this.

"Beautiful, love. But what happened to the red dress?"

Fiona stops mid-twirl and nervously plays with an errant curl. "Oh. I thought I'd wear this one tonight."

Joshua makes a tsking sound and shakes head. "I picked out the red one specifically for this night. Of course, you are gorgeous in anything you wear, but you would have stopped traffic in that red one." He turns to me, his perfectly groomed brows jumping conspiratorially. "There is a certain sensual danger about a woman in a red dress, don't you agree, August?"

I don't answer. I just stare at him, mentally picturing what a broken nose would do for his business. Or maybe some missing teeth would be better. He doesn't seem to notice. He turns back to Fiona and very literally shoos her away with a kiss.

This is my chance. With Fiona gone, I can really give Dr. Dunghole a piece of my mind, followed by some very serious threats of bodily harm. And if that doesn't work, I'll do what I'm best at. I'll lie. Joshua will be outraged, which will lead to his hasty departure, Fiona will return none-the-wiser, I'll tell her that he's just come down with a retched case of the BGs or crabs...whatever, then we'll blow this popsicle stand, grab a couple orders of Pho from our favorite spot, and get home in time to watch *Shark Tank*.

However, I'm not even able to put my plan into action when a busty blonde wearing nothing more than a crimson scarf struts up to our table and damn near aligns her massive tits with Joshua's face.

"Dr. King! I thought that was you!" she squeals, bouncing those jugs, which coincidentally, don't move an inch.

"Lisa! Great to see you, love!" He quickly jumps to his feet to greet the eager woman with a peck on the cheek. Hmmmm. He must be known for his bedside manner.

"I was just telling my friend about you. She has a photo shoot next month and I told her she *has* to come see you ASAP," she grins, waving towards the bar. And sure enough, an equally busty, long-legged blonde waves back.

"Is that so? Have her call Sue first thing Monday morning. I'm sure I can sneak her in," he replies with a wink.

"You're the best, Dr. King!" she trills, bouncing again. Only when one of her giant titties nearly knocks my drink from my hand does she notice me. "Oh? Is this your friend?" She smiles at me like it's cheat day and I'm a triple bacon cheeseburger with a side of curly fries. I may not be as flashy as Señor Choco Taco, but I have a face that women like.

"Lisa, this is August. He's a very talented writer, or so I've heard. He even wrote a book called *Tears of Sand*."

"*Tears of Glass*," I retort, shaking her offered hand. She lets it linger in mine for just a second longer than what would be deemed cordial.

"Really? So, what's that about? Is it like *Fifty Shades of Grey?*"

And there it is. Lisa should just pick up the shrimp fork used to eat the overpriced miso-sriracha glazed tiger prawns and stab me in the eye now. If I had a dime for every time I've been asked that, I'd probably be able to pay for this stupid fucking meal.

"No. It's nothing like *Fifty Shades,*" I try to say as politely as I can muster.

"Oh. Well, that's too bad. It's my favorite book, like, ever. Christian is *sooo* hot." She looks back at her friend who is staring at our table intently. "Anyway, my girlfriend, Lauren, and I were just about to grab a table. Maybe we could share one?" She looks at Joshua, then back to me, as if she can't decide which treat to choose at the candy shop. In the end, her gaze rests on Joshua.

"No can do, love. Maybe another time." He cushions the blow of rejection with a chaste kiss on the cheek, compliments her outfit, then reminds her to tell her friend to call his office. It's a successful brush-off, I'll give him that, but it's still not the same as letting this chick know that he's got a girlfriend who is probably freaking out right this fucking minute as she tries to figure out how to turn the goddamn faucet on in the space shuttle-chic bathroom.

"Clients," Joshua chuckles once Lisa returns to her friend at the bar, empty-handed. "She's been in for different procedures—but she's a big fan of our anal steaming, and our Right and Tight package. You'd like her. She's fun."

Now why did that just sound like, *Lisa has an ass that won't quit and is totally bangable. Trust me. I know.*

Fiona approaches just in time to save me from the shit show disguised as dinner, her face flush and her hair tousled.

"You okay, love? You were in there for a while," Joshua greets her, kissing her forehead.

Fiona nods. "Couldn't figure out how to turn the darn knob at the sink. Why do they make it so complicated? Not everything needs to be artistic and modern. I was starting to think only a Divergent could turn that thing on."

And there you have it, folks. The reason why Fiona Shaw is my best friend. And why she's too damn good for Joshua King, who doesn't have a goddamn clue what we're laughing about.

SHE WAS ON HER KNEES, *begging for reprieve. Whimpering her lust in short, panicked breaths. Ice blonde hair fell into her eyes, but she didn't dare brush it away. He did it for her. He did everything…for her.*

"Please, sir," she cried. "Please don't make me suffer any longer. I need you."

"No." His voice was cold. "You need to be obedient. Did I tell you to touch yourself?"

She shuddered in defeat. "No, sir."

"And did I tell you to entice him? Into tempting him with your body? Did I tell you to let him fuck you?"

"No, sir."

"You enjoyed it, didn't you? Letting him taste your defiance. You screamed when he pumped your pretty little cunt

with his betrayal."

Eh. Cunt. Now there's a tricky four-letter word. Too much? I look over at Bartleby, who is doing what he does best—taking up space and sleeping. He's no help at all.

"*...when he pumped your pretty little pussy with his betrayal.*"

"*No!*" *she cried out.* "*I wanted you! I always want you!*"

"*Lies! You came for him. You let him steal the orgasm reserved for me. Didn't you? Tell me you didn't cover his cock with your sweet nectar.*"

Blech. Well, there goes my breakfast. Why does it have to be sweet nectar? I have yet to have a woman that tastes like fresh-squeezed peaches.

"*I'm so sorry, sir. I want you. I want only you inside me.*"

"*You wound me with your deceit, my love. It pains me to do so, but you must be punished for your insolence.*"

"*No.*"

"*Yes.*"

"*Yes.*"

On his command, she climbed to her feet and he led her to the edge of the massive four-poster bed. She bent at the waist and buried her head in a pillow, offering the sacrifice of her smooth, steamed, bleached ass.

The fuck?

I read over my words. Did I really just describe an ass as *steamed* and *bleached?*

Oh, *hell* no.

I hit delete and try again, but I just can't get the words—the image—out of my head. Joshua has permanently skewed my view of the female backside. I've never considered myself an ass man, but shit, I've been known to perform a pretty badass rendition of *Baby Got Back* in my day. Sir Mix A Lot liked 'em round and juicy, not bleached and steamed like dry cleaning.

I rub my tired eyes and shut down the mean machine after saving my work, as awful as it may be. I've been going pretty hard all day in an attempt to cleanse my mind of that atrocious dinner last night. Joshua was everything I expected him to be—handsome, charming, stylish, and a complete douche. It's not even that he's a controlling, self-absorbed douche that makes him intolerable. It's the fact that he's clueless…totally oblivious to his douchiness. He's the type of man that doesn't see anything or anyone outside of his little realm of excellence. If you don't meet his standards, well, you just don't exist. And I can see that he's already begun to mold Fiona into his little prototype of perfection. The dress, the makeup, the hair. Shit, he's even making her eat kale! What kind of cruel and unusual punishment is that?

And I really should be pissed at Fi for even going along with his evil regime. I mean, yeah, I know her biological clock is a ticking time bomb, and she's practically had her wedding planned since she was six years old. But that doesn't mean she needs to cling to the first fucker with a decent head of hair and a good orthodontist.

Besides. She has *me*.

She's always had me.

"What do you think, Bart?" I ask the lazing cat aloud, currently perched on a stack of notebook paper on his side of the desk. He barely even flinches in my direction but his ears perk. "Should we call Fi and tell her what a giant, massive, catastrophic asshat her boyfriend is?"

Bartleby finally spares me a glance, his jade-flecked eyes slanted with the remnants of slumber, and answers with a purr before going back to sleep.

"She thinks she's in love with him, you know. She actually thinks this Dr. Dingleberry is the one. Like, I can see that shit in her eyes when she talks about him, as if he walks on water and turns Arbor Mist into a 2010 Grand Vin de Château Latour. Seriously, who does he think he is? With that stupid hair and those stupid dimples and that stupid fucking accent."

At that, Bartleby pulls an Exorcist, his head turning 180 degrees to give me the side eye.

"Yeah, I said it. He's stupid. *Stoooopid.* About as stupid as I feel talking to an overweight furball that licks his own ass."

Shit. I'm really losing it.

I need some air. I need some perspective. And as much as I hate to admit it, I need Fi.

Half an hour later, I am speeding down 1st on my Harley Davidson FXS Low Rider. Now I know what you're thinking—how very cliché of me to be a writer, or an artist in general, who rides a motorcycle. To be fair, it's a classic, and it belonged to my grandfather. So to not accept it would be a slap in the face to him—and all mankind—really. I've spent a small fortune keeping it in its original condition, probably way more than it's worth. But you can't put a price on nostalgia. And let's face it… it's pretty badass.

When I arrive at Durkin's, the Speakeasy-style joint aptly housed across the street from both our favorite bistro and bookstore, Fiona isn't there. I shouldn't care—I'm often late because...well, punctuality isn't my strong suit—but this is the second time, and Fi is that annoying person who always shows up five minutes early. I don't want to speculate, but there has to be a reason behind it.

I order an Old Fashioned from the hipster-stache'd bartender and settle into a booth. I haven't eaten yet, so I put in an order of Poutine, which is the Canadian version of Disco fries. Fi loves their Poutine. When we first discovered this place, she made me come here at least twice a week for them.

"Sorry!" she bristles, sliding into the booth beside me. When she leans over to kiss my cheek, I notice two things. One, she smells good. Not that that's a bad thing. But I can tell she's freshly showered and perfumed. The good shit too. Not the body spray from Victoria's Secret that litters her bathroom vanity.

Two, she's wearing a dress and heels. And not just any heels either. Fire engine red "Fuck Me" heels that are never meant to be removed when the actual fucking is occurring. I should know. Chapter 12 of *House of Noire* by Hope Hughes. The clothes come off but the shoes stay on.

"Interesting choice of attire for little old me, Fi. You really shouldn't have."

She smiles sheepishly. "I'm meeting Joshua a little later."

"Oh?" I try not to sound affronted. I really do. Come on, it's Saturday night. *Of course* she has plans. What young, attractive person doesn't?

Ding ding ding!

"About Joshua..." I take a sip of my drink while Fi orders a glass of wine from a passing server.

"Oh no. It was only a matter of time, wasn't it? I couldn't

escape this. Go ahead, August…lay it on me."

"Shall I start with the most obvious omission?"

"And that is?"

"Oh, I don't know. Maybe the fact that you failed to tell me he was a fucking Hemsworth!"

"A whaaa?"

"A Hemsworth! Australian. Alarmingly pretty. Looks kinda dumb…but isn't." I tack on that last part solely for her benefit.

"I told you he was from Australia."

"Yeah, but not *that* side of Australia!"

"What do you mean *that* side of Australia? Sydney?"

"Um, no. The small island off the coast where they genetically mutate their people to make us red-bloodied Americans look like Sloth from *The Goonies*."

"Oh, hush." She waves me off, but she's smiling, a rosy blush painting her cheeks. She knows Joshua is exactly that superhuman in the looks department, and maybe part of her feels flattered to be with him. I get it—in a world of plastic and pretention, Fiona's girl-next-door beauty isn't really appreciated. It was what set her apart in college. She would rather swath her slight frame in oversized sweaters and ankle boots than those teeny tiny booty shorts with the words *Juicy* written on the butt that girls in her dorm were partial to. And that's exactly what drew me to her all those years ago.

The first thing that gave me pause was her music. It was the era of 50 Cent when he was only a nickel, Bootylicious Beyoncé, and the Federline decline of Britney Spears, and she was listening to The Fray circa Grey's Anatomy. I only knew this tidbit of pop culture because Fiona's roommate,

Tami, was my current flavor of the week, and she was heavily into some guy named McDreamy. As luck would have it, my flavor of the week turned into my taste of the month, so I got to see Fiona more often than not. She was always the same—college sweatshirt three sizes too big, melancholy music, and nose stuck in a book. Not the usual required reading either. Most times it was cheesy romance novels, but sometimes she'd surprise me with books I had read, or would read. *Good* books. Books that made me want to know more about the girl who coveted them so passionately.

I only knew her name was Fiona because her roommate mentioned her once in a while. I never saw her at parties. I never heard any Neanderthal-esque locker room talk about her. And she never seemed to notice me. Which was odd. Because I *was* noticed, especially by the opposite sex. Even when I didn't want to be.

The first time I spoke to her, I'd decided she was deaf. I was waiting on Tami to get done with her study group down the hall so we could go on our date (which really meant pizza and cheap beer in my room followed by sex) and I had grown tired of watching the top of her head as she read. About as tired as I'd grown from listening to some guy whine on about saving a life. I asked her what she was reading. And I got… nothing. I cleared my throat and tried again, earning the same response. I was just about to chalk it up as an auditory dysfunction on her part when she looked up at me with tear-glazed eyes narrowed in annoyance.

"I'm pretty sure you can read. So why don't you do us both a favor and stop trying to act like you're actually interested."

Well…damn.

"I, uh, I am interested," I stammered.

"Really." She gave me a look that was the equivalent of calling bullshit.

"I am. I'm an English major with a minor in Creative Writing. It's my duty to know these things."

"Your duty?" She rolled her eyes. "Oh, please, spare me the whole valiant spiel about saving the world one passé trope at a time. I know you're an English major. We share most of the same classes."

"Oh. Yeah. I knew that." I did not know that.

"Oh really? Well, you've been boning my roommate for a few weeks now. Why haven't you said hi in—oh, I don't know—one of the half dozen times we cross paths on campus daily? But I guess when you're so grossly self-absorbed, it's hard to notice anyone that isn't you *or* presently screwing you."

I had no words. I had just spent my afternoon memorizing every honored Charles Dickens quote in existence for the Brit Lit Nazi, yet I had zero words to help me right at that second. The smug look on Fiona's face wasn't helping either.

"Ok. Fine," I said, admitting defeat. "But it's not like you were so eager to speak to me between trying to rewrite *The Virgin Suicides*."

"*Excuse* me?" She closed the book and let it slip off her lap.

"How is anyone supposed to talk to you when you hide in clothing that you obviously purchased at Big and Tall, and you play music that makes anyone within ten feet spontaneously menstruate?"

"Oh, you," she spits, shaking her head in disgust. "You… you…stupid jerk butt."

I died laughing. Like, seriously died right there on the squeaky-as-fuck twin bed situated right across from this mousey, brown-eyed girl who was the most intriguing person I had come across all day.

"Did you just say…?" Still dying. "I could have sworn we were in college, away from Mom and Dad. You do know it's okay to say bad words, right? No one is going to take away dessert for a week."

"Ha ha. I know where I am. But I'd rather not stoop to your level of fatuity. If one cannot express himself in a way that does not involve expletives, surely it is a reflection of his intelligence…or lack thereof."

"Or surely it just really gets his fucking point across."

We sat in the tiny dorm room, lit only by the desk lamp she used for reading, staring each other down. Silently trying to outwit the other until they broke.

I was the one to break.

"So… what are you reading?"

Fiona picked up her paperback from the ragged quilt that covered her sweatpants-swathed legs and opened it, flipping to find her lost page. "*Twilight.* Vampire falls in love with a fragile human. I'd tell you how it ends but you just interrupted me as it was getting to the good part."

"Oh good God. Tell me you're not into *those* books."

"Those books?" she said without looking up from her page. "You mean, entertaining? Inspiring? Bestselling?"

"I mean, corny romance drivel. A few days ago, you were reading *Anna Karenina.*"

She shrugged. "For the fourth time. I like to mix it up."

And that was how August and Fiona became Rhys and Fi.

Over the next twenty minutes, I found myself wanting to know everything about her. I asked her what she would consider the best books of all time, and I told her mine. She told me how she had spent her summers interning at a small press magazine solely centered on romance books. She wanted to be immersed in the culture as much as possible, even if it meant she didn't write. I told her I wanted to be the next great novelist, and there was nothing I could do on God's green earth *but* write.

When Tami finally arrived, I didn't want to leave. But not because I was hoping to get lucky with Fiona. I already had. I had found someone who *got* me. In this big, wide, lonely world, I had found my soul mate.

And now, as I look at this beautiful, bronze-cheeked being in a dress and heels that could inspire most men's dirtiest fantasies, I'm wondering what happened to that cute girl that would steal my sweatshirts and talk to me for hours about the lack of real courtship in modern books. The girl who would read with tears streaming down her face and make playlists for her favorite novels. The girl who fell so deeply in love with fairytales that she began to live her life on those pages.

Heartbreak after heartbreak with guys that could never measure up to her favorite literary heroes, and she had found the one person to make her live outside the pages. Yet, that person was not the hero of her story. He was the villain. She just didn't see it yet.

A server comes over with a heaping plate of Poutine and

Fiona's wine, breaking me from my reverie. I slide the plate over to her before taking any for myself.

"No, thanks."

"Why not? You love these things."

"I had a salad a little bit ago. I'm ok. And honestly, you probably shouldn't eat that stuff either. It's horrible on your digestive tract."

I grab a few fresh, crispy fries smothered in gravy and cheese curds and haughtily stuff them in my mouth. "You were saying?" I mumble around the scorching hot potatoes.

Fiona rolls her eyes and takes a sip of wine. "Your colon, not mine."

"Oh! Speaking of… how in the hell did you fail to mention Josh's specialty? Anal Rejuvenation? Holy shit, Fi, how could you leave something like that out?"

She heaves a sigh and looks down at her watch. "Because I know you. I would have never heard the end of it, and you would have teased me until I broke up with him and/or you put it in a book. It's really not a big deal."

"Not a big deal? The man plays with asses all day. Fi, at dinner, he described the butthole as a beautiful flower. No bullshit. A flower in shit."

"Can we not do this right now? I really don't need the visual, tonight of all nights."

That's when I notice that her wine is gone, and she's signaled for another.

"Something's wrong."

"No, nothing's wrong," she shakes her head. "Tonight is just…special."

"Special as in meet-the-parents or special as in wine-dine-and-69?"

"Special as in the 3 month anniversary of the first time we…*did it*."

I lift a brow. "Is that a thing? That people actually celebrate?"

"Apparently so. Joshua is getting a room at the Grand."

"Oh," I bristle. "Swanky. So what are you two gonna do? Reenact the first time? Ooooh, did he make a sex mixtape? Does he want you freshly shaven or would he like to scalp you once you get there?"

"Can you be serious for one second, please?"

"I am being serious," I insist. "Come on, tell me what you have planned tonight."

"I don't know."

"So it's a surprise?"

"Yes. No." She heaves out a heavy sigh, releasing her anxiety into a fresh glass of Pinot. "I don't know. He's so…experienced. And don't get me wrong; I've had my fair share of lovers. But being with Joshua kinda intimidates me."

That gets my attention. "Intimidates you? You think it's intentional?" I know some twisted fuckers—hell, it's kinda my job to know what's going down in the world of kink. If Joshua is into some BDSM shit, I can't say I'd be cool with it. In fact, I'd be downright pissed and I wouldn't hesitate to tell him so.

"I don't think he does. It's just… in person, he's this great, charismatic guy. He's gentle and sweet with me, and treats me like a princess. He even likes to dress me. But in bed… I feel like he takes on this persona. Like he's a stranger, and I'm nothing more than some slut on the street. And he keeps…

encouraging me to try things that I wouldn't normally do."

"He's not forcing you to do anything, is he?" I ask, my voice dark and gravely with the threat of violence.

"No, no. Nothing like that. He's just so *eager* to get me to open up. And I'm trying, I swear. I just feel like I'm doing it wrong." She downs her wine in three big gulps then checks the time again, sighing. "I better go. Joshua likes it when I'm punctual."

"Fuck Joshua." There. I finally said it. And it felt fucking fantastic. "We still need to talk about this. You shouldn't be made to feel inferior in anyway, especially in bed."

"August, can we please not do this now?" she rage-whispers, her gaze darting everywhere but on me. "I should have never said anything. It's nothing but my own insecurity."

"Insecurity that *he's* projecting on *you.* Seriously, Fi, fuck him. No decent guy should make a woman feel like no more than a blow up doll provided to fulfill all his dirty fantasies."

"Well, isn't that how you make all *your* dates feel? Like they're only good for one thing, and one thing only in your little bubble of detachment?"

She says it without blinking...without feeling...as if she's merely stating a fact, not trying to cut me to the bone. Yet, as I bleed out in a pool of my own denial, I know she's absolutely right.

I am that guy. That guy that keeps every woman at a distance, unless I'm inside of her. Or unless that woman is Fiona.

"Look, I gotta go. My Uber will be here any second. Let's just forget this whole conversation and talk tomorrow," she relents, slapping a twenty on the table and sliding out of the booth. And I'm going to let her. I'm going to let her walk out of here with my blood on her hands. And I'm going to pretend like what she said didn't matter…didn't sting. And a few days, weeks, months from now when the distance has grown so vast between us that I can't even remember the sound of her laughter, I'll tell myself that we just grew apart, like all people do.

I'm going to let Fiona chase her HEA. Even if that means I have to play the villain.

The fries go virtually uneaten and I order another drink, then another. I kill time by scrolling through my messages, searching for something. Something to ease the burn of Fi's words.

Within twenty minutes, I have company.

Within an hour, we're at her place.

I may be cold. I may be detached. But at least I'm honest.

No, I'm not even that.

It's half past eight, and under normal circumstances, I would be naked by now. But with any new "friend" you have to keep up with certain expectations until you learn each other's rhythm. And since I was raised to have some modicum of decency, I try to go along with the usual pretenses that come with any new "friendship."

Would you like to come up for coffee? How about a night-cap? A little Netflix and Chill?

Of course, there's usually never any coffee or Netflix, but somehow I find myself sipping French Roast and chatting about everything under the sun while episodes of The Office play in the background. And all I can think about is how I left things with Fiona. Or should I say, how she left things with me.

"Okay, dude. Spill it," April says, finally exasperated with my less-than-stellar conversational offerings.

"Huh?"

"You've been preoccupied all evening. Wanna talk about it? I promise you, I'm not trying to pry. Just putting the offer out there."

I look at her lovely face, and force myself to remember how it contorted in overwhelming bliss when I slid inside her. So full of expression. She wasn't loud, but she didn't have to be. It was written all over her face. And now that same face is painted with concern and a little bit of skepticism.

"I'm ok," I say, sipping my brew. "Just a spat with a friend."

"Oh. Sorry to hear that."

"Can I ask you something?" I don't know where the question comes from, and I don't wait for a response before I'm unloading all my crap onto her black Ikea coffee table. "If your best friend that you had known for years started dating someone that was all wrong for them in every way, even though they looked like the epitome of perfection and made your friend happy, would you interfere? Would you do everything in your power to break them up? Or would you step back and let things play out on their own, even at the risk of your friend getting hurt?"

April blinks, startled by my candor. She didn't expect me to actually tell her what was bothering me any more than I expected to spew my inner unrest.

I put down my mug, and prepare to make a mad dash for the door before I blow any more truth chunks. "I'm sorry, I shouldn't have—"

"No, no. It's fine. I'm glad you did. And you're right to

be concerned about your friend's happiness. That just proves that you care, even if it makes you unpopular."

"So you would tell the friend that they're making a huge mistake, right?"

She shrugs a shoulder, causing one side of her black tunic to slide down her arm. "Maybe not in those words, but I would definitely express my reservations. Your friend may not want to hear it, but you'd never be able to rest knowing that you could potentially stop them from making a huge mistake."

"That's how I feel. Like…my friend is going too fast and changing the person that they are for this…this shiny new toy that may look enticing on the outside, but is just rotten to the core."

April nods thoughtfully, listening to me go in circles about my Fiona crisis. After digesting my muddled diatribe, she looks up from her cold cup of coffee and asks me the million-dollar question that's undoubtedly been souring her tongue for the last several minutes.

"And this friend… are you in love with her?"

I knew it was coming, yet it stuns me just the same, instantly sobering me. "Me? In love with…"

"It's just the way that you talk about your…. friend… I know it's a woman. And you're so passionate and caring, and I can see the way you react just talking about—"

"I'm not in love with Fiona. That's preposterous. We're just friends. Always have been, always will be."

"Oh, is that right?"

"Absolutely. She's not someone I would go for. She's not even my type." That confession seems to ease her mind a bit, and I take it a step further, remembering tonight's task at hand. "April, Fiona and I are strictly platonic. If I were in love with her, why would I be wasting my time here with you? If I wanted to be with her, wouldn't I be sitting on *her* couch, drinking *her* coffee, wondering if *her* lips are as sweet as the last time I tasted them? Hoping *she* would let me help her out of her clothes so I could trace her tan lines with my tongue? And longing to feel *her* long, silky legs tighten around my waist and *her* fingers running up and down my back?"

April can't even respond, and I don't need her to. Her hungry expression is saying it all.

I'm a man of my word, and I do everything I promised to Fiona—I mean, April. April. Shit.

I'm doing everything I described to *April* and more. And by more, I mean, I am trying to overcompensate for the fact that I can't seem to stop thinking about Fiona, with the hope that submerging myself in sex will cleanse the impure thoughts I'm having about my best friend. But even as I part April's thighs and taste her, all I can think about is the way Fiona calls her pussy her love biscuit. And when I suck April's pert, pink nipples, I'm reminded of the way Fiona looked in that black dress last night. Even when I sink every inch of myself inside her, I can't feel April. I can only imagine Fi looking up at me with devastating ecstasy in her eyes.

My cell sounds from my rumpled jeans on the floor, and I nearly jump out of April like her vag is on fire. I'm so frazzled and distracted that I don't even check who it is.

"Hello?"

There's sniffling on the other line before a meek voice

plummets me back into my biggest fear. “Rhys?”

“Fi. Are you ok?”

She tries to say yes, but her voice cracks, breaking into a sob. “Something horrible,” and “It’s over,” are all I can make out.

“Fi, what’s wrong? Tell me what happened,” I bark out, not meaning to scare her, but growing more and more worried with every second that ticks by without me with her, knowing for certain she’s safe. “Are you hurt?”

“No,” she croaks, allowing me to find a tiny speck of comfort. It’s still not enough.

“Fi, I need to know you’re ok. Where are you?”

“Home.” Her voice is just a hoarse whisper.

“Stay put. I’m on my way.”

Only when I’ve hung up do I spare a glance in April’s direction. Her expression is about as limp as my cock.

“I’m sorry, I have to…”

“Yes, go. Whatever you need,” she nods, sitting up and covering herself with a blanket.

I grab my clothes and make a turn for the bathroom, when a foreign emotion strikes me just before I hit the doorjamb. I turn to her, feeling the need to say…something. To explain. To apologize. To just say *something.*

“It’s not what…” I don’t know if it’s what I mean to say, but it’s all I can manage. I’m a mess. “I didn’t mean…”

“Go to her. She needs you right now.” Her words are full of understanding and compassion, but the look on her face is all hurt and disappointment. Both of which I’ve caused. I just don’t have it in me to make it right.

I wash up in the bathroom as quickly as possible before racing into the night in search of clarity. Luckily, Fiona's apartment isn't far and cops are more heavily scattered around the bar district, so I'm able to make it there within minutes. I don't even remember the ride or the sting of the crisp air whipping my face. All I can imagine, as I take the stairs up to her apartment two at a time, is her tear-streaked cheeks, and all I can feel is the uncertainty that has constantly pummeled me in my gut all evening.

With my fist raised to strike, I pause at her door, forcing my brain to still enough to gain an ounce of perspective. What does this mean? If things are truly over between her and Joshua, do we just go back to how things were before? I mean, that would make sense, right? It's not like she is thinking of me the way I'm thinking of her. And all those insane thoughts of her, existing in spaces where someone else already exists, could all be just a fluke. They could very likely dissipate the moment I see her.

I expected tears, red cheeks and smeared mascara. What I don't expect to find is Fiona in an oversized sleep tee and knee high socks, holding a half empty bottle of wine.

"Oh, Rhys. Thank God you're here," she cries, pulling me into her apartment as if she's frightened of the world outside her window.

"What's going on, Fi?" I grasp her shoulders, searching her for any signs of harm. Her eyes are puffy and red, and her smudged makeup and wet hair are a mess. But other than that, she seems fine. Which leads me to believe that whatever trauma she suffered tonight has left its scars internally.

She twists from my grip and buries her face in her palm. "It was awful, Rhys. Mortifying! My life is officially over." She lifts her head only to take a swig of Pinot straight from the tap.

"Stop being melodramatic and tell me what happened," I demand as gently as I can possibly muster whilst wrestling the bottle from her clutches. Fi is a lightweight. In college, she used to think Malibu and pineapple was a stiff drink.

"I can't! I can't even say it!" More tears. A good amount of snot.

"Fi, there's nothing you can't tell me. You know that. Come on, have a seat and catch your breath."

I lead her to the sofa and cover her with her favorite quilt. She's had it since she was a kid and refuses to let it go, no matter how many patches she's had to mend. A few feet to the left and I'm in her tiny kitchen, which is no more than three feet of counter space, a refrigerator, a sink and a range. The rest of the wine goes into a glass for her and a few fingers of Macallan for me from my stash. And a box of tissues for the situation under her nose.

"Start from the beginning. I promise you it's not as bad as you think," I say handing her the glass.

"It's worse. It is absolutely the worst thing that could ever happen to me…to Joshua. Oh my God, Rhys! You should have seen his face! He will never speak to me again. And if this gets out, my reputation is ruined." She looks around at her tiny shoebox apartment with alarm in her eyes. "I'll have to move! Where will I go? How will I find a job on such short notice?"

"Calm down, Fi." I swap out her Barefoot Bubbly and replace it with my glass. She downs it like it's iced tea and not 25-year-old scotch.

“I ruined everything, Rhys,” she croaks through the sear in her throat. “It’s over.”

“It’s not over yet,” I assure her, looking down at my sad, empty glass. “Tell me the story, and maybe we can try to fix it.” Fix it. Yeah, let me get right on that.

“I don’t know, Rhys,” she shakes her head before looking up at me with brown eyes drowning in tears. “Just promise me, that no matter what, you won’t look at me differently. Please, don’t let anything I say change the way you feel about me.”

I gaze back, unblinking, my face of mask of my denial. Trying desperately to hide the fact that it’s already too late. “I won’t.”

"I'm nervous when I arrive, and he can tell. It's as if my fear arouses him. He invites me in, greeting me with a kiss that steals the very breath from my lungs. He tastes like alcohol. Maybe he's not the only one that's nervous. Or maybe he knows that we'll both need a little help for what we have planned. Or should I say, what he has planned for me."

"And that is?" I call out, grabbing my bottle of Macallan from the kitchen cabinet. I re-fill and settle in on the couch next to Fi, who is drawing comfort from her old quilt.

"I'm getting there. Don't interrupt. This is hard enough for me to even recount, you know. And this stays between us. No new material for your journal."

"It's not a journal, it's a notebook. But whatever. Continue."

"He pours me a drink—something dark and strong, but I barely taste it. I'm afraid to admit to him that my anxiety is bordering on fear. He's so sexy and confident and daring...I want to be all of those things for him too. So I force my inhibitions aside, take a deep breath, and undress for him without saying a word. He wants tonight to be special; I'll give him special. He wants me to be salacious; I'll give him that too."

"The surprise striptease. Nice touch," I force myself to say in the name of friendship.

She cracks a tiny grin. "Thought you might like that. Anyway...

"He watches me with a ravenous glare, his eyes probing my body like a starving lion. Only when I stand before him wearing only my shoes does he make his way to me, crossing the room in just a few eager strides. Every step brings me closer to my fate, and while I am a willing sacrifice, I can't ignore the roiling of nerves in my gut. I think to stop his advance—or at least make him slow down—but then I am in his arms, and his lips are on mine, and I am lost to him. He completely disarms me, and I let him. I want him to take it all away—all the doubt, all the fear. I want to live his world, if only for this moment. Even at the expense of my better judgment."

"Hmph," I snort, taking a sip of scotch to mask the taste of bile in my mouth. "Mighty poetic of you."

"I try. But it's true. I allowed him to push my boundaries, because being loved by him is all I've ever wanted. It's the type of love I've dreamed about since I was a little girl, watching my mom throw herself at scumbag boyfriend after scumbag boyfriend. It's what I wished to have for my future when my deadbeat dad left us in his past like we never existed."

I put down my glass and turn to face her, cupping her still-damp cheeks in my palms. "Fi, you can't settle for a man because you're still searching for the love your asshole sperm donor was incapable of giving you. We've talked about this."

"I'm not settling," she insists, pulling away. "I feel like Joshua was the one who was settling…for me."

"You're not going to say shit like that when I'm around," I deadpan, meaning every bit of it.

"It's true, Rhys. And once I tell you what happened between us, you'll understand."

"Fine. But I'm telling you right now—"

"Just listen, ok?"

I gesture for her to continue before refilling my glass. If she's going to go down this road and expect me to keep my opinions—no, *facts*—to myself, I'll need all the help I can get.

"*We kiss. We touch. I undress him. He lays me on the bed. We're hungry for each other like it's the first time, even though in the back of my mind I'm dreading what's next. But a part of me craves the thrill of him needing me in every way possible. He tells me he'll be right back, and that feeling in my gut returns…the anxiety, the uncertainty, the anticipation. But I don't have a chance to doubt myself any longer. He's back within a few moments, and the lust in his eyes isn't the only thing that tells me he's ready. He positions me onto my knees, then opens the small tube of gel in his palm…*"

"Wait a minute. Wait a fucking minute. You mean to tell me that all of this is about anal? You had me abandon a naked woman—mid-hump mind you—because you decided to give it up to the Booty Bandit? Holy shit, Fi! Why didn't you say so?"

"It's not just that! Plus, I had never done that...with *anyone* ever! I was scared, Rhys. And a part of me was kinda ashamed too."

"It's anal. Anal, Fi. What did you expect? The dude is ass obsessed. You don't become a butcher unless you love meat."

"I know that, and I know I agreed to it, but..." Flustered, she downs the wine in her glass and holds it out to me for a refill. She's already killed the entire bottle, so I hand her my scotch. There goes another $50 shot. "You don't understand. You're confident and gorgeous and women flock to you like you have a golden penis. You don't ever have to compromise to get what you want. And you're like Joshua."

"I am *nothing* like Joshua." My jaw is clenched so tight that it feels like my teeth may shatter.

"I mean, you're experienced. You've done it all...seen it all. And you're not searching for anything because you already have everything."

She's wrong, but I don't have the words or the heart to tell her so. I don't have everything.

"Look, it wasn't even the anal thing that freaked me out. It was..."

"Just tell me. Tell me what has you so mortified. Come on." I wrap my arm around her shoulder and she burrows her face into my chest. I know talking about sex skeevs her out, and there's no way she can look at me while recounting her dirty little tryst.

"It burns at first, but he knows what he's doing. He goes slowly, gently. He tells me it will feel good soon, but it doesn't, even after several minutes. I know something is wrong. I know

it's not supposed to be like this. And then I feel it."

"Feel what? Is he pierced or something? Does he have a double dick? That's a thing, you know."

Fi soldiers on, despite my questions.

"I try to bear down, try to clench as hard as I can. I can feel it coming, but I'm too horrified to tell him to stop. He's close... so close. But so am I. I can feel him throbbing with release, and all I can do is pray that it's quick. But when he thrusts in deep and hard, calling out his climax, I can't hold it anymore. And before I can stop myself and save him from the revulsion...it happens."

"What? You farted? Fi, you're not the first person to ever fart during anal. He knows that."

"No! I wish!"

"Then what?" I sit up and lift her head to face me when she doesn't answer. "Fi, tell me you didn't..."

"I did!" she sobs uncontrollably. "Oh my God! I pooped on him! With him still inside me! It was all that darn kale that had my stomach feeling funny. Do you know how much fiber is in kale? *A lot!* Oh my God. Oh my God, Rhys. It was like a chocolate fountain! It was everywhere! And Joshua... the look on his face...the horror! But that's not even the worst part. He threw up! He jumped away from me just in time to barf on the floor. I am so repulsive that I made a grown man toss his cookies all over a fancy suite at the Grand! There was poop and vomit everywhere. I tried to help him, but he told me to leave him alone and get out. I ran out of there in a bathrobe and high heels, leaving him sick and covered in excrement. I didn't even grab my dress. Don't you see? My life is ruined!"

I'm biting my cheek to keep from laughing, but it's futile. I die on the spot, eyes closed, cramped into the fetal position as I imagine the shitty situation that Fiona has laid before me. Serves Joshua right. He wanted Fi to eat kale, so she ate kale. She even shared some of it with him.

"Holy shit, Fi! Holy fucking shit!" I cackle between deep belly guffaws.

"It's not funny! It's humiliating!"

"And disgusting! Only you would shit during anal. Only you!" Tears are streaming down my face. Actual tears.

"Hahaha. I'm so glad you're amused by my misery. Happy I could entertain you while my life crumbles into ash."

"Awwww." I stop laughing long enough to sit up and pull her into my arms, placing her in the warm, safe spot between my bicep and chest. "Come on, Fi. You have to know this is hilarious. It may not seem like it now, but trust me; you'll look back and realize it. And when we're old and gray, sitting in our rocking chairs and talking about the good ol' days, we'll be able to reminisce about the day you shit on the butt doctor. You have to admit; it is rather fitting."

She shakes her head, but I can feel her smiling against my tee shirt. "God, Rhys. Why do I even try? Why do I expect to get a different outcome when I know it will all end in disaster?"

"Simple, Fi. You try. You try for something that isn't real...that doesn't exist beyond this fantasyland you've constructed in your mind. You have the heart of a heroine, but this world is full of villains where romance is tragedy and love is merely comic relief."

She heaves out a sigh that seeps into the cotton of my

shirt, warming the space encompassing my heart. "Maybe you're right. Maybe I need to stop trying."

My cheek rests against the top of her head as we sit in the silence of unspoken dreams. I hold her like she's water in my palms, and she holds me like she's trying to grasp an ocean.

"Maybe, Fi," I breathe into wisps of damp, matted hair that smell of lavender and tears. "Or maybe you're just trying for the wrong thing."

"So let me get this straight: she's a virgin who's pregnant."

"Yes," Fiona nods, grabbing another slice of pineapple and ham pizza.

"And she has two guys pining for her, one being the baby daddy."

"Correct," she answers around a mouthful of mozzarella.

"I don't get it."

"What's there not to get? She was accidentally artificially inseminated. And she's never had sex."

"I just don't get how she's still a 20-something virgin, and now a pregnant 20-something virgin. Isn't that like a free pass to just give that shit away to the highest bidder? And it's not like these dudes are bums either. How are they even cool with this? They are straight, right?"

"Totally straight. One is even married."

"Hmph," I grunt, reaching over for my third slice. "She must have a mouth like a Dyson then."

"No, no, it's not like that! She's a good girl. And she's writing a romance novel!"

I pause mid-chomp. "Hold the phone. A pregnant…virgin…*romance* novelist? What were the sitcom writers trying to do? Stack every ridiculous conflict they could pull outta their asses and try to make them cohesive? What is this… plot twist Tetris?"

"No, it's actually a good show! There's also a murderous crime lord amongst them, but they don't know who it is." Her eyes are glued to the screen, and she's on the edge of her seat.

"Oh, *of course,* there is. It wouldn't make much sense without a crime lord."

I'll give her this. After the tears and humiliation Fiona experienced this evening, tolerating a rom-com marathon on Netflix over pizza is the least I can do. Besides, the show isn't half bad. I'm not telling her that though.

The heroine has a revelation, resulting in one of the guys getting his heart broken. Fi is torn about whom she wants to win the girl—and the baby.

"You knew that was going to happen," I tell her. "They were trying to play the "just friends" card when it was evident they had chemistry. And this is why men and women cannot solely be friends."

"How can you say that?" she scoffs.

"Um, history. Experience. It's biologically impossible for two people to carry on a friendship under the current of sexual attraction. When you see the opposite sex, one question and one question only enters your mind: Would I sleep with him or her? Attraction is basal, not intellectual."

"Then how do you explain us? We're friends, and we've never hooked up."

"That's different, Fi. You thought I was repulsive and whorish when we first met, and I thought you were mute. This relationship was never built on attraction. It was built on snap judgments, sarcasm and a mutual love for books. We're the exception, not the rule."

"Not true!" she objects, throwing a stray piece of pineapple at me.

"How so?"

"Well…I was attracted to you."

A bite of pizza nearly gets lodged in my throat and kills me. "What?"

"I was attracted to you."

"You didn't even notice me. I had been damn near squatting in your dorm room for weeks, and you never even so much as looked at me."

"Rhys, it was *you* who never noticed *me*, remember? Of course, I looked at you. *Everyone* looked at you. You had this air about you—like you were already the person that you were meant to be. Everyone else was there trying to figure it out, and you already knew. You were totally nerdy in theory, but you didn't look it. You had this James Dean-meets-Jesse Eisenberg persona—sexy, dangerous and totally brilliant—and you knew it too. You knew you had the world on a string."

I shake my head in disbelief at her assessment. We've been friends for nearly a decade. Nothing like this has ever passed her lips. "Why didn't you tell me this before?"

"Why would I?" She shrugs like she hasn't just dropped a massive truth bomb on me. "You were dating…everyone. You knew what you looked like. You knew the effect you had on women. What good would it have done if I'd confessed that to you? It's not like your head could get any bigger than it already was."

"I know but…" How do I tell her that it would have changed *everything*? That Rhys and Fi could have turned out to be something completely different. But then again, what if it didn't work out? Nineteen-year-old August Rhys Calloway was an immature ass who only cared about himself and his needs. His only desire was to be worshipped for his words… praised for his poetic prose. He was in love with the idea of being great. How could he ever see past his own ego to show that same affection to her? In the way that she deserved?

"I guess you're right," I admit to us both.

"I know I am. Besides, I'm so glad I didn't. If I had, we wouldn't be here today."

"How do you know that?" I frown.

"Because I know you, Rhys. Sex is the proverbial period on relationships. Once the deed is done, you have no desire to move past the hook-up stage."

"So what are you saying, that I am cock blocking myself…with my own cock?"

"Um, yeah," she cringes. "I guess you can say that. So unless we were going to be born-again virgins, no good would have ever come from me confessing my attraction to you. Besides, once I actually spoke to you…you weren't all that cute."

"What?" I toss the rest of my slice back into the box and

tackle her onto her back. She squeals and squirms while I unleash a barrage of tickles from her arms to her belly. "Take it back or I'm going for the thighs."

"Ah! Stop August!" She giggles, trying to wrestle for control, but I easily outweigh her by eighty pounds. Still, she's a scrappy little thing. "You were not that cute! Your mouth made you a 6! Maybe even a 5!"

"Take it back right now! I'm warning you!"

"Never!"

I reach between us, aiming for the inside of her thigh, the area that makes her cry with laughter whenever I tickle her there, when I brush against soft, bare skin. She isn't wearing shorts under her sleep shirt. And my hands are between her legs. Instantly sobered, I jump from her body and completely off the couch, putting perspective and a good three feet of space between us.

"What's wrong?" she asks, sitting up. The concern painted on her face is a direct result of the shock on mine.

"Um, nothing. I, uh, need a drink." I do. I'm bugging out. We've wrestled and joked around more times than I can remember. I've seen Fi in her bra and panties, and she's seen just about every part of me. There are no secrets between us. So why do I feel like I've just stumbled upon some great mystery that completely alters *everything*?

"Pour me one too," she calls out as I stalk to the kitchen.

I scour the kitchen in search of bottled clarity in the form of cinnamon flavored whiskey. I take a shot, grasping the counter, trying to hold onto weightless reality. Trying to slow the tempo of my heartbeat that's currently serving as the foreboding music that sets up a character's impending doom.

When the confused haze of lust clears, I grab the bottle and two shot glasses. Macallan is exceptional, but this is a job for Fireball.

"What'd I miss?" I ask, aiming for blasé. I pour us each a shot, and we tip them back with ease. This is the most I've seen Fiona drink since the big breakup of 2013. I swear, she survived only on an IV drip of Pinot Grigio and chocolate, salted caramel cupcakes for a solid week.

"The baby's father wants to start things up with the virgin mom, but his ex-wife is psychotic. Love makes you crazy."

That's my cue to refill our shot glasses. "You can say that again."

Somewhere between Catholic nuns and hot lesbian sex, eyelids grow heavy with exhaustion and booze. I don't even realize I've nodded off until I jerk awake, finding Fiona curled into my chest like a sleeping kitten, her deep, slumbered breath a purr of contentment. I should go. I've slept over in the past, but now I'm not sure that's such a good idea. Not when I am relishing the feel of her warmth pressed into my skin. Not when I'm leaning in to smell her hair and kiss the lavender-scented crown of her head. Not when my arms ache at just the thought of not holding her all night.

I shift, forcing myself to do the right thing by her—by us—and it causes her to stir. She grasps my tee shirt tight, refusing to let me go. Somewhere in the distance, or maybe just in my head, The Fray's *"Never Say Never"* begins to play, and she's begging me not to let her go.

And I won't.

I don't.

"Stay," she whispers, still on the verge of oblivion. "At

least until I fall asleep."

"I will." I exhale, feeling the weight of my tangled affections fall from my shoulders. I hold her tighter, telling myself it's all an illusion. I drift away, dreaming it will become tangible.

I'M GONE BEFORE FIONA WAKES — which won't be for some time, considering she drank enough to make the Colonel proud. Back in his day, he was known to enjoy a nice scotch, which is probably where I picked up the affinity. After publishing my first romance as Hope, I splurged on a bottle of Macallan 25 and shared it with him. This was right before my grandmother passed, and the last memory of my grandfather being truly happy.

Since brunch is totally off the agenda for the day, I decide to grab some omelets from the Colonel's favorite diner and head over to the senior village—after a shower and fresh clothes, of course. I'm too wired to sleep, and considering I can't even close my eyes without imagining the silken feel of her inner thigh against my fingertips, I need a good distraction.

I expect to see the Colonel in the entertainment room watching pregame reports and working on new jokes when I arrive. He's been an early riser since as far back as I can remember, and thinks seven a.m. is sleeping in. However, when I don't see him, Nurse Tabatha informs me that he's in his apartment.

"Is he ok?" Alarm eclipses the confusion I was feeling just moments before.

"He's probably just tired, sweetie," she answers, patting me on the back. "Go on and wake him. I'm sure he'd be thrilled to see you this morning. Might lift his spirits some."

I nod and thank her, eager to see my grandfather for myself. I've never known him to be tired. And he's the hardest-working man I've ever known.

The senior village is made up of dozens of bungalow-style apartments that give their residents a sense of privacy and independence. They house patients that require more care and attention inside the main building, while the rest are scattered throughout the property. Fortunately, the facility is within walking distance from my apartment, so I'm never too far away.

The Colonel has lived in his studio apartment for nearly six years, but he hasn't decorated or made it a home. The small living room space only houses a TV stand, flat screen and a couch, and the few pictures he has up are the family ones I put up for him. He keeps his framed photo of Grandma Lee on his bedside table. Other than that and a short bookshelf filled with his favorite titles, the place is pretty bare.

"Morning, sir," I smile when he answers the door, still

wearing his flannel pajamas. It's been years since I've seen him in something other than slacks and a button-down shirt.

The Colonel grumbles a greeting and waves me in. "You're up early."

"Thought I'd bring you breakfast. Omelets and hash browns from Frank's." I conveniently leave out all questions about him sleeping in. The Colonel is not one to be interrogated. I've received the *"I'm a grown-ass man, dammit,"* response enough times in the past to know better.

He looks down at the plastic bag dangling from my grip and raises his bushy gray brows. "Egg whites?"

"No, sir. Got the good stuff," I answer, holding it up to give him a whiff.

"My boy. I'll grab the juice."

We sit at the small round table he uses for his meals. While our visits are mostly spent in the community entertainment area in the main building, the Colonel is an introvert who prefers to be alone. His only concession is when football is on. He'd much rather watch the game on the big screen so he can cheer on the 'Hawks in HD.

"Something on your mind, son?" he asks after a few silent moments of eating. The Colonel doesn't mess around. He's already halfway done with his meal.

"No," I lie, stabbing a chunk of country ham with my plastic fork. "It's nothing."

"There's an *it*. That doesn't seem like nothing to me."

The Colonel has always been incredibly perceptive, and while I can serve the world bullshit in a pretty bow, I cannot fool him. Which is why I can't tell him how I've been feeling when it comes to Fiona. Hell, I don't even think I can define it. Admitting it to him would be admitting it to myself. And honestly, I don't think there's much to admit.

"Really, there's nothing to say," I reply, shaking my head, before attacking my eggs with gusto.

I can feel his eyes probing me the way a scientist dissects his specimen. However, he doesn't pry. He knows it'll only make me withdraw even more. We're a lot alike in that respect.

"I decided to go out to LA next week," I say, trying to shift the mood.

"Oh yeah? What are you hoping they offer you?"

I shrug. "I'm not hoping for anything. I'm not moving. But I figured a free vacation wouldn't be too bad. Any thoughts about joining me?"

"Nah," he shakes his head. "Old timer like me has no business trying to keep up with models and movie stars. How about Fiona?"

"Fiona?" I don't mean for it to come out like a dirty, four-letter word, but it does. Maybe it's because she's been on my mind. Maybe it's because I don't want her to be.

"Yeah. Why don't you take her?"

"No," I shake my head, even though the idea wouldn't be half bad. Some time and space from Joshua could be what we both need. "She probably has to work, and it's too late for her to try to get time off."

"Or you probably haven't told her yet." Sly amusement shines in his knowing eyes.

"It's complicated. I'll tell her though."

"Better sooner than later, son. You won't have your window of opportunity forever. Every rosebud eventually blooms and gets picked."

The Colonel's words echo in my head long after the Seahawks whoop the Lions 13-10. And even as I try to jump back into my manuscript, I'm plagued with endless doubt, wondering if I'm completely destroying our friendship from the inside out. Because the more I think about Fi, the less I want to be around her. Having her in my proximity would only cause my anxiety to intensify. And I'm a writer, for fuck's sake. Anxiety kinda comes with the territory. It's like when the Big Guy upstairs was passing out gifts, he looked at all the writers and said, "And here's a little mental illness for thou wordy mofos. Now go forth and write thy book!" He knew what he was doing too. His was a pretty well-known bestseller.

I pour a cup of coffee to go with my sarcasm, and force myself to focus on the screen. The heroine has somehow morphed into April, and while I've slept with more tall, leggy blondes than I can remember, this tall, leggy blonde has invaded my thoughts more than I care to admit. She's a cool girl—sweet, charming, and understanding as hell. Maybe I need to focus more on her and less on Fi.

I make a note to call and apologize, then return to the task at hand: putting all my frustration on paper and making this story my bitch. Or maybe that's the other way around.

She called out to him from the bed, moaning in exhaustion. She shouldn't be here. If he knew she had come once again, after promising to stay away, their relationship would not survive. But the promise of danger and delight was far too strong to ignore.

"Does he make you happy?" a voice asked from the door-

way.

Startled, she covered her bare breasts with sheets made of fine Egyptian cotton that felt like silk over her nipples. Her first instinct was to lie; she knew he would not like her answer. But she also knew that he was a master of every one of her senses. Every shift of her bright blue eyes…every inflection of her voice…he could read her like a book. Lying was futile. Lying would only make him angry.

"Yes," she whispered, her voice barely audible.

"Does it pain you to have to deceive him?"

"Yes."

"Does it pain you that he deceives you?"

"Yes."

"And do you want to stay? With him?" His expression was blank, as always. She couldn't tell if this was a trick question, and she didn't want to risk offending him. But she needed to be honest. She needed him to know that this…this arrangement… was killing her. And as much as her body craved the raw violence only he could provide, her heart was being destroyed in the process.

"Yes. I do. I love him."

He stalks to her, his strides as swift and severe as his strike, and pulls her up by her wrists. "Then prove it…"

Arms crossed over my chest, I lean back in my chair and read over everything I've written since I got home. And would you look at that…I don't completely hate it.

The clock cat's short whisker is on the six, meaning my ass has been fused to this seat for four hours. I need a break. I need a drink. I need food.

I need Fi.

Nope. Thinking like that won't get me anywhere but in a cold tub of water with blue balls.

"What do you think, Bart? Thai food or Mexican?" I ask aloud, searching takeout menus for my favorite spots. Bartleby mewls a response that oddly resembles *"Cuuuuurrrry."* Thai it is. It won't be like Grandma Lee's, but it'll hit the spot.

As I sit at my desk, which moonlights as a dining table when I'm too lazy to move, I think about my grandfather. Imagining him living the rest of his days alone, eating his meals alone, sleeping alone, watching TV alone… it makes me realize something.

That will be me in 50 years.

I've grown so accustomed to hiding beneath my own bullshit hang-ups and insecurities, that I've enclosed myself in a fortress of denial. I keep telling myself that I was built this way, that some people were just made to be reclusive. But the glaring realization that I will be living, eating, sleeping, and eventually, dying alone, well…it fucking terrifies me.

I nix the delivery idea and grab my coat. I am who I am, but that doesn't mean I'm perpetually doomed. That's the beauty of words. I can rewrite the story.

I show up to Fi's apartment with Styrofoam containers of shrimp Pad Thai (her favorite), Panang Curry (my favorite) and enough spring rolls to sustain us through an Inland Northwest winter storm. After our night of drinking—and the massive hangover she sustained after—some fried noodles are exactly what she needs.

"My hero!" she rasps, spotting the bags of food. She hurriedly ushers me inside. "I'm starving! I haven't moved from my couch all day."

"Yeah. I can tell." The empty bottles of booze, glasses and old pizza box are exactly where we left them last night. Fortunately, it appears that Fi has showered and washed her face, if only to put on more pajamas and tie her hair into a messy bun.

"Everything is such a fog. Please don't tell me we polished all this off."

I clear the coffee table and replace the stale pizza with fresh Thai cuisine. "We did. And you encouraged it."

"Oh my God," she grimaces, covering her face. "Was there crying involved?"

"Plenty. Plus pregnant virgins and secret crushes."

She parts her fingers and peeks out at me. "Secret crushes?"

"Yup. You admitted you had a thing for me in college. And this was pre-Fireball so you can't even blame it on the booze. You're attracted to me, Fiona Shaw."

"Ugh," she groans. "Great. Just what the world needs. August Calloway with an ego the size of Texas."

I laugh, making light of the situation. I grab a spring roll and bring it to my lips. "It's no biggie. You were young. And I was pretty irresistible."

"Oh God," she says, grabbing the crispy morsel from my fingertips just as I was about to rip into it. "Irresistible, my butt. Thank God age and maturity has vastly changed my taste in men."

"So you're no longer attracted to me?" I frown.

"You're handsome, Rhys. You know that. Looks have never been your issue."

"My *issue?*" Who the hell said I had an issue?

"Let me break it down in a way that you'll understand... You know how there's always some hidden motivation that spawns the main character's conflict? He had a meager upbringing so he's a workaholic who neglects his wife. His mother abandoned him as a child, so he plays girls like fiddles. He was abused so he keeps people at arm's length in an attempt to spare him from any more pain. Rhys, you have no motivation for the way you are. Your parents are still happily married. You were raised in a nice house. And you've always been brilliantly talented. You have achieved everything you've ever wanted in life. I don't get why you insist on rejecting love."

I stab a curried potato with my fork. She's right. But she's also very, very wrong.

"I'm a writer," I shrug. "We're fickle fuckers. There's no rhyme or reason."

"Maybe. Or maybe you're just afraid someone actually will tap into your motivation, so in order to keep it under wraps, you remain unattainable."

I smile and lightly flick the tip of her nose. "You got me there, Fi."

"Yeah right," she sighs, digging into her noodles. "It's probably something petty like you have a weird fetish or you're a germaphobe. Either that, or you're really gay, and I'm your beard."

At that, I actually do laugh. Jeeeesus. How tight are my fucking pants? The girl at Nordstrom said they were sexy. Especially as she peeled them off me in the dressing room.

"Not a chance, Fi. Not a chance."

We turn our attention to our food and don't come up for air until we're engaged in a Mexican standoff over the last spring roll. Forks and chopsticks drawn, we stare each other down until one of us breaks.

And just like the day we first met, I break.

"Yes!" she cheers, pumping it in the air like a Jersey Shore fanatic. "Victory is mine!"

"That's because I let you have it," I grumble.

"Awww, Auggie-poo. Don't be such a sore loser," she mocks, pinching my cheek. "Besides, it's been a rough week-end. I've earned it."

"No word from Dr. Pooper Scooper?"

"Shut up!" she shrieks, slapping my arm. "He called. A lot. Left a ton of messages. Should I call him back? I shouldn't, should I? It's too embarrassing. What would I say? What if he wants to officially dump me? What if I made him seriously ill?"

I take a beat to deliberate my choices.

I could

A). Tell her to let bygones be bygones, and forget about him. Not many people could come back from an incident like that unscathed mentally. Intimately, they'd be doomed. Hell, in his case, maybe even professionally. Obviously, they're not sexually compatible, and maybe this was the wake up call she needed to let the relationship die.

Or

B). Resist feeding her bullshit, and for once in my life, act selflessly. Be a good friend. Give to her what she's given to me for the last decade.

"Call him back. If he wanted to dump you, he would

have done it over text. I think he wants to work it out." I'm so fucking stupid for this, but it's the right thing to do. And no one ever said being right was easy.

"Really?" she asks, her voice filled with hope. I'm already regretting my answer. "But I don't know if I can deal with what happened. I don't see how I could ever look him in the face again."

I take a deep breath, conjuring more words of reason and optimism. They're buried way deep down in there somewhere. "He's a doctor. He's seen way worse. Just look at this as a funny story you guys can look back on and laugh about. Because if he still wants to be with you after all *that,* he's got to be in it for the long haul."

Before I can brace myself, Fiona attacks me with hugs and face kisses. "Thank you, Rhys. I've been going out of my mind all day! You're the best!" She hops off the couch with renewed zest in search of her phone. "I'm going to call him now."

I know that as soon as her fingers graze that touchscreen, she'll be lost to me. It's now or never.

"Fi, I'm going to LA."

She stops dead in her tracks and turns back towards the living room. "What?"

"Wednesday. I'm going to LA to meet with the studio execs that want to adapt that show about me. I'm going to hear them out."

"Why didn't you tell me?" she asks, taking her place at my side.

"Just haven't had the time. Besides, it'll just be a few days. I'll hear them out, enjoy the cushy suite they've arranged for me, get some sun. A change of scenery will be good for my writing."

"So just a few days?"

"Yeah," I nod. "We meet Thursday. I have until Friday to accept or decline. I'm staying through Saturday."

"Oh. Good. That's not too bad then." She kisses me on the cheek and grasps her cell phone to her chest. "Let's talk more about this. I want to call before it gets too late."

I leave Fiona to her devices after pushing her back into Joshua's arms. Part of me feels encouraged by the fact that she doesn't want me to leave. The other part of me feels like an idiot because I know I never will.

Los Angeles. The city of angels. Where stars live and die under palm trees, smog and endless summer. I'm actually pretty glad to be here, away from the doom and gloom of my life back in Washington. I was right about Joshua. He wanted to put that unfortunate anal issue behind them (no pun intended) and move forward. And Fiona was more committed than ever to be perfect for him, meaning she had no time for me.

"Lunch?"

"Can't. I'm going to the gym."

"Since when do you go to the gym?"

"Since Joshua asked me to join him during his workouts."

"Dinner?"

"Can't. We have plans with one of his colleagues and his

wife. Our first double date!"

"Want to read a few chapters?"

"Can't. I'm exhausted. Between social events and exercising, I'm beat."

That was how our last few conversations had gone—me trying to find a way for us to connect like we used to, and her inserting Joshua into every facet of her life.

I couldn't blame her. Objectively, I had her to myself for a decade. Even when she was dating, she was still my girl. I still came first to her. Which, in hindsight, is probably the reason those relationships didn't last.

Maybe some distance will be good for the both of us. I can gain some perspective, and she can figure out what's really important to her. Even if I'm not part of that equation.

"Kerrigan, you know what I look like. You don't have to stand near baggage claim holding a sign," I say, shaking my head at my agent. She flew in from New York City to ensure the meeting went smoothly, and to negotiate the terms of the deal. Of course, she totally stands out like a sore thumb. She's dressed in black from head to toe, heels and a no-nonsense air that makes her thin, 5'2 frame seem frightening. Plus she's a fast talker, which is like speaking a foreign language on the West Coast.

"I know, but I didn't feel like looking for you." She goes to grab my carryon, the only piece of luggage I brought aside from my laptop bag, and I quickly jerk it away.

"What are you doing?"

"Taking your bag." She tries it again.

"Kerrigan, you're not holding my bag. Knock it off. I'm a big boy."

"Suit yourself," she shrugs as we make our way outside where a car and driver await. "Ok, so strategy for tomorrow is just listening. Don't tell them what you want—or what you don't. Just listen. I'll be there to chime in with anything non-negotiable. What are your hard limits?"

I hadn't thought about that. Moving was a big issue for me, but I know that's unavoidable. I want to be portrayed as honestly as possible without giving anything away about my identity, so casting is important. And I don't want them insisting on anything cliché or cheesy.

However, none of this matters, because I'm not taking the job. No way. No how.

"Nothing I can think of."

"Good! I'll drop you at the hotel to relax. I've got errands and meetings for the next few hours."

Being a sought-after talent definitely has its perks, one of them being the accommodations. It's not enough to be staying at the Beverly Wilshire, which has lodged everyone from Jay-Z to John Lennon. But the fact that the studio actually sprang for one of the specialty suites has me feeling like Pretty Woman.

After calling down for room service, I take advantage of the quiet and open my manuscript, hoping to get some work done. But everything is falling flat. It's a story about a woman torn between two loves—the one she was meant for and the one that was forced upon her. Why does she love them? Why has she put herself in a position that compromises her future…her sanity…her body?

What's her motivation?

I'm sinking fast. The words are there, begging to be written, but it's like trying to funnel a million jumbled thoughts through a pinhole with the hope that they'll somehow make sense on the other side. I don't get it. I just had them a few days ago. For once in forever, I didn't cringe through every fucking line of dialogue. I didn't feel like gouging my eyes out every time the heroine felt conflicted about who she needed, versus who she wanted. Why can't I focus? Why does the thought of stringing together a bunch of meaningless sentences all in the name of romance physically repulse me?

"Fuck it," I growl after staring at the blinking cursor for more than an hour. I wish Bartleby was here to listen to me babble. I had to drop him off with the Colonel for a few days. The old man tried to play it cool, but I could tell he was happy to have the company.

I change into some shorts, grab my shades and Moleskine, and head out to enjoy the balmy Southern California fall weather. The Beverly Wilshire pool is a lot smaller than I expect, but when you have beaches and privately owned pools in every backyard and terrace, it's no big deal. Shit, it's 40 damn degrees in Spokane right now. I may go into shock from all this Vitamin D.

I swim laps, I laze in the sun, I drink frou frou tropical drinks, and eventually, I pull out my notebook to jot down some notes. But when I put pen to paper, I find that my head is not in my manuscript. I can't even remember my character's names or what they look like. My mind is captured by something—and someone—else entirely.

The warmth reminded him of the time the AC died the spring of junior year, forcing her to shed the armor of oversized sweaters and knee high socks. They had finals approaching, and the library was transformed into a hot box of hormones, poor diets and bad decisions. She wore frayed denim cutoffs—not too high above her mid-thigh but short enough to make him take notice the way they rode up when she sat down.

"I feel ridiculous," she said, opening up the mammoth sized textbook containing the material they were to cover for the next six hours.

"Why's that?" he asked, pretending not to stare.

She looked up from the study guide just as he was looking away, feigning indifference. "I look like a twelve-year-old on the first day of summer camp. All that's missing is the braces and bad skin. Can we just go back to your dorm to study?"

"It's even hotter in there. Trust me." His room had been deemed the official meet up point after things with her roommate had gone sour.

"But I feel like people are staring at me. Oh my God, Jimmy Lepito looks like he wants to lick the sweat from my brow. You'd swear I was wearing a coconut shell bikini." She wrapped her bare arms around her chest, shielding them from view. It was a good thing. She didn't have on a bra under her sleeveless tee, and Jimmy Lepito wasn't the only one that was looking.

"He looks at everyone that way. I think he's just stoned."

"Surprise, surprise." She pulled a paperback novel from her bag and slid it over to him. The Color Purple by Alice Walker. It was required reading, and although they had read it ages ago, she didn't mind revisiting their favorite passages. "Read it to me, please."

"But you can practically recite it verbatim."

"I know. But I like the way you read it. You relate every word as if you believe them. As if they were birthed from your

very tongue. You have such a way with words. Even the words that aren't yours."

"That's all I have—all that I am. I'm just words."

Shadows dance across the page, and I look up to find that I'm not alone. A bikini-clad brunette stands over me, watching me with brazen fascination.

"What are you writing?" she asks.

I squint up at her, my Ray-Bans no match for the California sun. "A story."

"Oh really?" She takes the lounge chair beside me, as if my answer was an invitation. "What kind of story?"

"The maddening kind of story that sneaks up on you when you have no time to write it."

She giggles at that, and I take a beat to let the sound move through me. She's gorgeous. Not just Hollywood gorgeous, but sincerely attractive. Straight brown hair, flawless skin, and a body as long and languid as a desert palm.

"Seems like quite the dilemma."

"It is. But it could be worse."

"And how's that?"

"Well, I could be out here, enjoying this beautiful weather and scenery alone."

She blushes, pressing her lips into a sly smile. "Yeah, that would be unfortunate."

"So I guess I should be thanking you for helping me out today."

"Maybe you should." She chuckles again, and looks back to where her friends are gathering towels and flip-flops. "Look, I actually have to get going, but for some reason, I couldn't leave without talking to you. I'm Michelle. If you're staying here for a few days, you should call me...let me show you around. I'm a pretty good tour guide."

I'm intrigued by her candor, and I can't say I'm mad at the proposition either. Not mad at all. "Nice of you to offer, Michelle. I might just take you up on that. I'm August," I say, extending a hand.

"August. I like that name," she replies, running her delicate digits over my exposed palm. "I think I'll like getting to know you too."

She gives me her number, which I quickly scribble down on a blank sheet in my notebook. Before she turns to rejoin her friends—who are now waiting for her with amused expectation—she says something that instantly turns my curiosity into interest.

""*If a story is in you, it has to come out.*""

"Faulkner," I nod, impressed.

"Good luck with your writing, August. Hope to hear from you sooner than later." Then she turns and struts away, leaving me with the pleasant view of her pert backside.

A new story and a new friend. So far LA is shaping up to be pretty damn great.

The meeting goes exactly how I expect it to: Kerrigan talking and me trying to feign interest. I hear what they're saying, but I just can't get over the fact that I'd be separated from my grandfather and Fiona. I couldn't pay the Colonel to move out here, and Fi can't just pick up her life and follow me out here. Not when she's trying to share said life with someone else. Even the thought of asking her to goes against everything I've ever believed in…everything I've ever told her.

"I wouldn't want you to devote your life to a lie."

Is that really what I'm reluctant about? Or am I afraid that she'll see right through me?

I fish out my cell, in need of the sound of her voice to ground me. I came out here to gain some perspective, but maybe that was already at home.

"Please tell me you're having a horrible time, and you can't wait to come back."

"I'm having a horrible time, and I can't wait to come back. Oh, and I got a tan."

"Jerk."

"And I'm currently strolling Rodeo Drive, resisting the urge to buy you something annoyingly gaudy and expensive after having the best Benedict in history while someone in a suit tried to throw money at me. Times are hard all around."

"I'll say. I'll create a hashtag for you. Social media should know of these harsh conditions."

"Finally, someone who feels my pain."

We share a laugh, something we haven't done in almost a week. I've missed her. Even when I'm there, I miss her.

"So how much money *did* they try to force upon you?"

"Enough to buy you a lifetime supply of Pinot and spring rolls with extra dipping sauce."

She whistles her response.

"But I'm not taking it."

"Why not?"

"Because I'd have to relocate, at least for eight months

out of the year. And if it's picked up for another season…"

"Oh," she whispers.

"Yeah."

"Well, if that's what you want to do…"

"Leaving you and the Colonel is not what I want to do, Fi."

"I know that. But this is *your* life, Rhys. You can't keep living it for others. Especially not for me."

I want to tell her that she's wrong. That *she* is my life—her and my grandfather. I have no one else.

"Let's talk about this when I get back, ok? Tell me what's going on there. Any anal-free plans this weekend?"

"Oh, shut up. Actually I do have really exciting news. I got tickets to see Train at the Gorge!"

"I thought that show was sold out weeks ago?" Fi had been kicking herself for missing out. Even I had scoured the web for seats that weren't in the stoner section on the grass.

"Well, Joshua just proved that he is the best boyfriend ever and somehow got me tickets! Floor seats, too! I can't even tell you how stoked I am. I'm taking a half day and driving up tomorrow to make it in time for the show!"

"That's great, Fi. You'll have a blast." Ugh. Joshua. I'm happy for her but annoyed that it was him that made it happen. In an effort to play nice, I ask her, "Does he have any idea how much of a freak you are about them? I feel like I should properly warn him."

"Well, he's not going, actually." The disappointment is all too evident in her voice. "He has a medical seminar this weekend and has to fly to Portland. So unless I find someone to go with, I'll be going stag."

"I don't know about that, Fi. You shouldn't be going out there alone."

The Gorge is a massive outdoor amphitheater near the Columbia River in Washington. Never heard of it? Probably because it is smack dab in the middle of nowhere. It's a gorgeous venue, but it's also breeding ground for modern day flower children and squatters. Meaning, Fiona and her rose-colored glasses definitely should not be going sans cohort.

"Well, I don't know anyone who would be willing to suffer through four hours of *"Drops of Jupiter"* and *"Hey, Soul Sister."* Well…no one but you."

It's true. I took her to see Snow Patrol two years ago, and I was probably the only one on earth who could tolerate her for at least three weeks afterward. I can't even hear *"Chasing Cars"* without slipping into a musically induced coma.

"Sorry, Fi. If I was there…"

"I know you would. But it's fine. You're off being amazing and famous. I'll figure something out. If all else fails, I'll just resell them."

"No…no, we'll figure something out." I don't miss the use of the word "we" as if we're in that space right now. Especially with an entire state physically separating us.

"Don't overthink it," she sighs, as if reading my mind.

"I'm not. I won't…" But I am. However, before I can even begin to pick it apart like a desert vulture, a familiar face pops into view. "Hey, Fi, let me call you back," I find myself saying, deciding to trade confused frustration for fun and friendly.

"Oh…ok." She sounds hurt, but quickly tacks on that she has to get back to work anyway. This isn't the time or place for me to question whether or not she's being genuine. Not when I'm genuinely tired of questioning her.

"Hey," I smile after pressing End on my cell. "I've only been in LA for a day. I didn't expect to have a stalker already."

"Well, I'm just taking a break from accosting other random dudes at hotel pools. A girl needs her caffeine, you know. The stalker life can be exhausting." Michelle smiles back and brushes a lock of chestnut hair behind her ear. She's wearing a white gauzy sundress and wedge sandals that remind me of cork. Minimal makeup. She's stunning. But I think her svelte frame would look equally gorgeous in a burlap sack.

"Headed to get coffee?"

"Yeah. There's a shop I like right on the corner. What are you up to? Plotting stories you shouldn't write?"

"Something like that," I shrug.

"Ah. Well, how about you walk with me and tell me all about it."

As we stroll side by side on a crowded Rodeo sidewalk, I'm flooded with the sights and sounds of this little slice of paradise. The people are beautiful, if not a little sad. The weather is amazing, yet blinding. The shops are grand and extravagant, but only for those that fit a certain social class. There's a story here, embedded in the Palm-adorned cement under our feet. How many stars have walked these streets by day, only to crumble to them at night? How many have sold their souls in search of something to fill the void within their hearts?

"Check out that lady," I say, nodding towards a woman decked out in pink from head to toe, holding a tiny dog wearing a Prince-worthy ruffled shirt and suit. "What do you think she…" I stop in my tracks, remembering where I am and whom I'm with. This isn't an afternoon stroll in Riverfront Park creating fabricated backstories for strangers. And this isn't Fiona.

"What was that?" Michelle asks, obvious confusion furrowed on her brow.

"Oh, um…check out her dog. Do you think he actually enjoys wearing those outfits? He looks like he's on his way to a canine production of *Purple Rain*."

"Oh, he does. He's quite the celebrity too."

As we pass, I notice a few paparazzi snapping photos of the odd couple. While I'm awestruck that something so ridiculous could be newsworthy, Michelle hurriedly maneuvers through the crowd, as if it doesn't bother her in the least. We're at the coffee shop within the next few minutes and, as I expect, it's outrageously elegant for a place that literally serves coffee and those little French cakes that look like tiny gifts. However, Michelle insists that they make a mean cup of Joe. And for someone who is widely versed in all things coffee, I'm interested in putting her theory to the test.

"Not bad," I say after my first sip of java. "But it's no Thomas Hammer."

"Thomas Hammer? Is that some coffee lingo I don't know about?" Michelle questions before sipping her iced caramel latte-something-or-other.

"No. It's a Spokane coffee roaster. Crazy good coffee, locally owned. I swear, they sponsored my entire senior year of college and most of my books."

"Oh, so you don't just go around penning random tales? You're a writer?"

"I am," I nod. "Either that, or I'm a psycho serial killer, and I was just documenting the daily patterns of my next victim when you met me."

"I'm hoping for writer. Murder has never been my thing—too messy. And I've always been attracted to writers."

We have that moment. You know, the moment when we both lock eyes and smile at each other before she blushes and looks away.

"You're from Washington?" she says, changing the subject as she tries to feign interest in her straw.

"I am."

"So what brings you to LA?"

"Business meeting."

"Oh. So you're not actually hawking your books out of the trunk of your car?" She seems impressed. What is it that makes most people imagine some dirty granola-gritty beard and Jesus hair sleeping in coffee shops when they think of a writer?

"Not really," I chuckle.

"Wow. What genre do you write?"

I struggle between the idea of telling the truth or lying my way out of this like I do everything else. She doesn't know me, or my story. And after this trip, I doubt I'll ever see her again.

So in an impulsive act of defiance and insanity that goes against all my better judgment, I give her just a small taste of honesty. "Romance. I write romance."

"I have a date tomorrow. An actual date," I say over the phone while flipping through the channels. The Seahawks aren't playing, but Thursday Night football is on.

"A date, huh? With who?"

"A nice girl I met here yesterday."

The Colonel grunts, and I can imagine him giving me one of those infamous looks of disbelief, one bushy brow cocked higher than the other. He's not one for talking on the phone, but it's seldom that I'm out of town. Also, it's Meatball Thursday, and I'm sure he'd rather be talking to me than chatting with crazy old Helen.

"She really is nice. We had coffee today too."

"Coffee and…"

"That's it. Just coffee. She works nights, so we just talked for a little while. Like I said, she's a nice girl."

"What kind of nice girl works at night?"

"The kind of nice girl that's a DJ. I'm serious. She's nice."

"I'm sure she is." I know it's killing him not to say it. I can hear the restraint in his voice. *I bet she's not nice like Fiona.* And for some reason, that annoys me more than usual.

"Everything going ok with Bart?" I ask, hoping to steer the conversation away from Fi.

"Of course. He doesn't do much more than sleep and lick himself. He's a fat S.O.B. too. What have you been feeding him?"

"I don't know. Cat food?" And leftover Chinese. And bits of turkey on rye. And his personal favorite, pizza. Honestly, the little dude eats whatever I do, or whatever drops on the floor when I'm trying to write and eat simultaneously. I'd be surprised if he *wasn't* overweight.

"Well, you need to think about switching his diet. This stuff that you brought with him isn't cutting it. He keeps trying to swipe human food."

Probably because he's never tasted dehydrated cat kibble. "Yeah, I'll head to PetSmart when I get back."

"Good. He'll need to get in shape for the LA pussycats. They'll want a fit feline."

"I don't think he'd like it much here. Too hot. He belongs in Spokane. We both do."

"Here you go with that. Son, you need to do what's best for you and your career. But if you won't do that, at least do what's best for your love life."

I resist sighing heavily into the phone out of respect for

the Colonel. But I'm truly sick of talking about this. "I'm doing the best I can with both, at the moment."

"Bullshit."

"Seriously, I went to the meeting and gave it some thought. I don't know, maybe I'll kick it around some more."

"And your love life?"

This time I don't resist releasing an annoyed breath. "Love life would suggest that I am actually a procurer of love. And since that's not the case…"

"Yeah, yeah. I'm not buying it. I've seen a lot happen over the last three quarters of a century. And believe me, son, I know bullshit when someone is trying to feed me bullshit. You know what your problem is? You actually do believe in love. You want it for yourself. But you're afraid. Of what, I don't know. But you are scared shitless that love will sink its hooks into you and never let go. So you run from it like a pansy, hoping you can screw your way through the innate need to devote yourself to one person. Because you think Fiona—"

"I'm sorry, Colonel. I hate to interrupt, but I have to go." I'm desperate, searching for any reason to get off this damn phone before I say something I'll regret.

"Hmph. There you go running again. Truth hurts, doesn't it?"

What hurts is lying to him. It really does. But just as he taught me, sometimes pain is necessary. "Really. My agent just arrived to talk numbers. I promise I'll give what you said some thought."

He's quiet for a beat, like he's debating whether or not to call me out for being a lying sack of shit. "Ok. You do that."

He says the words as if they're weightless, just like my promise.

I sit for a long time, replaying our conversation in my mind. And when I'm sick of myself, I go down to the hotel bar in search of perspective at the bottom of three fingers of scotch. It's fairly crowded for a Thursday night, and there are plenty of women that look like good company, but I honestly don't feel like going through the motions. My heart's not in it. Maybe it's somewhere else entirely.

I'm still a bit wasted the next morning, but not so wasted that I make any rash decisions. After a much needed shower and an order to room service for enough food to sustain a small village, I call up Kerrigan to give her my answer. I was born to be a writer. And in my quest to write epic shit, I have to be true to the stories in my head and the characters that demand to be heard.

"You're making a huge mistake!" Kerrigan trills, no doubt chain-smoking like a chimney. This would have put cash in her pocket, especially since her firm handles movie and TV deals in-house.

"Maybe so. But I have my reasons."

"And those are?"

I open my mouth to answer, but not a word escapes. My life is in Washington. My grandfather, the only family I've got left on this side of the country, is there. And Fiona… no matter what, she'll always be in my life.

The thought of not hitting Santé for Sunday brunch or Durkin's for drinks and Poutine or my favorite taco truck for late night munchies, just doesn't seem normal. Not being able to scour the shelves of Auntie's Bookstore for my next read amidst the comforting smells of coffee and old books isn't an option for me. Trading the marijuana tinged air and winding paths of Riverfront Park for the beautiful Boardwalk of Venice Beach would be a dream for some. But it's not for me.

It's not home.

It's not my story.

"You can't hide behind Hope forever, August," Kerrigan says, her gritty voice almost gentle. I say *almost* because I'm pretty sure she came out of the womb fisting a Virginia Slim. "Eventually, someone's going to see you for who you are."

"Yeah, I know." And I *do* know. That's the part that scares me.

"Look, let's put a pin in this. I'll let the studio know that you need more time. Give it a week or two, and if you still want to nix this opportunity, we'll pass. Plus, this'll add pressure for them to offer more money."

I agree just to get her off the phone. My date with Michelle is this afternoon —before her gig at some exclusive nightclub that caters to the likes of Hiltons and Kardashians—and I want to get some writing done. However, when I open my manuscript, I'm left uninspired once again. Instead, another story has planted roots in my mind. A story with characters that are as tangible to me as the pen and paper in my hands...

They became accidental best friends. It was not his intention to grow attached to the unsuspecting girl who wore her brown hair in a messy knot and clothes three times too large for her slight frame. She wasn't his type. And his type was... well, pretty much every attractive girl in town. Not that she wasn't attractive. He just didn't see her that way.

Well, not since before the heat wave.

Since seeing her in those tiny cutoffs and tank top, a sheen on fresh sweat dusting her nose as she fanned herself with notes from her Romantic Age course, he couldn't stop thinking about her in the way he thought about other girls. Still, it was different. She would always be different to him, even if the warmth jutting up his thighs was very familiar.

"Why are you staring at me?" she asked, breaking him from his thoughts.

"I'm not."

"You are. We were supposed to be reading chapter eighteen. Do I have spinach in my teeth?"

"No."

"A bat in the cave?"

"No."

"Then what is it?"

He wanted to tell her, but he couldn't find the words. Aside from her, the words were his only comfort, his only weapon, yet they had dissipated before his eyes as if they never truly existed. He was left defenseless and utterly alone. And that was a feeling he had grown all too fond of.

Time falls away from me, and I realize that I've got twenty minutes to get showered and downstairs in the lobby. Michelle offered to pick me up, and since this is her hood, she's planned the entire day. I've been looking forward to it. Not only spending time with her, but also trying to actually date. It's a novel idea, I know, but one that I'm intrigued by. But before I can even make it to the elevator, I get a text from Fiona that has me rethinking my plans.

-Can't find anyone to go with. Looks like it's just me.

-No, Fi. Not a good idea.

-But what else can I do? Joshua is gone for the weekend, and I don't want to miss this chance.

I try to compile a mental list of people that would be potential candidates, but come up short. All my suggestions are women I've slept with, and none of them would be the type to sit through hours of Fi's tear-filled singing. Which leads me to my next revelation: I don't have any friends. All my empty relationships, all the Hope readers and fans around the world…and I can count the people that truly know me on one hand, with fingers to spare. If that's not a sad state of affairs, I don't know what is. It's my own doing, of course, and I'm not one to dwell on popularity or lack thereof, but shit… when did I trade a life for loneliness? When did I say *I do* to a lifetime of late nights and paper cuts? When did words become my only love and misguided fame my mistress?

I'm getting older. The biological yearning for companionship echoes within those long, cold nights spent pouring over wrinkled Post Its and ripped notebook pages. Maybe that's why I'm here, boarding an elevator that'll lead me to a beautiful girl with an enigmatic smile. Maybe that's why I want to tell her all my secrets.

Maybe that's why I know I can't.

"Ready to hit the town, handsome?" Michelle smiles at me when I step from the suspended steel. She's lovely in a flannel shirt that's fashioned as a dress and ankle boots. I laugh inwardly. Flannel is like the city-wide uniform for the lumbersexual population in Spokane. The guys in their collared plaid, manbuns and beards. The girls in oversize checked tops that they've stolen from boyfriends, and boots. Fiona had been into that style long before it became popular. And once it caught on, she vowed to steer clear of flannel until her dying day.

"I have to go," I say, not really meaning it, but knowing I have to. I don't want to disappoint her, but if I don't do this, I could be losing more than her interest. I could be losing the thing that matters most to me.

"What?"

"I have to go. I'm sorry. Something came up, and I have to get back to Spokane."

She's confused, hurt even, but she nods. "Oh, ok. Everything alright?"

"It will be if I get there in time."

I kiss her on the cheek, thank her for her hospitality, and promise to call. Then I run upstairs to grab my shit and get the hell back home. I'm getting in a cab fifteen minutes later when I receive another text.

-I'm not going. I wish you were here. I don't want to go with anyone but you. Why'd you have to run off to LA again?

I'm coming, Fi. I'm coming back to you.

I want to tell her, but the writer in me wants to make it a surprise. The look on her face when I show up on her doorstep, the way she'll jump into my arms... I'm not sure what it all means in the grand scheme of things, but it'll make for one helluva story.

The fates are on my side, and there's a flight leaving in forty-five minutes headed back up North. According to the flight plan, I should arrive just after 5pm. The concert starts about an hour and a half later, but we can at least catch the main act. None of that will even matter to Fi anyway. She'll just be grateful and overjoyed that I came...that I was there when Joshua wasn't.

I shoot her a text with some generic "Stay positive" message before putting my phone on Airplane Mode. When we're in the air, I pull out my MacBook Air and open a new .doc. A new story has taken flight in my head. Time to make it official.

Unwritten: a novel

Chapter 1

I write the words that have embedded themselves on my psyche. I breathe life into the characters whispering in my ear. And then I tell the tale that's been scrawled on my heart.

I write about her.

4678 WORDS.

4678 stitches of my patchwork soul.

4678 reasons why I'm falling for my best friend.

I land in Spokane and with plans of heading straight to Fi's apartment, but when I switch on my 4G, I see that she's sent another text message, probably while I was airborne.

-Found someone to go with! Andrea from work. We're headed there now. Can't wait! Wish you were here!

I shuffle off the plane in a fog, wondering if I made a huge mistake by leaving LA and a perfectly normal, uncomplicated girl. Someone who didn't possess the power to completely alter my universe with just the sound of her laughter.

But for that reason alone, I know that I did the right thing. Michelle, as cool and beautiful as she is, would have never been able to reach the pedestal that I had placed Fi on. And that's my own fault. I created my own little monster. I formulated such a perfect image of her in my mind that not even I was worthy enough. And here I am, trying to convince myself that maybe I can be. Maybe I can be what she's wanted all these years, when I've done everything in my power to rage against that very same ideal.

Since I hadn't even told the Colonel about my plans to return early, I don't bother going by to pick up Bartleby. Plus I don't feel like subjecting myself a bunch of questions about my motives. Admitting this shit to myself is confusing enough. I'm not ready to say it out loud.

After stashing my luggage at my apartment, I find myself at the lower level bar at Durkin's. So much has happened since we last sat in one of the booths, laying harbored resentment on the table alongside a plate of Poutine. I wish I could go back to that evening—to the conversation—and tell her how I really felt.

Fuck Joshua, because he's a prick who doesn't deserve you.

Fuck Joshua, because he's not the one you should be wearing high heels and your best perfume for.

Fuck Joshua, because I'm not him.

As if karma has some sick, twisted sense of humor, I hear a familiar, accented voice behind me, chortling through a convoluted story about his days as a young, brilliant med student. He boasts of the great work he's done to a chorus of *ooohs* and *ahhhhs*. He spins webs of heroic feats in the operating room, mending nature's physical ills with his gilded scalpel.

My surprise doesn't stem from seeing Joshua surrounded by scantily dressed adoring fans who worship him for the golden-haired surgical god that he is. It's rooted in the fact that he's here—in Spokane—when he should be in Portland, suffering through a dreadfully boring medical seminar. And it doesn't seem as if he's all that upset that he's not with Fiona right now, watching her sing along to some of her favorite songs, and smiling because she is utterly adorable when she gets that starry look in her eyes while hearing her favorite bands. And believe it or not, I'm not even shocked at the way some classless chick in a catsuit is damn near sitting in his lap while running her fingers through his hair.

"You look positively homicidal. Someone you know?" the full stached-and-suspendered bartender inquires, jutting his chin toward the crowd in the back.

I down my Old Fashioned and shake my head before climbing to my feet. "Not on purpose."

Joshua doesn't even notice my approach, and neither does his entourage, consisting of three cleavage-bearing women and two equally well-dressed, smug-smiling men. When his eyes finally land on me standing before their table, a noticeable hush falls around the room. It echoes strongly of guilt.

"August," he nearly gasps, quickly scooting away from his companion and batting her hands away. "Nice to see you, friend. I thought you were in California."

"And I thought you were in Portland." I don't waste time with a fake smile or handshake. Besides, my hands are balled so tightly at my sides, all I'd be able to muster is a fist-bump… to his face.

"Ah, yes. Change of plans last minute. Decided to grab dinner with colleagues. Join us?"

I see right through his phony invitation and shake my head. "No thanks. I came back early to try to catch Fiona before the concert. She was disappointed you couldn't make it."

"Yes, unfortunately, I couldn't. Certainly she'll still have a good time." At that moment, he realizes that his friends are following the conversation intently, their curious eyes ping-ponging from him to me. "Where are my manners? This is August Calloway, Fiona's mate from college. August is a writer here in town."

"A writer, eh?" one of the men at the table ask. I don't even bother acknowledging him. "I consider myself well read. Anything I may know?"

"Doubtful," Joshua answers, shaking his head. "I believe August's book is self- published, so not at the *real* book caliber that you're used to. *Tears of Water,* right? Cheeky title, eh?"

I don't even bother correcting him. I'm much too furious at the fact that he's insulted not only me, but indie authors everywhere. "*Real* book? As opposed to what? A fake one?"

Joshua waves me off like he can't believe my absurdity. "Oh, don't be sensitive, Auggie. You know what I mean. You're more…down to earth. You're not a Dean Koontz or Stephen King. Hell, you're not even a Nicholas Sparks, and *that* guy writes *romance.*"

He spits out the word romance like it's poison on his tongue—bitter, stereotypical, cringe-worthy poison. And you know what? I'm fucking offended. The man thinks panty sniffing and snatch shaving is romantic. What the fuck does he know of the genre?

I can talk shit because I live romance. I breathe romance. Romance is my bread and butter. And it took this moment—right here amongst Lord Douche and his loyal subjects—for me to see that, shit, I don't hate romance. I *am* romance. And it's my total lack of self-awareness that held me blind from that fact all this time.

Amidst all my soul searching, I've missed all the little digs Joshua and his cronies have taken at my expense. But you know what? I really don't give a fuck.

"I've always believed writers are just people too narcissistic and insecure to get a real job," the other guy says with an air of condescension. The girls laugh with equal parts phoniness, probably wondering what the hell *narcissistic* means.

"Ah, come on. Famed writers helped shape this great nation," the other guy pipes up. "Of course, none of them were self-published… But I guess beggars can't be choosers."

"Now, gentlemen. Let's be cordial. According to my Fiona, Auggie here is very good at what he does."

I laugh. I laugh so hard that it startles them into silence. Then I take a deep breath and show them the power of my words.

"Narcisstic and insecure?" I say, turning to the asshole on my right. "That's rich, considering you haven't stopped looking at your own reflection in your girlfriend's eyes for the last ten minutes. Don't worry, bro. The hair plugs look great. And I bet your friends can't even tell that you're wearing Frankenstein platform shoes to make yourself appear taller."

I make a gesture toward the floor where, sure enough, he's desperately trying to hide loafers that have been enhanced for height. "Hmmmm, I wonder where else you're lacking a few extra inches..." I remark, giving his girlfriend a wink, who responds with a sheepish grin.

Next up, the well-read dick to my left. "And you're right. Many famed writers have shaped this great nation. And since you seem to be so knowledgeable on the literary market, it's probably no surprise to you that independent publishing is a multi-million dollar industry, with most of that money going straight into our pockets. See there's a little thing called royalties, buddy. And self-published authors get to keep the largest slice of the pie. So trust and believe, no one is begging. Now you, on the other hand...you will probably be begging to get out of the doghouse later tonight." I angle my gaze on the strawberry blonde woman tucked under his arm. "The tan line around his finger is from a wedding ring, sweetheart. And that Rolex on his wrist is a swap meet special. The second hand glides, not ticks. You'll have to brush up on your gold-digging skills."

Flustered, both jerk-offs sputter unintelligibly, looking to their blonde god for guidance.

"What the hell, man? What was that for? We were only having a laugh."

I lean over, fists pressed into the table and glare trained on the lying, cheating bastard known as Joshua King. "Of course, you are. This is my laughing face. Can't you tell? Don't be so sensitive, Joshie."

"Look, whatever you think you saw or know, it's not what you—"

"What? Not what I think? Now what would give me the crazy notion that I had witnessed something that would be significant to me? Is it Botox Barbie damn near giving you a hand job under the table? Or could it be the fact that you lied about a make believe business trip and sent Fiona out of town so you could have a night of debauchery?"

"Now, you just wait one minute, August—"

"Oh! So you *do* know how to pronounce my name. Apparently, you're not just a pretty face that likes to steal women's dirty panties."

"You're out of line," Joshua grits, giving me his angry face. It oddly resembles *Zoolander*'s Blue Steel. "You need to leave right now before things get ugly."

I straighten up and hold up my palms in mock defeat. "My apologies. Didn't mean to ruin your evening. But FYI," I say to his female companion, my voice loud enough to be heard over the bustling roar of the bar. "Crocodile Dundee digs poop play. I hope you're well stocked on your fiber."

Two raps on the tabletop serve as the proverbial period on this conversation, this night, and soon enough, he and Fi's relationship.

"FI, CALL ME WHEN YOU get this. It's important. And don't talk to Joshua until you do."

It's the second voicemail I've left since I hit the exit of Durkin's along with my four text messages. When she finally calls me some time after midnight, I'm still wired from my run-in with Joshua.

"Oh my God, Rhys. Is everything ok?" There's panic in her voice, and I instantly feel bad for the dramatics. But there's no way I could have let him get to her first.

"Yeah, but you need to listen to me. Come straight to my apartment tomorrow morning. Don't even go to your apartment. I have something really important to tell you, and it's time sensitive."

"Wait…won't you still be in LA?"

"No, I flew back early. I'm home."

"Oh. Is this about the job?"

"No, nothing like that. But promise me you won't talk to Joshua until you see me. Promise me, Fi."

"I promise, Rhys, geez. You're scaring me."

"Don't be. Just come see me, ok? Come straight here."

"I heard you the first time. I wish you would just tell me now. I won't be able to sleep tonight knowing something is wrong."

"Don't worry, Fi. Everything is about to be exactly how it's supposed to be."

Sleep is a struggle, and I pass out some time after penning over 5000 words on my new story. I don't even know where I'm going with it or what I'm even planning to do with it. It's not a Hope story, that's for sure. No insta-love or surprise pregnancy. Not even a stitch of clothing has been lost in the second chapter. It looks, smells, *feels* like romance, yet for some reason, it doesn't. It's just…*real.*

After I wake from slumber sponsored by scotch, I make a concerted effort to tame the anarchy that is my apartment. You know those stories where the bachelor is some neat freak weirdo, and everything must be pristine, including his women? He also works 80 hours a week and has time to cook gourmet meals, work out daily and wash his dirty gym shorts. Yeah. That's not me.

I'm not a slob, per say, but my neurosis requires a certain level of chaos to thrive productively. So there are a few dozen sheets of rumpled paper lying about, along with multi-colored sticky notes claiming most flat surfaces. I'm grown up enough to throw away my empty food cartons and pizza boxes, but there is a fair amount of used coffee cups cluttering the kitchen counters. And there are books. Everywhere. Books on shelves, books on tables, books on the sofa, books stacked on the floor. I'm a writer, but I will always be a reader first.

My buzzer sounds a little after noon, and for the first time in all the years I've known her, I'm nervous to see Fi. A few weeks ago, I would have answered the door in whatever I had on when I rolled out of bed, chin unshaven, teeth unbrushed and hair uncombed. But here I am—showered, smelling good and wearing actual pants. This just seems bizarre to me, and apparently to Fi too.

"Whoa. Going somewhere?"

"No," I shake my head. It looks like I'm trying too hard. This is Fi. She doesn't care what I look like. Shit, during the last leg of a deadline, she's used to me moonlighting as one of those Duck Dynasty guys.

"Oh. Well, you look nice." She steps inside and looks around, visibly stunned by the tidiness of my place. "Ok, Rhys, spill it. You had me race back here like my car was on fire. What's going on? I'm worried."

"How was the concert?" I ask, stalling for time. I planned on telling her about Joshua, but I didn't factor in hurting her. Fuck. This isn't going to be as easy as I initially thought. What did I expect? Of course, news of Joshua's deception will crush her.

"How was the concert? It was great, you know that. But we can talk about that later. Please, Rhys. Tell me what's going on."

"Have a seat," I offer, leading her to the living room. "I'm thirsty. Want a glass of water? Mimosa?"

"Whatever," she replies, rolling her eyes. "Just get on with it. Joshua was able to fly back early and wants to meet up in a couple hours. Said he has a surprise planned for me, and I still need to get home to get ready."

Joshua. Fucking Joshua. Of course he does.

"I thought I asked you not to talk to him until we spoke. What did he tell you?"

She winces at my erratic behavior and shrinks back. "Nothing, geez. He sent me a text. I just replied with *Ok*. Seriously, Rhys, you're acting crazy. What's going on?"

I have to do it now. I have to tell her the ugly truth, no matter how it'll crush her already fragile heart. Luckily, I'm here to pick up the pieces.

"Fiona, I saw Joshua last night."

"What? Wait, how did you… but he just got back in this morning."

"No. He didn't, Fi. He was at Durkin's last night, and he wasn't alone. He also seemed shocked to see me."

"What are you talking about, August?"

"I don't think Joshua ever went to Portland, Fi. I think he wanted to get you out of town so he could hide what he really was up to. And with me gone, he'd be able to go out freely. He was drinking, laughing, acting as if he didn't have a care in the world. And there was a woman hanging on to him as if she was comfortable with his body. Touching him the way a woman touches a man that she plans to sleep with…or already has slept with. Are you getting what I'm saying?"

She's silent, unmoving, maybe even unbreathing, as she processes the information I've just given her.

"Fi, say something," I whisper, sliding an arm around her shoulder. Her body is as stiff and tight as a board. She swallows through the lump in her throat.

"I'll take that drink now."

I jump up to retrieve a glass of water and a tumbler of scotch. I'm not entirely sure what type of drink she's seeking, but the way she swipes the amber liquid is all the answer I need. She downs it like it's a shot of tequila during Spring Break in Cancun.

"More," she demands, her voice raspy from the liquor. I hurriedly refill and place the glass back into her eager palms.

"Fi, I know this is difficult for you to hear—"

She cuts me off with a raised hand, signaling me to stop. She sips her drink, —slower this time—but within minutes, it's gone.

"Better?" I ask, looking for any indication that I should refill. She simply nods and sets the glass down.

"This woman… was she pretty?"

"Fiona, you don't want to hear—"

"Just answer me, please." Her voice is barely above a whisper, but the pain is boldly evident. "Was she pretty? Tall? Slender? Glamorous?"

I started this conversation with truth. I can't deviate now. "Yes. She was." *But she wasn't you.*

"And did it seem like he wanted her to touch him?"

"He did. I'm sorry." I don't know why I'm apologizing for that prick, but I just can't stand to see the dark shade of dejection painted on her porcelain face.

"And did it seem like he was open to do more than just touching with her? Like, maybe he was hoping, willing, trying to *fuck* her?"

The word *fuck* from her lips sounds harsh and foreign to me, and I reflexively pull her into my arms to shield her from her own wicked tongue. She breaks in two, releasing a flash flood of tears that drowns the words from her quivering lips. So I speak them for her as I hold her close to my chest. I murmur them into her soft brown hair. I whisper them along her neck and earlobe. And I draw them onto her tear-streaked cheeks with the slightest graze of my mouth.

"Fi, I'm so sorry. I'm so sorry. I didn't want to tell you. I didn't want to hurt you."

Her sobs rip me open, and I'm unable to feel anything beyond her pain. There's no joy in this. No sense of victory or validation. There is no satisfaction in destroying Joshua. Because in the process, I've destroyed her. She is merely a casualty of war.

She holds onto my shirt, pulling me as close to her as I can get in hopes of sharing the hurt. It's too much for her to bear. And if I could go back to just minutes ago, I would take it all away. But then where would that leave her? In that lying fucker's arms.

It's several minutes before her body stills and her tears dry, yet she doesn't let go of me. I'm in no hurry to let her go either, so I angle my body so I can lift my legs onto the couch, pulling her with me. My back to the armrest, I position her damp cheek against my chest so I'm able to wrap her in my warmth.

"It's not fair, Rhys," she whispers. "I thought he actually liked me for me…possibly even be in love with me. But nothing changes, does it? It's not fair."

"I know it's not, honey. But the real injustice is you wasting your time on some smug asshole with a black card who looks at you as an accessory. You made him look like a decent human being, Fi. You asked me to find one tolerable trait in him, and I did. It was *you*."

"Hmph," she snorts in manufactured jest. "Well, since it was all just an act, that doesn't count."

I rub her back from her neck to the bottom of her spine. "Hey. Don't say that. Maybe he does really care for you, yet has commitment issues."

"Then why get into a committed relationship?"

"Did you two ever sit down and say that you would be exclusive?" Her silence speaks for her. "Fi, you can't expect someone like Joshua to figure out the rules unless you spell them out for him."

"I just thought… we're together all the time! Every day! When would he have time to date other women? And considering all that we've done, all that I did for him—because of him—why would he want to?"

I pull her up so her face is aligned with mine, so she can see the truth in my eyes. "Because he's a selfish, self-absorbed dick who doesn't know what he has right in front of him. Because if he did, he would have no need for other women. He wouldn't have to question whether or not he loved her, because it was physically impossible not to. And every second he suffered trying to fight against that fact would be an act of self-inflicted madness, because deep down, he always knew he was in love with her. Right from the start. From the top of her messy bun to the toe of her knee high socks. She was his muse, his soul mate. She was the beauty in his world of heartbreak."

Big brown eyes, glassy with fresh tears, stare at me as if trying to unearth the message in my words. But I stare right back, unwavering. Unwilling to take it back. I won't take it back. Not anymore.

"August…" She doesn't say it with its usual tinge of annoyance. My name is light and breathy on her tongue, like a feather caressing her lips. I brush my fingertips over her mouth, mimicking my thoughts, and she leans into the touch.

Her hands tremble against my chest, saying, "*What are we doing?*"

Mine rake through her hair to the nape of her neck, replying, "*Everything we should have done before. Rewriting our story.*"

I guide her lips to mine slowly, waiting for her to resist. Expecting her to slap me across the face and tell me I'm crazy, that I'm just imagining the bold electricity causing sparks between us in jagged, neon strands. But the assault never comes, because she wants this. She wants *me.* In the way that goes beyond friendship, beyond attraction, and beyond the pages.

Tongues collide in an erotic tussle of pants and licks. Her lips are softer than I expect, yet as sweet as I've imagined. Her warm breath sustains me, lending me life as I sink further into her kiss. She fists my shirt in a haze of hunger, her nails lightly scoring my chest. My hands grip her ass and hips, and I pull her in closer to me, desperately trying to mold her body with mine. She gasps into my mouth at the sensation of me throbbing against her, the quiver of my cock radiating through denim and cotton. She feels me there…wants me there. And I have every intention of taking her there.

Fiona whispers my name as my tongue slides down her neck, finding the sensitive spot that every hero in every book seems to know like the back of his hand. Her hands pull at my short-cropped hair when I tease it, nipping her flushed skin with my teeth. Her body is so responsive to me; I can feel her nipples harden through her light knit sweater. It feels like a thousand pounds of wool right now. I all but rip it off her and fling it across the room before doing the same with mine. Her bare skin sears against mine, the friction of our hunger causing every nerve ending to burn bright in radiant cobalt and vermillion and merigold. I feel her in my bones, aching in delicious pangs of need. Desire is wet heat that seizes my joints and ligaments, making it impossible to do much else but kiss her…hold her…love her.

I'm on my feet and she's in my arms, my waist tucked safely in the warmth between her legs. I move us through the living room where we once sat cross-legged eating take-out and listening to music, down the hallway that she helped me paint Hale Navy, and into the bedroom where her back meets my bed for the very first time. Her ankles are still locked around my ass, giving me perfect access to the fly of her jeans, so I slide my fingers down the flat expanse of her belly to battle the metal lock of her denim captivity. I go slow, giving her the chance to back out. Giving her the chance to tell me no.

She doesn't say no.

I lean forward, kiss her jaw and her neck. Leaving her mouth free to tell me to stop.

She doesn't say stop.

I hook my finger into her belt loops and slide her jeans down her thighs, taking my time, deliberately giving her the opportunity to tell me we can't.

She doesn't tell me we can't.

I'm on top of her, working my own jeans down my legs and kicking them off with more gusto than I've ever felt within these four walls, plastered in secrets and painted in lust. I'm so eager to feel her, to fuck her. No, not fuck her. To love her. To make love to her. Make love like I've never loved before. Because I haven't. Before this moment, before me and her. Before kiss-burned thighs and peach-tipped nipples and honey-flavored lips, I'd never known love. Because to me, love was a fantasy. A fairytale. And Fiona is and always has been the happiest of ever afters. She's my ghost. My reason for trusting in something as intangible and lucid as the air whistling through my clenched teeth as I push inside paradise. And, as I dip my head to kiss her through the pleasure of drowning in her ocean, the pain of letting go of all my inhibitions and insecurities, I know that for the first time, I irrevocably, intensely, insanely believe.

I HEAR MUSIC.

Fiona is naked and lying beside me, the sheets are tangled at our feet, and I hear music.

In movies, music is the backdrop to every pivotal scene, especially love scenes. But for me, music is the scene. It attaches itself to a memory and inks itself on your heart, so every time you hear that particular song from that point on, you're instantly transported back to that moment. You relive it. You breathe it. You feel it like you're right there, gripping the headboard, sliding inside her, hearing her whisper your name over and over.

However, the music is slightly skewed.

Sex in romance resembles your standard Bedroom Mix tape back in college. Sometimes it's light and fun and flirty like "Your Body is a Wonderland." Or maybe it's racy and enticing like "Sex on Fire." On a good day, it's the epitome of eroticism like "Freek'n You," or if you're lucky, just downright XXX-rated like the cult-favorite "Closer."

However, it is never, ever—under any circumstances—supposed to be like "One Minute Man." I'm a fan, but hell no… I don't need Missy Elliott pouring salt in the already festering wound of my ego. Bad (quick) sex doesn't happen in romance. So what the hell just happened here?

I count down from twenty as I study my bedroom ceiling, hoping that by the time I reach one, the last five minutes will be less mortifying. I'm being liberal with five minutes. Maybe to Fiona, it'll feel like more. Maybe like the best five minutes of her fucking life.

"That was… interesting." Nope. I was wrong.

I turn to look at her, but she doesn't move. Apparently, she also finds the ceiling riveting. "Interesting?"

"Yeah. Um. It was nice."

"*Nice?* That's even worse!"

"I'm sorry."

"You're sorry? Sorry that you said sex with me is nice? Oh my God, Fi. I swear, this never happens to me."

"It's fine. I know you've been under a lot of stress…"

"I'm good. Like, *really* good." Holy shit, I need to stop talking, but I can't. My dick may have given out like a two pump chump, but apparently my mouth is the Energizer bunny.

"It was nice, Rhys. Honestly."

"I'm not nice, Fi. I'm good. Great, even. Some say I'm the best they've ever had."

She finally turns to face me only to pin me with a skeptical cock of her brow. "Really?"

"Oh, for fuck's sake! We're doing it again. I'll show you. Just give me twenty minutes. And let me stretch this time."

"No!"

"What? Was it that bad? That you can't even stand to try it again? Oh, fucking hell…"

"No! I mean, yes. I mean, no it wasn't so bad that I can't stand to try again. But also, no, I don't want to do it."

That sobers me. "What are you saying?"

"Rhys…" She touches my bare arm, not with passion or lust, but in an act of comfort. Pity. "What we just did… it was a mistake. It should have never happened."

"Yes. Yes, it should have happened. It should have happened a long time ago."

"No!" She shakes her head and closes her eyes, as if trying to erase our reality. "We're friends. We're not…whatever this is. We're not the kind of friends that sleep together."

"Well, apparently, we are," I remark, motioning between our naked bodies, still damp with passion.

"Oh, hardly."

"Ouch."

"Sorry. I'm just really freaked out, and I don't know what to think right now." She covers her face with her hands and rolls onto her back. "Oh, God, what have we done? I have a boyfriend!"

"A boyfriend that cheats and lies," I remind her.

"Allegedly." As if the thought of being naked beside me repulses her, she jumps out of bed, shielding her body with trembling arms and hands, and begins collecting her clothes.

"I gotta go. I shouldn't be here. This isn't how it's supposed to be."

"Just wait a minute, Fi," I insist, sitting up and tugging on my boxer briefs.

She's running around my apartment, collecting her panties, her jeans, her shoes, like it's an erotic Easter egg hunt, and I'm right on her heels. "No! I need to get out of here! Don't you see what we've done? We just ruined everything!"

"Or we just made things right. You're freaking out, Fi. Come back to bed and we'll talk about it."

"I don't want to talk about it, August!"

"Oh, so I'm August now." In retrospect, it's petty, but it still stings.

She stills her search for her bra and shakes her head while running her fingers through her hair in frustration. Just mere minutes ago, I had that hair in my fists as I pumped into her.

Well… it only happened for a second, but it still happened.

Fiona looks up at me with tearful eyes, donning the same expression she wore when I told her about Joshua. "I didn't want this to happen. You mean too much to me, and I can't lose you. I'm sorry."

"But you won't lose—"

"This was a mistake!" she cries, all but running to my front door. I follow her, but she's already halfway down the stairs when I reach the frame, and I'm still in nothing but my skivvies.

"Wait, Fi!"

"I can't. I can't do this."

"Let's talk about this." Mrs. Roswell from across the hall

pokes her head out to investigate the commotion, but I don't give a damn. I shoot her an apologetic grimace and try to stretch my nearly naked body over the stairwell, just in time to see Fi reach the bottom landing.

"I'm sorry, August!"

Funny how three words can sound like *goodbye*.

I slink back into my apartment, leaving an amused Mrs. Roswell to gawk at my bare back alone. I had her. I had her where I've wanted her for so long. I didn't even realize that this was what had been missing from my life until I had held it in the palm of my hand. And now she's gone. Gone back to him as if all is forgiven and I'm left forgotten.

Maybe she was right; maybe this was a mistake. Maybe I've been fooling myself into believing we could be anything more than Rhys and Fi, BFFs. Shit, now I'm not sure if we're even that.

My mind is clouded with confused chaos. My body aches with the ghost of her touch. I feel like I'm losing my mind, and the one person who made me feel grounded just walked out the door. I get it. The sex was bad. Really, really bad. And that shit just doesn't fly in the world of romance. But this isn't a novel. And this damn sure doesn't feel like hearts and flowers. This feels like defeat.

Her scent is madness on my skin. The taste of her is torture on my tongue. Every thought of her makes every part of me throb in turmoil.

Disgusted with myself, I head into the bathroom to draw a bath. Usually, when I'm stuck on a scene or blocked, I like to take what I call a Brainstorming Bath. There's something about soaking in a tub of hot foamy water that makes my thoughts more fluid. I feel serene and weightless within the safety of those suds. And right now, I need to wash away the dark and dirty. I need to cleanse myself of the doubt and fear.

I sink into the nearly scalding water, allowing the heat to warm my tense muscles into submission. With my eyes closed and head propped on the tiled edge, I try to remember a time when Fiona wasn't the first person I thought of when I woke up. Or after I completed *Tears of Glass*… she was the one who held my hand when I hit Publish. And when it crashed and burned, she was right there, enduring a long whiskey weekend complete with my favorite comfort foods. Fiona was the one to put the pen back in my hand when I wanted to give up on writing, and she's read every word since. She's been my therapist, my confidant. She's shared my joys, my pains, my accomplishments, my failures.

I once told myself that I wanted to write something that made Fi fall in love. And now that I see that it wasn't the words I wanted her to hold so dearly that she couldn't help but weep as she read. I wanted to write something to make Fiona fall in love with *me*. Not my pretty words or my pretty face or any of the other inconsequential bullshit I had deemed important. I just wanted her to love me, her Rhys.

With a sense of clarity, I cup water with my hands and let it run over my face and chest. I have to do something to make her see—to make her believe—that what happened between us wasn't a fluke. I jump out of the tub renewed in my conviction and get dressed. If she won't come back to me, then I'll have to go to her.

I shouldn't be surprised that she isn't home, but for some reason, a pang of disappointment stabs my gut as I lay on the buzzer for the fourth time. I use my key to let myself inside, hoping like hell she isn't actually in there… and occupied. However, I find her place quiet and still, albeit a bit messy, as if she was in a hurry to leave. This shit should not bother me, but I'd be a fool to say it doesn't. A fool or a liar, and I've already mastered the art of the latter.

I text her to let her know I've come by. I leave her a voicemail. Another text. I pace the floor until the wood laminate runs thin. I curse myself every single second I'm here, hating her for not answering, and loving her because I can't fucking help it.

It's approaching midnight when I realize that I've spent an entire day pining and waiting. My only comfort comes in the form of scribbled notes on in my notebook. Even in my haste to get to her, I still managed to grab it on the way out the door. Old habits die hard. My sudden stimulus spark isn't surprising. Nothing is more inspirational than real life angst. Genius is bred in the darkest, loneliest parts of our minds.

I send one last text before I head home, asking her to meet me for brunch. She reads it, but she doesn't reply. Still, she reads it.

Some time after copious amounts of whiskey, followed by a vat of coffee to dilute the booze, I sit at our favorite table in our favorite bistro, waiting on a much-needed Bloody Mary from our favorite waitress. And while the tomato and vodka may start a riot once it hits the murky slurry currently simmering in my gut, I need something to drown the anxiety.

"Rhys."

I hear her before I see her. I must have dozed off while

staring at the words scrawled on the paper in front of me. I close my notebook and look up, hoping the mere sight of her would make this better. That *she* would make *me* better.

"Fi."

She stares at me without a hint of recognition. We've somehow become strangers overnight.

"Sit. Please," I say, as if coaxing a kitten from a high ledge. I want to touch her, hold her. I want to take her away from here and make her mine over and over again, the way I should have done yesterday when I had the chance. What can I say? Anticipation is a bitch.

On timid heels, she takes the chair across from me, and I swear I don't breathe until her backside meets the Tulip Bentwood.

"I'm glad you came." A day ago, I would have never said something like this to Fi. *I'm glad you came?* I would have greeted her with a hefty dose of snark. She would have given me that stern, sexy teacher look. Then we would have fallen into a seamless, easy banter. That was our love language.

Our server returns with my drink, temporarily relieving us from the overwhelming awkwardness. Fiona gives her a tight smile with her own order before reluctantly turning her eyes on me. I can see her battling the urge to flee. She's uncomfortable here with me. *Me.* A guy shaved her, sniffed her dirty drawers, and made her shit herself, yet *I'm* the one who makes her uneasy. Un-fucking-believable.

"Look, let's stop tip-toeing around the big ass, sequin-studded elephant in the room, shall we? We slept together, Fi. And while it didn't go as I would have planned, it happened. Now, I don't know if it meant something to you, but it damn sure meant something to me." I take a deep breath to conjure my nerves. If I want to make this work, I have to go there. I have to go to that place inside me where the vulnerability of truth hides. I have to drop the act and show her who I am…who I'm willing to be. For her. "Fiona, we've been best friends for a decade. There's nothing I wouldn't do for you and there's nothing you can't tell me. I don't regret what happened. The only thing I do regret is that conflicted look on your face. Tell me what I need to do to fix this. Tell me what I need to do for us to move forward. Because I want this, Fi. I want what you've—"

"He proposed."

"What?"

"Joshua. He proposed last night." She says it like it pains her to utter the words.

"Wait… what?" She couldn't have just said what I think she said. I refuse to hear it.

"He's moving his practice to Seattle, and he wants me to come with him…as his wife. When you saw him last night, you saw him celebrating with his new business partners. He was slated to appear at that seminar, but a last minute meeting with the investors came up. He said he had been planning to propose for a while, but that news just solidified his decision."

"Get the fuck out of here." I shake my head and down half my drink in just two gulps.

"And he told me how rude you were to him and his colleagues. He said you were out of control, and he's never been so embarrassed before in his life."

"*I* was out of control. *Wow*. Ain't that fucking rich." The rest of the drink goes down, and I lift my empty glass to signal for a new one. I won't even mention how Joshua and his *colleagues* tried to have a go at me. *Tried* being the operative word.

"And even with your outrageous behavior, he said he forgives you. He was even oddly grateful that there was someone who looked after me so fiercely. He understood how things may have looked, and felt there was even a sliver of validity in your reaction."

"You've got to be shitting me. It looked the way it was. Like he was being a fucking creep while you were gone, and the arrogant jackass didn't think he'd get caught."

"No, August. You misinterpreted what was happening."

"So I guess the chick in the lace catsuit trying to jerk him off was just giving him a handshake to seal the deal, huh?"

"See. There you go. You revert to being crude instead of trying to see both sides." She lifts her hand to pinch the bridge of her nose, as if even trying to explain this to my daft ass is giving her a migraine. And that's when I'm momentarily blinded by the small boulder resting on her left hand.

"You said *yes*."

The fire in her glare dies to embers, and she quickly hides her hand under the table.

"You said yes."

Fiona nods like she's ashamed of the gesture, or maybe afraid of my reaction. "Of course, I did. It's everything I've ever wanted. *He's* everything I've ever wanted."

"But what about..." I can't even bring myself to say what is so boldly etched on my heart.

What about Netflix marathons and pineapple and ham

pizza?

What about Saturday night secrets over French toast and mimosas on lazy Sundays?

What about make believe backstories and food truck fare?

What about texting at three a.m. about absolutely nothing?

What about bookstore treasure hunts that end with us reciting our favorite passages on the threadbare floor?

What about listening to emo rock book playlists over takeout followed by whiskey-sponsored singing?

What about history? Chemistry? Destiny?

What about *us?*

"You knew I wanted a life, August. I wanted a husband, kids, a house. I wanted someone I could grow old with, make memories with. Fifty years from now, I want to have someone to share a scoop of ice cream with in the park."

"You can have all those things with me." I don't even think. I just say it.

Fiona shakes her head. "You don't mean that in the same way I do."

"But, I do, Fi. I want what you want. And I want it with *you*." I'm hanging by the tiny, thin thread of my dignity, exchanging the safety net of my denial for her heart. "What happened between us wasn't a fluke. It was exactly what I've wanted since that day in your dorm room. It's what I've wanted every day since, but was just too stupid and stubborn to admit it."

She goes silent for a moment, digesting my confession. However, when she meets my earnest gaze, none of the expected affection rests within her bourbon brown eyes. Not even a hint of tenderness, or even gratitude. Actually, she looks downright pissed.

"This is so typical of you, August. You just couldn't let me have this, could you? You just couldn't let me be happy."

I grimace at the sting behind her words. "What? Of course, I want you to be happy."

"Really? On whose terms?" She throws her hands up in exasperation, nearly knocking over her still full mimosa. "For once, I'm not all about you. You're not the center of my world. I'm not just August Rhys Calloway's hopeless, loveless gal pal—his one-woman cheerleading squad. I actually have a life of my own, and you can't handle it. Ten years, August! Ten years I've been at your beck and call, watching your revolving door of hook ups, telling you every detail of my relationship misfortune. And not once did you deem it appropriate to tell me your feelings before now. But that's right… you didn't know up until now, did you? Until a handsome, successful man that wasn't *you* showed genuine interest in me. Tell me the truth, August: Had it not been for Joshua's presence in my life, would anything have even changed between us? Would you have been honest about your affections for me?"

I take a beat to consider my next words. I want to give her the truth, but not at the expense of what's left of us. "Eventually, I would have…"

"You would have what? Come to your senses to see what was right in front of you all along? Admit it, August. We would have been right where we were ten years ago. Me making myself embarrassingly available, and you seeing me as nothing but a pathetic sap that you hang out with when you have no one better to do."

"Bullshit," I spit out before she can even complete the blasphemous sentence. "You know as well as I do that I always put you before any women I date."

"You date? Since when is fast food and meaningless sex dating? And considering your track record, what would make you think I'd be ok with being just a part of your rotation? I guess you would call me Brunch, huh?"

If she were anyone else, I would have already given her a tongue-lashing so harsh that she'd be crying into her spiked OJ. "You're being ridiculous, and you know it."

"Whatever. Maybe I am." She finally takes a sip of her mimosa before pursing her lips in irritation. "It doesn't matter anyway. It's not like you'll want to pretend much longer."

"Pretend? What the hell does that even mean? What the hell does *any* of this mean?"

"Yesterday… what we did. Didn't you say sex was your only objective when it came to women? That you had no interest whatsoever in anything deeper than that?"

"Yeah, but—"

"Then that's it for me—for us. You got what you wanted, right? You came, you saw, you conquered. Someone like you wouldn't have much use for someone like me anyway. And that's fine. I'm not looking to be someone's occasional nightly entertainment. I want substance, August. And while you have the ability to create magic, I fear that you are completely empty inside. And that…that is truly a tragedy."

It takes everything in me not to get up from this table, seething with ire and passion, and tell her in vividly colorful detail just how wrong she is, just before pulling her into my arms and kissing her with so much conviction that her knees weaken under the weight of our love.

But that only happens in fictional worlds erected on an onyx-inked canvas. And this is by far the realest shit I have ever felt.

"Fuck you, Fi," I spit out in frustration before pushing away from the table, the chairs legs cutting angry slits into the hardwood. She looks up at me dumbfounded, confused by my reaction. Wondering why the hell her words could have affected me so deeply when all she did was serve me cold truth on a silver platter. I don't bother to set her straight or defend myself. I don't even look at her. I do exactly what's expected of me. What I've done to every person who has ever told me something I didn't want to hear, nonfiction or not.

I turn and walk away as if the last ten minutes, the last ten hours, the last ten years never existed. I leave it all behind on the white linen tablecloth of my once favorite table at our once favorite bistro with my once favorite girl. She is merely a memory of my best friend, and I a ghost of hers. Trouble is, she doesn't believe in me.

Maybe Fi was right. Maybe I do self-sabotage. Maybe people like me and her can never be more than friends. Shit, maybe I'm not meant to be more than friends with anyone. Because as I retreat into the safety of my detachment—where I lick my wounds doused in scotch and nurse my sorrow-scrawled scars—I can't think of one good goddamn reason why I thought I could be capable of more.

"WANT TO HEAR A JOKE?"

In the fog of dejection, I nod. I'm hollow inside, allowing words and thoughts and emotions to float disjointedly in my head. So I say nothing, in hopes that soon, I may feel nothing.

"What's a Dallas Cowboys' favorite pastry?" the Colonel asks, his eyes still fixated on the screen. My gaze is trained ahead, but I haven't see a thing. I didn't even realize the Seahawks were playing the Cowboys.

I barely open my mouth, and answer without breathing. "What?"

"A turnover!"

I nod again, the only sign of coherency I'm able to muster. I wouldn't have even come if it weren't for having to pick up Bartleby. Plus, I promised the Colonel, and I always try to keep my promises. I'm a liar, but I try to at least be a loyal one.

Several quiet minutes tick by before my grandfather speaks again, yet he still stares intently at the televised violence that uncannily resembles the mish mosh of turmoil in my empty gut.

"Something on your mind, son?" He knows the answer. He knows I'm not myself, that I've strolled in here this lovely fall afternoon just a fraction of the man I was just yesterday. Fiona cut me to the quick, and I've been left a bleeding, severed carcass. Incomplete in every way.

Yet, and still, I answer, "Nope."

"Sure about that?"

"Yup."

He doesn't pry. We've learned to communicate with the words that go unspoken.

He grunts, *"I'm here when you want to talk about it, son."*

I nod, *"I know, Colonel. Thank you. I just can't. Not now."*

I'm two seconds from throwing in the towel on the charade when we hear the familiar foghorn cackling and windbreaker sweat suit swish of Hell-On-Wheels Helen. I roll my eyes and heave a heavy sigh, sinking further into the couch, wishing like hell it would swallow me whole. I can avoid the Colonel's questions, but I have no patience or energy for Helen's incessant prying.

"Benny! Lovely to see you, darling. And with August here as well. Look at that! April was just telling me what a splendid time you two have been having."

I look up to find not one but two pairs of blue eyes vying

for my attention. I must look like shit, yet they're both nearly salivating all over Helen's cheap nylon jacket, which is fittingly decked out in orange and black for Halloween.

Shit. Where have I been? It's almost November already, meaning my deadline is much closer than I mentally calculated.

"Nice to see you, Helen. April." I force myself to my feet to greet them both with kisses on their cheeks. I owe April that much. She was totally cool about the way I left things with her. And for what? To rescue a girl who didn't need rescuing? Who didn't want it? From me? "It's good to see you," I tack on when I pull away and sit back down, moving over to indicate that she should join me, leaving Helen to torture the Colonel on the other side of the couch.

"Didn't expect to see you here, August," she smiles stiffly, reading the tension around my eyes. "Everything ok…with your friend?"

"Yeah, um, everything's fine. Sorry I haven't called in a while. I was out of town. Just got back Friday night."

"Oh. Well…I'm glad to hear it."

"Thanks again," I say, scrubbing the back of my neck, feeling like a complete jackass. I feel like I've let her down, like I owe her something. An explanation, an apology, a do-over—something. But before I can offer the tiny bit of fuck I have left, she beats me to the punch.

"Hey, how about dinner some time this week? I make a mean chicken parm."

"Oh, yeah?" I don't have the heart to turn her down, yet what's left of it—the tattered, bloody mess that beats raggedy within my chest cavity—is just not feeling this. Not feeling her. Not feeling anything but confusion and frustration and, shit, fucking rage for putting myself out there and revealing the only honest part of my soul only to have it mocked and derided for an audience of bemused diners enjoying shirred eggs and scones.

They say there are five stages of grief. Well, I think I'm tackling at least two of those fuckers simultaneously with all the grace of a bull doing ballet.

"So…dinner?" April pipes up quietly, pulling me back to the conversation, the room. Back to sanity. She watches intently as I chew my bottom lip, pondering the best way to explain my predicament.

I'm tragically in love with my best friend —whom I've just slept with—however, she's in love with a cocksucking, cheating scumbag with a great head of hair. So while yes, I'd ordinarily love to eat your chicken parm and whatever else you're offering, I'm much too fucked up in the head to see past anything that isn't Fiona Shaw, as much as I hate her right now.

"Hey, son. Let's go to my apartment to get that thing you came for so you can get back to work. I know your deadline is approaching," the Colonel says, climbing to his feet and throwing me a lifeline. I nod my appreciation. Nodding is good. Nodding keeps me from blurting out something I'll regret tomorrow.

"Yes sir. You're right about that." Turning to April, I offer her the consolation of a regretful smile. "I'll… I'll see you." I don't when or how or in what capacity. I don't have any pretty lies to warm her heart or her bed tonight.

Her eyes lower to the floor, refusing to let me see the hurt in them, and I'm grateful. I don't care about her pain. I can't. I'm too consumed with my own.

"You're talkative today," the Colonel remarks tersely when we've made it to his apartment. Bartleby clambers down from his spot on the couch and greets me at my feet, rubbing his fluffy body against my ankles.

"Yeah."

"Everything ok with the book?"

"The book is fine," I reply flatly.

"And the deal out in Hollywood… still haven't decided?"

"Nope."

"And things with Fiona are good?"

Bingo.

My answer is my non-answer, and I busy myself by stalking over to the kitchen and gathering Bart's things. And by gathering, I mean throwing them unceremoniously in a grocery tote bag with enough force to punch a hole in the flimsy canvas. Food, bowls, brush, treats. At one point, I think I tossed in a dust bunny that the cleaning ladies must've missed.

"August, is Fiona ok?"

I suck my teeth in distaste. "She's fine," I spit out while gathering Bart's bed and toys.

"You two having a fight?"

"No." Technically, we're not. We're not having anything, for that matter. Not even a friendship according to her theory.

"Hmph. Is that right?" he grunts, feigning nonchalance. But the pitbull in him just won't let it go. He just won't let me dry swallow my rage, letting it shred my insides on the way down until I'm retching my bright red denial. He won't let the hollowness take me to that place where fiction reigns and truth is burned at the stake for its black magic audacity, charged with domestic terrorism on the homeland of my heart.

Goddamn that truth. Goddamn the Colonel. Goddamn his wisdom, his insight. Goddamn my inability to ever amount to the man he was—the man he is today.

"She said yes," I sputter. I look away just as the whites of my eyes are colored in red-inked rejection.

"What?"

"Fiona. The doctor asked her to marry him. She said yes."

"You're kidding."

"No," I reply darkly. "He's moving her to Seattle. And she said yes. Yes to marrying some asshole she hardly knows. Yes to leaving her home, her job. Yes to leaving her family and friends." *To leaving me.* "She said yes to all of it like she never even gave a damn. Like her life here was merely a holding pattern, and she was just waiting for her white knight to sweep her off her feet and fly her far away from mediocrity. She said yes."

My grandfather is a logical man. A thinking man. And instead of regurgitating his disdain as I have so eloquently done in the past, he grows quiet and still for a beat. Then he looks up at me with an expression that borders and sympathy and shock.

"How do you feel about that?"

Words bubble up my throat so quickly that I nearly choke. "How the fuck do you think I feel?" I grimace. I should apologize, but I'm tumbling recklessly through the

Anger stage, hoping to get to the sweet detachment on the other side.

"I think you're mad at the wrong person, that's what I think," he says softly, yet sternly.

"Oh, don't you worry. I'm plenty pissed at her too."

"I don't mean Fiona, August. I mean *you*."

I stop stalking around the room in search of invisible cat toys, and turn to look at him. "What the hell is that supposed to mean?"

I can see him fighting with his patience at my tone. Even Bartleby has good sense enough to retreat behind the sofa. "It means the real person you should be directing that anger at is yourself. August, you've had Fiona for ten years. Since the day you met her—"

"Had her? I've never had Fi."

"You had her. From day one, she was yours. But you were too blind and too stupid to see it. You thought chasing every skirt in town somehow made it less true. But every night, it was her you were calling, divulging all your secrets. It was her that waited patiently at home while you ran the streets at night. Her that listened to your ideas, your dreams, your fears. And you didn't see her, August. You didn't see what was right there in front of you all along. Not until someone else had eyes for her."

I shake my head. "Now you sound like her."

"Am I wrong?"

"You are," I lie. "It's not like that. We're friends. I'm just disappointed she was so desperate for marriage that she settled for the first guy that came along with a Jared credit account. I thought I knew her better than that."

"No. You thought she would always be there, waiting in the wings until you deemed your wild oats sufficiently sowed. And now you're upset that she decided to chase her own happiness. You can't have it both ways, August. You can't have her, yet refuse to let her have you."

"You don't know what you're talking about."

"I know a lot more about life and love than anything you could ever write in your silly little books, young man."

I snort sardonically and shake my head again. "Whatever. I have to go."

"Fine," the stubborn old man barks.

"Fine," my equally stubborn younger self retorts.

We trudge off in opposite directions, me towards the couch to scoop up Bart, and him to his bedroom. The Colonel and I never argue. He talks and I listen. But today, I've heard enough. From him, from her. I've heard enough.

Begrudgingly, I have to go through the main building to exit the grounds, and I'm in no mood to play it coy with the residents. So when Helen catcalls me from the crochet table, it takes everything in me not to tell the blue-haired biddy to fuck off.

"August! There you are. April apologizes for her hasty departure, but she has to work today."

"That's fine," I grumble, trying to escape. Bart squirms uncomfortably in my arms. Even he can feel me tick-tick-ticking closer to a category 5 explosion.

"I have to tell you..." she rambles on, "I am absolutely delighted about you dating my granddaughter. I never pegged you for the romantic type—you're almost as rigid and reticent as your grandfather. But April is more than a little smitten with you. I guess it's true what they say. Love finds you when you least expect it."

My mouth says, "I guess so." But my mind is screaming, *"Oh, please shut the fuck up about love."*

Love is what got me into this mess. Love is the reason I snapped at the one man I've looked up to since I was a scrawny ass kid. Love is the reason I tried to be someone I clearly am not, only to make a fool of myself.

So fuck the fairytale. Fuck trying to conform for the sake of someone else's view of happiness. I create the fantasies. I don't live them. Not anymore.

Chapter Seventeen

I CAN'T STAY HOME.

I can't look at these walls and pretend like she's not embedded in every crack and fissure. I can't sit on the couch and not smell her scent of lavender shampoo on the leather. I can't listen to music without hearing her favorite songs torturing me on repeat. I can't watch TV without wondering if the pregnant virgin had her baby or conjuring memories of vegging out with Law and Order: SVU marathons. And I can't write without every word—every fucking syllable and vowel—being about her.

To avoid going to prison for arson, I grab my coat and a cab and head down to the bar district. It's Sunday, so it's quiet. But I'm not here to socialize. I'm here to forget.

"Well, isn't this a pleasant surprise," Maureen, my artsy bartender smiles before licking her cherry lips. "Been a while, August. I thought you had forgotten all about me."

"How could I ever do that, Mo?" I smirk, sliding onto a barstool.

She wipes down the counter and places a cocktail napkin in front of me. "What'll it be, handsome?"

"Scotch neat. For now."

"For now?" she coos as she makes my drink.

"Yes. For now. What time do you get off? Or should I say, what time am I getting you off?"

The blessed thing about Sundays is that it's dreadfully slow after there are no more football games to air. So after a few drinks and unholy confessions, Maureen and I are making abstract art between the sheets of her queen-sized bed. She licks lazy strokes up my thighs until heat gathers at the base of my spine. I paint pretty pictures on her soft, pink canvas. I shatter her into a million pieces and scatter her ashes amongst a sky full of neon colored stars. I do to her what I should have done to Fiona.

"What's wrong?" she asks, halting her tongue's advance down my torso.

"Nothing," I insist, gently pulling the magenta curls at the nape of her neck.

"No. I felt you flinch. Am I hurting you?"

"Of course not. I'm just ticklish there." The lie rolls off my tongue like butter. There's no way I could tell her Fiona was responsible for pulling me out of the moment. Just the thought of her makes me feel…I don't know. Inadequate? And that's not a feeling I'm used to.

To scrub her from my mind, I flip Maureen over onto

her back, and reach over for another condom from the nightstand, slipping it on in five seconds flat.

"Again?" she breathes, her eyes wild with lust.

"Hell yeah," I all but groan as I part her legs and slip into her.

I need this. I need to rage fuck her into the headboard until all thoughts of Fiona are purged from my mind. Even if I can't feel her, hear her, taste her...at least I won't have to constantly be tormented with the remembrance of another woman.

I'm pumping into to her viciously, chasing the high of orgasm that seems so close yet somehow unobtainable, when Maureen presses her glittery blue tipped fingers to my cheek. It's too tender, too soft. Too much of what it felt like to be artificially loved by Fi. I try to turn away and focus on the feel of her warmth wrapped around me, but she guides my face to hers.

"Hey," she whispers with too much sweetness on her tongue.

"Yeah?"

She frowns, and the whites of her eyes glaze with emotion I refuse to acknowledge. "Where are you?"

I dig into her hard, relentlessly, causing her breath to stutter, but she doesn't give up. "Where are you, August," she mewls through waves of pleasure.

"I'm here. Don't you feel me?" Another deep stroke that makes her shiver underneath me.

"No, you're not," she moans. "I feel your body, but I can't feel your soul."

I pull my face out of her grasp and gather her wrists

above her hands. Then I bury myself deep inside her, as far as I can go. Until I'm hidden in the safe arms of denial.

I don't come. I can't. I have nothing left in me to give.

"Don't go," she begs when I sit up at the edge of the bed. Her fingernails carve glittery trails on my back. She's still panting, and so am I, but I have to go. There's nothing here for me.

"Have to write," is all I offer her before pulling on my jeans. She sighs when I stand up to finish dressing, but I don't look at her. I'm too ashamed to face the disappointment in her eyes.

"I'm glad I saw you tonight. I needed to talk to you."

"Oh yeah?"

"I met someone. A nice guy. I really like him."

"Congratulations," I remark flatly.

"Things are getting serious."

"That's nice."

"So… maybe we should just be friends. He's a good catch. Good job, dependable, attentive. I want to make it work with him."

Somewhere in the world, Alanis Morrisette is dusting off her red beanie and phoning home to 1995. All I can do is chuckle darkly before leaning over to place a final kiss on Maureen's still damp forehead.

"Take care of yourself, Mo." When I pull away, she looks affronted.

"Wait. So you don't even care?" she stammers. "That's it?"

I shrug on my coat and turn for the exit. "That's all it ever was."

My skin is crawling by the time I hit the frost-kissed sidewalk. I tell myself that I'll just walk up the street back toward the bar district to catch a cab, but the feeling of cool air against my face is a refreshing reprieve from the burning in my gut. I feel sick and grimy. The ruse of momentary passion as I filled Mo with my dirty lies was regrettable at best. Sex once inspired me. By freeing my body, I was able to open my mind. And I was a man of many muses, each of them willing to do their part to arouse my psyche. But that—what I'd just done with Maureen—didn't feel like inspiration. It felt like a transaction. And I didn't even have the decency to leave the money on the dresser.

Before I know it, I'm halfway to my apartment, so I say *fuck it* and keep going. It's cold tonight, but I don't care. It's a welcome distraction—focusing on nothing more than the frigid bite of late October on my cheeks over the hollow ache in my chest. Fiona said I was empty, and my actions tonight proved her right. And as I approach my apartment building, the vacant space in my chest expands with the remembrance of her scent wafting over me as she kissed my lips. A tangible ache blooms within the void, clinging to my ribs like thick, sticky tar as I remember the sound of her moan when I entered her. The achiness evolves into searing burn as it slides like sludge through my bloodstream at the memory of the way her body felt beneath mine. Her warmth…her softness…is my torture. And every thought is a stinging lash across my battered heart.

I expect to walk into my cold, desolate apartment, pour a few fingers of scotch, and stare blankly at my manuscript while Bartleby licks himself from his spot on my desk. But what I don't expect is someone sitting on my living sofa, the same sofa I had been contemplating burning. And I damn sure don't expect that someone to be the very same person I had been obsessing about all damn day long.

"August."

I stalk towards her, pain and anger carrying me to my self-made torture chamber.

"Oh, so I'm August now?"

WE DON'T SPEAK. WE HARDLY look at each other. I take off my coat, wishing I had showered before leaving Maureen's apartment. I wonder if she can smell the sex on me. I wonder if betrayal singes her nostrils and disgust roils her stomach. I wonder if she would even give a fuck.

I retreat to the stainless steel sanctity of my kitchen for a much-needed dose of liquid fire. The good stuff stays on the shelf. I need JD to have my back on this one.

"I'm sorry."

Her voice fills the silence and pierces right to the empty pit of my stomach. Shit. When was the last time I'd eaten a decent meal?

"You said that before. But according to you, you have

nothing to be sorry for."

"I know, it's just… I'm sorry. It seems appropriate."

"False remorse seems appropriate?"

"It's not false. I truly am…sorry. For what I said."

"Are you still engaged?"

Her brown eyes dart around the room nervously as if the answer lies somewhere within the scattered books that rest atop almost every surface. "Um, yes." It's like being punched in the gut.

"Then you're not sorry," I reply, schooling my features to keep from wincing.

"I am. I'm sorry for hurting you."

"Who said I was hurt?"

"August…"

I let myself really look at her for the first time since I arrived. She's wearing a blue turtleneck sweater dress and knee-high boots. They're her clothes, not something that was bought or picked out for her. She came without the armor.

"I'm not hurt, Fi."

"But what you said… about feeling for me…"

I down my drink in a swift gulp. "Forget about it. Must've been the Bloody Mary talking. It's no big deal."

She climbs to her feet and abandons her spot from the very same couch where we shared our first kiss. "You don't have to lie to me, August. I know you, and I know you don't say things you don't mean."

I laugh so loudly that it makes her take a step back. "Seriously? I don't mean *anything* that I say. Or have you already forgotten?"

She shakes her head, refusing to acknowledge the badge

of truth that I've worn so boldly for years. "I don't believe that."

"How can you not?" I ask, throwing my hands up incredulously. If my glass wasn't already empty, it would be now. "Fi, you know better than anyone on earth what type of guy I am. I write romance, for fuck's sake, and I not only reject the notion of it, I loathe it. I just tell people what they want to hear. Women especially."

"Yeah, but that's different," she asserts. "*We're* different."

"How so? You said so yourself, Fi—I have no interest in women unless I'm sleeping with them. And that's the *only* interest."

"Yeah, but..." Her eyes grow wide and glossy as she tries to sift through all the reasons why that theory shouldn't apply to her. In the end, she relies on her heart. "You said I wasn't like those other women...that those other women weren't me."

I should tell her she's right. I should put her out of her misery and reassure her that the last ten years were as real and meaningful to me as they were for her. That even though I may sling gift-wrapped bullshit for the general public, only she knows the true, honest parts of my heart. But with my tongue possessed by the taste of her rejection, I play the petty card, and do just the opposite.

"I guess I was wrong, especially considering yesterday's events. Maybe you're no different from them. And maybe you were right about me...that I do sabotage with sex to keep people at arm's length. Because in the end, that's all I want anyway, right?"

"You don't mean that."

I nod. "Yeah. I do."

"So what are you saying?" The hurt is so thick in her throat that I can barely hear the words.

I suck in a breath, and scrub a hand over my forehead. "You were right about me. About *us*. We shouldn't have done…what we did. And we can't move on and pretend that it didn't change us. What's done is done."

"I agree," she nods, with a tinge of hope in her voice.

"So, maybe we should just see this for what it is—the end. You're starting your life with Joshua and moving away, and I'm going on with mine."

"Wait, August. No, that's not—"

"You didn't actually think we'd be able to keep this up, did you? What, you thought we'd turn out to be the modern day Cathy and Heathcliff? I'm not some *swoony*, literary hero, Fi. I'm not here to rescue you from your shitty love life that stems from your shitty childhood."

"I never said you were—"

I'm rambling, spewing verbal diarrhea all over her blue cashmere, but I can't stop. I can't shut off the bile that has been choking me since this morning when she disclosed her impending nuptials. "You have Joshua. He's the one you chose. He's the one you want. You made that perfectly clear. So what the fuck do you need with me?"

"I thought we were friends, August. I thought you and me were—"

"Well, I guess you were wrong. Friends don't fuck each other and then five minutes later get engaged. And why would you want to be friends with some empty, misogynistic prick like me anyway?"

"I-I didn't mean," her voice cracks, and the first tear escapes. She quickly dashes it away, refusing to let me play witness to her weakness. But I've already seen it. I share that very same weakness that has her bottom lip trembling. I'm just too much of a coward to show it.

"Look, I'm sorry. I think we just need a break."

"A break. Yes," she nods, dashing away tears. "You're right. We both said things we shouldn't have. Let's just take a few days to…"

"No. A break from this," I clarify, gesturing between us. "From us. This isn't working anymore."

"You're being melodramatic, August. We've had fights before. We've said things we didn't mean, and we always were able to work it out."

I shake my head and look away, refusing to acknowledge the dejection on her face. "But I meant everything I said."

It's quiet for a moment too long. I want to turn to her. I want to take it all back, but I can't. This isn't me being stubborn. This is me trying to save myself.

I sense her before I feel her. Her soft, petite hand grazes my jaw with the lightest of touches. I turn into her palm and catch a glimpse of the pain set deep in her eyes. All it would take is one second. One single moment to make this right. It'd be so easy fall back into the comfort of her arms. Easier than it is to pretend that I don't want her.

But then what?

She'll still go home to him, and I'll still be alone. She'll get married, and I'll chase the empty thrill of casual sex. She'll move to Seattle and I'll still be here, going to our once favorite bistro, sitting at our once favorite table, and scribbling notes about the girl that just didn't get away, but the girl who *ran* away.

I pull back from her touch, knowing that a second longer will only cost me hours, days, weeks of torment. "You should go home to your fiancé." My voice is as cold and icy as my heart.

"You don't mean that." She reaches out to touch me again, but I grip her wrist before her hand meets my cheek.

"I do. Go, Fiona. Go home to him. I have nothing for you."

"But, August, I—"

"Just go! Leave me alone! You said so yourself—I'm empty…that once I get what I want from a woman, I'm done." I tip my head down so my eyes are aligned with hers. So she can see with crystal clarity that I mean what I say. So she can feel the heat of my rage fan over her face. "I've gotten what I wanted. So unless you plan to be naked and splayed across my desk in the next two minutes, we're done here."

She just stands there, horror and humiliation splotched on her pale face like twin bloodstains. She doesn't move. She doesn't speak. At this point, she doesn't even cry.

"Ok. If that's what you want."

I begin to undress, starting with my shirt. She doesn't want to look at me, but she can't help but stare at my bare, rippled torso. Or maybe she's looking through me. It's hard to tell if she's even aware of what's happening at all.

I work on my jeans next, taking my time with the belt and zipper. I'm stalling—for her and for me. I want her to come to her senses. I want her to tell me to stop. I'm still soiled with the remnants of my time with Maureen, and no matter how pissed I am with her, she doesn't deserve that.

Fiona flinches when my jeans hit the hardwood, the belt buckle slicing into the moment with a piercing clang. It's enough to wake her from her trance and realize what's happening. She blinks rapidly, taking in my tense, nearly naked body and the obvious erection bulging in my boxer briefs. She sucks in a breath as she stares at it, bites her bottom lip as she remembers it, and shakes her head as she collects herself.

"You're disgusting," she sneers.

"Am I?" I smirk, sliding a finger under the waistband of my underwear and running it along the rigid V of taut muscle. Her eyes follow the movement in an act of betrayal.

"Why are you doing this to me?"

"Baby, I'm not doing anything to you. Not yet," I taunt.

"August, stop it. Put your clothes back on."

"Is that what you really want me to do? Because considering the way you're looking at me, I'm betting you're just itching for me to take everything off."

"No, I don't want that," she quavers.

"No? So if I do this..." I pull down one side of my briefs, exposing a chiseled hip and my upper thigh. "You don't like that?"

"No." Her expression is hard, but her body disagrees. She shifts from one foot to the other in an act nervous arousal, and the flush of her cheeks blooms bright red.

"Oh. Then maybe it's *this* that you want."

In a boorish act of desperation, I slip a hand down the front of my shorts and palm my cock. It throbs in my hand, and without even meaning to, I moan at the tight feel around it. The sound is like a jolt of electricity in her veins, and she gasps at my sordid audaciousness. Her reaction is exactly the motivation that I need, and even though I want to hurl at my own repugnance, I begin to stroke my cock slowly inside the barrier of thin cotton, my unrelenting gaze trained on her. She covers her mouth as she realizes what I'm doing and takes a step back. Angry, devastated tears rim her reddened eyes. I answer the sight with a haughty groan.

"Stay away from me!" she shrieks as she rushes to escape my apartment.

"Wait, don't you want to—"

"Leave me the hell alone!"

The last thing I see before she slams the front door is a blur of cobalt-streaked tears and tousled brown hair. I drop the act and sag onto the couch, my mind and body too exhausted to even bother redressing or showering. It wouldn't matter anyway. I'll never be clean again.

I'M NOT SOBER UNTIL THURSDAY.

It's not by choice though. Thursdays are reserved for meatballs, and even though I haven't even bothered to check in with the Colonel since our argument Sunday, which will also be known as the day I lost my ever-loving mind, I know he'll be expecting me for Thursday night football and homemade Italian. So after a much needed shower, shave and about a gallon of water to flush away the whiskey and remorse, I reluctantly trudge down to the senior center. However, I realize within seconds that I should have stayed my ass home.

"You look like shit," my grandfather says in greeting. He's sitting on the couch in the entertainment room and staring at the TV with a plate of untouched meatballs on his lap.

"Nice to see you too," I remark, taking the space next to him.

"I didn't think you were coming. Had I'd known, I would've waited."

"That's ok. I'm not hungry."

He looks down at the hunk of meat and sauce on a Styrofoam plate and blanches. "Yeah, me neither." He sets down the flimsy platter on the coffee table.

We go without speaking for several minutes, both of us pretending to be wholly engrossed in the match up between Green Bay and Arizona. I know he was just trying to be helpful and objective, but I'm too stubborn to admit it. And he knows I was just being frustrated and overly sensitive, but he's too thoughtful to say it. So we sit and pretend like we're not silently suffering, letting the silence build mountains and stretch valleys between us. We've never fought like this before, but then again, I'm on a roll.

"I think I'm going to turn in early," the Colonel states right around halftime. He struggles to stand up, and when I reach out to help him, he waves me away. To say the Colonel is prideful is an understatement.

"Let me walk you back to your apartment."

Again, a wave. "Nonsense. I'm a grown man. I got myself here, and I can get myself home. Go on. I'm sure you need to write."

"Yeah," I remark, running a hand through my thick brown hair. I'm in serious need of a haircut. And with the touch of Asian blood in my genes, my hair has begun to curl around my ears and forehead.

"I'll see you later, son," he murmurs.

I stay for a minute too long to watch him walk to his place. Had I hightailed it out of there, I would have missed Helen and her granddaughter, April, who I still haven't called. Luckily, April doesn't seem too nonplussed about my communication skills, or lack thereof.

"Nice to see you," she smiles. "Looks like I got here just in time."

"Yeah, uh," I stammer. "I was just leaving, actually. The Colonel is tired, and I have a deadline."

"Oh." Disappointment dimples her brow. "Well, ok. Maybe we can get together this weekend?"

"Yeah. Maybe." I don't even bother sugarcoating it with some lackluster promise.

"I've got a thing for work this Saturday. A Halloween party. Maybe you could come?"

"I don't know," I grimace. "Usually I just sit around and watch really awful horror flicks and OD on candy corn and caramel apples on Halloween." *With Fiona.*

"Oh. Well, maybe we could meet up after?"

She seems really pressed, and clearly not picking up on my less than amiable vibe, so I put her out of her misery and nod. "Sure. Sounds good."

The light in her baby blues flicks on instantly, so I lean in to leave her with a peck on the cheek before she starts picking out the color scheme of our wedding. I have to get out of here. But there's honestly nowhere I want to go.

I stick to my guns and resist the temptation of scantily clad women donning bunny ears and cat tails in 30 degree temps, and resolve to staying in. However, nothing is going as planned, and my company for the evening has zero interest in Scream or The Human Centipede.

"Brad from my Contracts class asked me to go to some stupid party tonight. He even tried to entice me with the promise of a keg. Seriously, how did half of those dumbasses even make it into law school? When they're evidently still latched on to their mother's tit?"

Denae sips her Malbec and runs a bare foot along my leg. I hate it. I hate it with the fiery passion of Lucifer in a sauna with a red-hot poker rammed up his ass. I down the rest of my scotch, in hopes I will hate it less.

Nope. Still hate it.

"And he even expected me to dress up in lingerie like some half-wit bimbo who thinks Red Lobster is a fancy restaurant. Did I tell you I let him take me to dinner once? And *that's* where he took me? He thought I was a sure bet because I ordered the Endless Shrimp. Fucking inbred hillbilly."

Exasperated by the grating sound of her voice, and her overall attitude, I push her feet from my thigh, and turn to her. "Let's go fuck."

Denae blinks rapidly before polishing off her wine. "Ok."

It takes less than sixty seconds to get her in my bedroom and naked. There's no sexy shimmy out of her panties. No dirty talk, no roleplaying, no costumes. Shit, there's hardly any foreplay. I push her gently onto the bed, and position myself between her thighs. My tongue teases her nipples briefly just before pushing into her without prelude. I'm immersed in her to the hilt in one swift, unapologetic thrust, causing her to scream out with shock and pleasure.

"God, August, you're ruthless," she shrieks, pulling my

hair.

I grab her hands at her wrists and yank her hands up over her head. "Shut up."

"What?"

"I said shut up," I grit between clenched teeth.

"Ooooh, you wanna play Dom tonight, huh? Oh, yeah, I'm into it."

Without warning, I pull out and flip her onto her stomach. She squeals with delight just before I cover her mouth with my palm and reenter her, just as viciously as before. At this angle, there are no words. No taunts, no praise, no judgment. No shrewd stare picking me apart. No soft gaze falling in temporary love with me.

I fuck her hard and fast, all with my hand muting her muffled moans. I crawl to the deepest part of her and bury my shame again and again, wishing it would go away. But even as I release myself into the sheath of latex while her body quivers and convulses around me, it still doesn't relieve the sense of overwhelming failure that trembles my frame. If anything, I just feel even more disgusting.

I roll out and off of her, and trudge to the bathroom to take a shower. I take my time to wipe away the remnants of my deep-rooted depravity, but I know I'll never be clean enough. I secretly hope she'll be dressed when I return, but of course, she's made herself at home under the covers with a cigarette. How very *Mad Men* cliché.

"You know, you should really get an iPad," she remarks as I reach over for my notebook after throwing on some sweatpants.

"Huh?"

"An iPad. Or a Kindle," she explains, tipping her head toward the pages in my hands.

"I'm writing, not reading, Denae."

"I know that. I'm not stupid. You could get one of those stylus thingies. Would make your after-sex ritual easier. I don't even know how you can form coherent sentences, let alone write them. After that, all I want to do is sleep for a solid twelve hours." She yawns right on cue to bring her point home.

"I'm not tired."

"Of course, you're not. You're Superman. And let me tell you, you seriously proved you are the Man of Steel. Where the hell did that come from?"

"I don't know," I reply absentmindedly, scribbling my disjointed thoughts onto paper. "Wanted to switch it up a bit."

"You certainly did," she coos, scooting over to curl into my side. She rests her head on my shoulder, causing my pen to leave a jagged, black line down the page. I resist the urge to push her the fuck off the bed.

"What are you writing?" Denae asks, trying to peer over and read my messy scrawl. I quickly close the notebook and toss it on the nightstand with an annoyed sigh.

"Nothing."

"Didn't seem like nothing. Did I just read my name?"

I scrub a hand over my face. "I write about people and things in my life. Coincidentally, you're in my life." For how long, that's the question.

"Oh, so it's like a diary?"

"I don't write in a fucking diary," I deadpan.

"Ok, ok. So a journal."

I roll my eyes. At this point, I'd say just about anything to get her to shut up. "Sure."

"Cool."

"Yeah. Hey, do you want something? A glass of water?" I offer, sitting up. Water means we're done. Alcohol means keep the party going.

"No, I'm fine."

I grab my phone from the living room before padding into the kitchen to grab myself a few fingers of scotch and some ice water. Of course, there are about two dozen new text messages, voicemails and emails. I'll check them when I check them. They're all the same anyway.

-Call me.

-Need to talk to you.

-When can I see you?

-I miss you.

-Let's hook up.

-Where are you?

Blah blah blah.

It's funny how so many people want a part of you, yet they don't even know you. And if they did, they wouldn't want to.

I return to the bedroom with my drinks and a still naked Denae, who looks at me with exuberant expectation. If she's hoping for a double header, she'll have to wait for a few minutes.

"So... you said I was in your life," she remarks out of the blue. Dammit. Not *this* shit. I haven't even had a chance to hydrate yet.

"Uh. Yeah."

"So what does that mean exactly?"

I turn to her, trying to conjure my most sincere, earnest expression. "It means that we're close. That we see each other."

"And is there anyone else in your life that you see?"

Fucking hell. I guess I just stepped right into this steaming pile of shit, didn't I? "You know I'm a busy guy, Denae, and you're a busy girl. We both have so much on our plates. If I could, I'd see you on a more permanent basis."

"I know, I know. I'm just thinking... we've been hanging out for a while, and we have a lot on common, and the sex is phenomenal. It's just...don't you ever wonder about giving it a shot? You know, trying to make it work?"

"Well, uh, like I said, it'd be kinda hard considering—"

"I know we're both crazy busy, and our schedules are insane, but maybe if we tried to take a little time every week, just the two of us..."

"I can't."

Denae flinches as if I've just slapped her. "You can't or you won't?"

"Both," I shrug. "Look, you're a great girl and—"

I'm just about to go through the whole *"you're awesome and any man would be lucky to have you"* spiel when an even better segue presents itself.

"Is that the door? At this time of night? Are you expecting company?"

I damn near jump out of my skin. "You might want to get dressed. Excuse me."

I'm completely calm and cool as I open the door and greet April with a kiss on her shimmery candy apple lips. She's dressed in barely a fraction more than a bustier and garter. The only thing that makes it Halloween-ish is her dramatic makeup and fake fangs.

"I came," she grins, stepping inside and removing her coat. She takes in my naked torso and swallows. "You look... comfortable."

"I am. Drink?"

"Sure. What do you have?"

"Let's see... wine, scotch, I probably I some vodka left, soda—"

"What the hell is going on?"

April and I both pause just before hitting the kitchen and turn around to a fuming Denae. She didn't get dressed like I told her. Instead she wrapped a sheet around her body like a bath towel.

"Well? Someone want to tell me what the hell is going on?"

I step towards her, putting myself between the two ladies. April looks confused and even a little frightened, even though she has at least half a foot on Denae. But the shorter girl has psycho in her eyes as she sizes up the tall, leggy blonde dressed in black lace and satin.

"Denae, this is April. She's a makeup artist. April this is

Denae, a law student. April and I were just about to get a drink and watch some TV. Join us?"

"Join you? Are you fucking kidding me?"

I play clueless. "No. You're welcome to. Want another glass of wine?"

Poor April looks like she's contemplating grabbing a broomstick and pole-vaulting to the door. "August, maybe I should go, and we'll talk later."

"Yeah, maybe you should," Denae spits, edging closer. I pin her with a stern look.

"Excuse you, but April is my guest. She's not going anywhere. Now I said you could stay too, but if you're going to be hostile, maybe we should say goodnight."

Denae stares up at me with angry tears brimming her eyes, searching for a reason, an explanation. I give her nothing.

"Wow," she whispers in disbelief. She shakes her head. "Wow. You are…unbelievable."

"So is that a no on the drink?" I ask, my demeanor the perfect picture of peace.

"Oh, I wouldn't want to intrude," she says slowly backing up. "I've had my turn, and my time is up. Please…go have your drink. I insist. I'll just get dressed and be on my way."

Her voice is cold, yet her ire is palpable. Still, she disappears into the room to dress. I try to remember if I have any sharp objects lying around back there.

"August, I should go," April insists once Denae is out of earshot.

"You just got here. At least let me pour you a drink. We didn't get to talk much Thursday."

Denae emerges fully dressed just as April and I make some lackluster toast. She almost appears bemused, yet I can clearly see she's pissed. However, she grabs her purse, and leaves quietly.

"Well, that was awkward," April remarks.

I shrug. "It happens."

"So…who is she?"

I step in close to April, close enough that the bare skin of my chest and abs grazes the soft satin of her bodice. "Nobody special."

No one is. Myself included.

"HOW LONG?" HE ASKED, LOOKING out at the sparkling city spread out before them. "How long have you been going to Joseph? How long have you been selling your body for my freedom?"

She paused at the doorjamb, her shaky legs unable to carry her any further. "Darling, please understand, I didn't—"

"How long have you been fucking him? Tell me!"

The silence felt like a splinters on their tongues. She knew of his transgressions, and he knew of hers. He was just unaware how deep and depraved they festered. She had committed the ultimate act of betrayal, yet she didn't even know it.

"You know I never meant to hurt you." But she did it anyway. She was his wife, his heart, his soul, and she had given away the part of herself that had been reserved for him and

only him. Yet, she was comforted in the fact that she was not alone in her transgressions. "You're no saint yourself, Adam. You are just as responsible for this as I am." Maybe even more.

She'd found out about his affairs long before she met Joseph. Long before Adam's business dealings had gone sour and he had to borrow money. Long before Joseph had to bail them out from the threat of prison, or worse, murder. Adam would undoubtedly argue that the stress and pressure had pushed him into the arms of another woman. He was still good to her, still loved her, still fucked her crazy. He just failed at fidelity.

She wanted to leave him. She wanted to separate herself from the predicament he had put them in, but she couldn't. She loved him still. And he wouldn't survive without her, she was sure of it. No matter how he had hurt her, she could not turn her back on him in his desperate time of need.

With his back to her, and his hands gripping the rail of the eleventh story balcony, he uttered something she could not quite understand. His voice was low and broken, much like her spirit.

"What?" she asked, finding the strength to take a step forward. She had never been afraid of her husband…before now. Still, she loved him in his madness. She wanted to shoulder the very same pain she had caused.

"And the Lord said unto Cain, Where is Abel thy brother?" *he uttered, each word a piercing dagger in her heart. Ice-cold dread began to race in her veins.* "And he said, I know not: Am I my brother's keeper?

"And he said, What hast thou done? The voice of thy brother's blood crieth unto me from the ground.

"And now art thou cursed from the earth, which hath

opened her mouth to receive thy brother's blood from thy hand;

"When thou tillest the ground, it shall not henceforth yield unto thee her strength; a fugitive and a vagabond shalt thou be in the earth.

"And Cain said unto the Lord, My punishment is greater than I can bear."

The gravity of his diatribe hung heavy in the cold air. He turned to face her, his expression unreadable. He waited... waited for her to realize the weight of her sins. The weight of their sins.

"He's...he's your brother. Joseph is your brother." Her voice was merely a strained, raspy whisper.

"Yes."

"What? How...? How is that possible?" She couldn't believe it, couldn't accept it. There were no pictures of Joseph at his parents' home, no recognition of him during family functions. He had never mentioned having a brother. How could they be related by blood?

"Joseph is the product of my mother's affair years ago. My father couldn't stand to raise another man's child, so he was given to his own, and my mother relinquished all parental rights. I watched her suffer every day for her choice, but she never spoke of it. She felt it was her punishment, her penance for her infidelity. She was never whole after that."

She tried to think back to all the times she had interacted with Adam's mother—Joseph's mother. She never seemed particularly forlorn, although a bit flighty. Nothing in her demeanor indicated she was an adulteress. However, the same could be said for herself.

"Joseph's father is Cosimo Fanelli."

It felt like a bucket of ice had been dumped over her head. Terror seized her joints as she realized just how far she had fallen. Cosimo Fanelli was the crime boss her office had been investigating. She had been a DEA agent for almost a decade and most of that time had been spent chasing the infamous criminal's ghost.

"No," she whispered.

"Yes. The man you know as Joseph Farris isn't some mysterious businessman from overseas. He's Jiovanni Fanelli, son of the most notorious mafia boss on the east coast since Gotti. You've been fucking the main link to solving the biggest case of your career, and he happens to be my brother."

"Why didn't you tell me?" she shrieked, suddenly furious. He knew. He knew all along, yet did nothing to stop her...did nothing to save her.

Adam stalked toward her, allowing the overhead light to fall over him like freshly fallen snow. That was when she noticed the gun in his hand. "You never asked," he muttered. Then he brushed past her without a second glance. She didn't breathe until she heard the front door slam.

I sit back in my chair and release a breath. I even almost smile. I'm here...that sweet spot in a story where words are flowing and everything is aligning as it should and the characters are creating just the right amount of friction as to not seem fake or overdone. This is the part that I live for. The part I kill myself for every day that I sit down and spread out my soul like an All-You-Can-Eat Buffet.

What is it about anguish that makes us thrive? That makes us see beauty in the bleakest of places? How can I possibly twist intricate tales of spun sugar and gold when my personal life was going to hell in a hand basket?

I haven't spoken to Fi in nearly two weeks, ever since I humiliated and disgraced myself in my living room with the scent of another woman's sex embedded in my skin. I haven't spoken to the Colonel since our frosty, yet brief encounter two Thursdays ago. I made up some sketchy excuse as to why I had to skip Sunday afternoon football, and he decided to pass on meatballs the following Thursday. I didn't ask why. I was just grateful I didn't have to pull another explanation from my big bag of lies.

This is the longest I've gone without any interaction from the outside world. Even my parents had tried reaching out after I sent a short email about flaking out on Thanksgiving in Florida. They offered to come here, but I was armed and ready with an ironclad alibi as to why it wouldn't be a good idea. Because when it really comes down to it, I just don't want to see them. I don't want to see anyone really. I am very nearly done with my manuscript for my publisher, titled *The Good Girl*, and I'm making serious headway with the idea I had started toying with in Los Angeles. It's no wonder I'm kicking ass professionally. I have nothing else.

Days pass in a blur of unanswered text messages, rumpled notebook paper and empty takeout cartons. I don't even know what day it is until an alarm goes off on my phone, alerting me to the signing I agreed to do for Auntie's Bookstore. I set the alarm because I knew I would forget, and while I would rather not subject myself to any more deprecation, I won't let them down. When no one else in town would carry

Tears of Glass, Auntie's didn't hesitate, and for that I am genuinely grateful. I may have failed everyone else in my life, but I won't fail them.

Getting ready takes more effort than usual. In the words of the Colonel, I look like shit. I'm one unshaven day away from yeti, and my hair is way too long to be combed into any particular style. While beards and longer hair might be considered fashionable now, it's never been my thing. I guess I always wanted to debunk the writer stereotypes. No full tattoo sleeves (although I do have one on the inside of my arm—a single bluebird as a nod to Bukowski. Fi has the same one on her hip). No crazy, eclectic wardrobe or neon-colored hair. And believe it or not, I won't burst into flames or twinkle like a disco ball if I step into the sun. Some people have actually questioned whether or not I was being honest about being a writer. Said I looked too normal. Go figure.

I'm greeted by the comforting scents of aged paper, fresh coffee and nostalgia when I step into the sanctuary of Auntie's Bookstore. I'm early. Amazing, since I'm never early to anything. But there's something exhilarating about being among those dusty shelves and cluttered tables. I feel at home. I feel like this is the only place on earth where I belong.

"August! You made it!" Delores exclaims, bounding towards me with all the exuberance of a kindergarten teacher. She waves towards a row of foldout tables and chairs that they've set up in the periodical section across from the cash registers. "We've got you seated right over here. Want to grab coffee first? It's on the house."

"Ok, great. Thanks, Delores."

"You know, Fiona was in here earlier this week," she remarks while walking towards the café with me. There's something conspiratorial about her tone, like maybe she was told not to mention it, but knew I'd want to know.

I nod, feigning interest. "Oh, really?"

"Yeah. Grabbed tons of wedding magazines and checked out the new romance releases. I mentioned the signing to her, thinking she was definitely attending with you like she's done in the past. However, she acted like she knew nothing about it."

"Oh?"

"Oh yes. But it probably just slipped her mind with all the wedding stuff," she muses. "Hard to believe she's gone off and gotten herself engaged. How are you holding up?"

I occupy my expression with the daunting task of stirring cream and sugar into my coffee. "Just fine. Why do you ask?"

"Oh. Well, you know."

At that, I look up, perplexity etched on my brow. "No. I don't."

"Well…it should've been you."

"What?"

"August, it should be you she's marrying," Delores explains. "Everybody thinks so. We were all completely shocked that she hooked up with that doctor. I mean, he's handsome, I'll give her that. But you and that girl were made for each other. That guy is nothing more than a temporary placeholder…for you."

I don't know what to say—what *can* I say? Have I been that transparent about my feelings, even though *I* didn't even really know they existed until recently?

"I don't know about that," I mutter, pushing away the thought.

"It's true, August. Just sad you two couldn't get it together."

Part of me wants to tell her she's wrong, that only saps and dreamers believe in such things as fate and soul mates. That we didn't miss our chance because we never truly had one, because the universe had deemed me its ugly stepchild and stripped me of the ability to open myself to silly notions like love and forever. We were all temporary—slaves to our own selfish desires and wicked lust. Eventually, the wind would blow, and the love we thought was built on brick and concrete would come tumbling down like a house of cards.

But I don't say it. Somewhere deep inside, maybe I didn't believe it.

"I better get my seat," I say with an apologetic smile. Sometimes the best explanation isn't one at all.

The signing goes much like I expect: Crickets.

We're all local authors, struggling to get our book in the hands of the masses. Some of us are more desperate than others (I'm looking at you, Tom from two tables down. No one wants to see a cardboard cutout of you holding your own book). I score a few pity buys which is more than what I've sold all month, so I consider it a good sale day. After a few hours, I decide it's time to pack it up and get home. I'm eager to get back to my manuscript, and that feeling is like pure crack cocaine in my veins.

"Excuse me, would you mind signing this please?" a familiar voice asks, as I'm bending down to stack the leftover copies of *Tears of Glass* into a cardboard box. I sit up straight and blink, hoping that I'm just seeing things. Praying that lack of sleep and staring at a computer monitor for two weeks straight have finally begun to eat away at my retinas. But that would be too easy for the universe. She likes to have her fun with me.

"Denae, what are you—"

"What am I doing here? Oh, I just thought I'd come and get my book signed." She holds up a copy of *Heat Wave…* by Hope Hughes. That's when I notice the flash and whirl of several cameras pointed in my direction. The press is here.

"I think you have the wrong book," I deadpan, taking in the dozens of patrons and staff looking on in curiosity.

"Do I? So…" She opens the book and flips to the first chapter. "*Denise*, a law student with a penchant for dirty talk and role play, actually isn't me? Funny. I compared some of the notes you made in your diary to the scenes in the book."

That's when she pulls one of my notebooks out of her purse and tosses it on the table in front of me. "Maybe you can sign both for me."

I'm at a loss. A complete loss. I never anticipated this happening. I didn't even think Denae had heard of Hope Hughes. Well, after today, everyone has.

I snatch up my notebook, grab my bag, and try to make my way around the table, but I'm blocked in by cameras and onlookers. "Get out of my way," I demand to a guy in a hoodie who's got a Nikon shoved in my face.

"Where are you going, August?" Denae taunts. "Or should we call you Hope? Do you wear dresses when you write? Makeup and wigs to really channel the essence of your readers?"

"Get the fuck away from me." I'm beyond being cordial. At this point, I'm just trying to survive. In two seconds, hoodie guy and his camera will be crumpled on the floor if they don't step aside. Reading the threat on my face, he reluctantly steps aside, yet continues to snap pictures. I hurriedly rush towards the front doors.

"You owe me! You owe me, August!" Denae calls out from behind me. "I was your muse! I inspired you! You need me!"

I escape the probing eyes and whispered questions, and hop on my Harley. I have nowhere to go, nowhere to find refuge in this shit storm of accusations and judgments. I'm naked out here, violently shivering in the freezing cold with no shelter in sight.

I find myself in front of Fi's apartment building. I know I have no place here, no reason for her to accept me, no hope of her shielding me from the cruel world of deceit and lies. The very world I created.

I sit and watch her window from the curb. There doesn't seem to be anyone home, since it's Saturday. On Saturdays she likes to hit the Farmer's Market, do some shopping, or read in the park if the weather's nice enough. But just as I'm about to kick on the engine, I hear music—*her* music. And seconds later, I see movement between her curtains. It's Fi, singing along to one her favorite songs, smiling, twirling around in a dress adorned with watercolor flowers. She's so gorgeous, so radiant that the sight of her hurts my eyes. I find myself smiling through the pain, and simply relishing the image of her truly…beautifully…happy.

I watch as her audience of one for a few minutes before

I notice her expression change. She touches her cheeks, as if she's bashful, and then shakes her head. And then she lifts her chin, eyes closed, lips pursed, and prepares to be kissed.

I see red as I watch Joshua fit his mouth with hers, pull her body into his, tangle his fingers into her head, and take what was meant for me. I can't watch it, yet I can't look away. I can't bring myself to rev the engine and ride away. I stand helpless and watch as he robs me blind, yet I do nothing to try to stop it.

The kiss builds and evolves into something too intimate for me to stomach as he dots kisses down her throat and across her shoulder. He slides down one strap of her dress and ravishes the skin with lips and teeth. Fiona tips her head back in ecstasy and I swear I can hear her moan his name over the music. His name. Not mine.

Just as he relinquishes her body of her other strap, I find the strength to crank up my bike and ride away. I didn't think it was possible, but somehow, I'm even emptier than when I arrived.

MY LIFE HAS BECOME ONE big Delete.

Constant calls and voicemails asking how I'm holding up, and if any of the stories are true. Delete.

Nonstop text messages from ex-lovers, demanding I compensate them for their part in my stories. Delete.

Incessant emails asking for interviews, exclusives and statements. Delete.

I delete them all, because I have nothing to say. And even if I did, I'd have no one to say it to.

They've had to add extra security to my building, which I'm sure will be added to my rent. My neighbors were especially thrilled with having our trash picked through my overzealous press and fangirls. I haven't even been able to order from my favorite restaurants since the pizza delivery guy tried to bring me my pie wearing a Go Pro.

"You have to talk to them, son. Set the record straight," my grandfather said when I finally got the balls to call him.

"Why didn't you tell us?" my parents wondered when I answered one of their many calls.

"This changes everything. Time to strike while the irons hot!" Kerrigan trilled, when we discussed strategy.

People assume my reclusion is a sign of guilt or shame. In all honesty, I just don't know what to do. My life—the life I had so artfully constructed—is over. And while it may sound melodramatic as fuck, I don't know how to be just August. I no longer have a secret to hide behind.

Bartleby needs litter, and after ransacking the questionable canned goods and freezer-burnt entrees, I know I have to venture out into the world. It's been a week, meaning some other train wreck has stolen the limelight and given the media sharks another hapless story to swarm around. Still, I don a ball cap, shades and dark, inconspicuous clothes, and stay far away from the tabloid mags.

"August?"

I'm in the cat aisle, headed for the checkout, nearly home free when I hear it. *Just keep walking,* I tell myself. *Maybe she'll go away.*

"August, wait a minute. Hold on."

I turn around slowly and find Fiona standing at the end of the aisle, holding a bottle of cheap wine and a plastic container of rotisserie chicken. She begins to smile, then thinks better of it after taking in my disheveled appearance.

"Um, how are you?" she asks, walking toward me slowly

as to not spook me. I look to my right and my left to see if anyone's noticed us.

"I'm fine."

"I see you're growing your hair out," she muses, nodding toward the wisps of brown curls peeking from under my hat.

"Haven't had a chance to get to the barber."

"Oh. Yeah. Right." She tries to fiddle with her hair, her tell for nervousness, but her hands are full. "So did you meet your deadline?"

I nod. "They pushed it back with everything going on…"

"Oh. That makes sense. Sorry," she grimaces. "So how are you holding up?"

I shrug. Obviously, she can see I'm a mess, and I've been a mess since our falling out. Still, I answer, "I'm great."

"Are you?"

"Yeah."

Her wide, brown eyes take in my baggy sweats and unshaven jaw. She tries to smile. "Ok. Glad to hear it."

"Hey, I've gotta go."

"I better get going."

We stumble over each other as we both try to retreat from the most awkward encounter since Kanye snatched the mic from Taylor.

"It was good seeing you," Fi says as she backs away.

I start to turn towards the exit, and momentarily consider dumping my shit and making a mad dash out the door. "Yeah, you too."

I watch a stranger walk away from me like I'm diseased. I watch her go back to her lovely life of lavish dinners and beaded dresses and kisses in the sunlight. And for one small beat, I remember what it was like to know her and to love her. I remember the sound of her laughter and the warmth of her embrace. And even though I tell myself I don't miss them, I can't help it. I can't help wondering if that stranger misses me too.

Seeing Fi is the motivation I need to get my shit together. It takes some time, but I finally pull my head out of my ass and make it through all the emails and texts marked Urgent. Well, the emails and texts I didn't delete.

"So far, two women have threatened to sue for defamation and damages. However, they're just threats. They have no case. Each Hope book was fiction and under copyright laws, your intellectual property is protected. However, I suggest you talk to your lawyer so there aren't any surprises," Kerrigan suggests over the phone.

"On it," I reply, as I scribble a reminder on a pad of Post Its.

"And People want to do an expose on men in romance, featuring you. I told them it was highly unlikely that you'd be up for anything face-to-face, but I did mention the prospect of a phone or email interview."

"Sounds good."

"And your little shit stirrer, Denae, will be appearing on The View this week. Surprisingly, she's not suing. However, she is capitalizing on her fifteen minutes with a tell-all book deal and a special on MTV. How this has anything to do with music is beyond me."

"Not surprised. Anything else?"

"Yes." I hear her suck in a lungful of lush, toxic smoke

and exhale. "The network still wants to work with you. They've even thrown more money your way. And with news of your identity, they want to get a jump on it ASAP."

"What's ASAP?"

"As soon as January."

"January?" I run my fingers through the top of my freshly clipped hair and begin to pace the floor. January? It's November. January is right around the corner, and I'm in no way ready to pack up my life and move. However, the prospect of escaping Spokane and the random whispers and stares whenever I leave the house is looking sweeter every day.

"I know it's soon, but development will take some time. It's not like you need to leave tomorrow."

"I know, it's just..."

Fiona.

And the Colonel.

Although, it seems like they're doing pretty well without me. I'm just not doing so well without them.

"Hey, Kerrigan, let me think it over. I'll get back to you on it, I swear."

"Ok, kid. No matter what you may think about all this, I think it's a good thing. All publicity is good publicity, am I right?"

"Sure, boss."

"Boss? Pretty sure I work for you."

I chuckle genuinely for the first time in weeks. "I highly doubt that, Kerrigan."

In the spirit of turning over a new leaf, I make an impromptu visit to see the Colonel. It's Saturday, and it's been way too long since I've visited. And to the elderly, a few weeks seem like a few years.

"August? August, is that you?"

"Hey, it's the Colonel's boy! He's back!"

"Good to see you, young man! It's been a while."

"Well, aren't you a sight for sore eyes. What's it been—a month?"

"Only about three weeks, ma'am," I say to the fifth resident since I walked through the doors. You'd think I'd just come home from war or a Gary Busey retreat or something equally tragic.

"Well, I'm sure seeing you will definitely lift the Colonel's spirits," Nurse Tabatha chimes in. "Go on and see him before he turns in for the night."

I look at my watch. "It's only 7:30."

"I know. The Colonel has been a little tired lately. Probably just misses you."

That lights a fire under my ass, and I hurry to my grandfather's apartment, successfully bypassing Helen and her snow-capped Cheetah Girls.

"Colonel?" I call out, entering his apartment without knocking. The lights are off and it's completely still.

"In here," he grumbles from the bedroom. I follow his voice and find him lying in bed, watching television on an old tube television.

"What the hell are you doing here?" he asks, his expression both perplexed and surprised. I take the wooden chair beside his bed, one of the very few pieces of furniture he has in his room.

"Thought I'd come see you, since my schedule's been so crazy. I finished the book."

"That's great, son. Proud of you."

That makes me smile. Hearing those words from him means the world to me. "Thank you, sir."

"So…what's next? Anymore thought about that television show?"

"Actually, yes. The network is still interested, even despite…"

"Ah. Yes. I heard. And you're ok?"

I nod, really, truly meaning it this time. "I am. Things have simmered down, and I haven't received any weird letters or packages in the past week. I think everything is pretty much back to normal now. Hope Hughes was a chapter in my life, and that chapter is over. I'm looking forward to just being August for a change."

"Good. I liked him better anyway," the Colonel quips. He even almost grins.

"So…what are you doing in bed so early? Don't tell me you're getting old on me."

"Getting old? Boy, I've got gray hair in places I didn't know could sprout hair. I've been old. But don't be fooled—I can still kick your ass."

We both share a chuckle, and for once in a long time, I'm having fun. It feels good—different, but good.

"Hey, can you grab my glasses off my dresser," he asks, waving toward the chest of drawers across from him. "I've been looking at the TV, but can't tell if I'm watching M.A.S.H. or a penguin documentary."

"Sure." I flip on the bedside lamp and walk over to the dresser where the Colonel keeps a few toiletries and books. The small area, which is usually meticulously neat, seems a bit disorganized, so I take a few seconds to tidy up scattered papers and mail. That's when I see an embossed cream envelope made of thick stock paper.

"What's this?" I ask, running my fingers over the calligraphy on the front.

"Oh, that. It's nothing. Go ahead and toss that back on the dresser."

"It's not nothing. People don't waste expensive paper on nothing."

"August, it's not what you think."

"I think it's exactly what I think."

"You've been going through a lot lately, and I didn't want to burden you with—"

"I'm fine. Ok? I'm a big boy. Now, what is it?"

He silence is all the answer I need. Still, I have to see if for myself. I pull out the embellished, blush-colored card and instantly wish that I didn't. The lettering is elegant although ostentatious, and when I see their names together, like miniature bride and groom atop a wedding cake, I'm overcome with defeat. They fit together. On paper, they sound like the perfect couple.

"January 23rd. Fiona is getting married January 23rd. In two months." The thought, the date, the very words in my mouth seem foreign to me.

"I don't understand why it's so soon. I asked her about it when she dropped it off earlier this week. She said it's because that doctor is moving her to the coast, and needs to be there by spring. Still, I think it's too soon. What about her job? Her apartment?" He's rambling. The Colonel never rambles.

"January 23rd," is all I can say.

"Why can't he go on to Seattle and set things up first? Why not deal with that first instead of trying to juggle a new marriage and a new city all at once?"

"January 23rd."

"I know, son. It's too soon. I wanted to tell her, but it just didn't seem appropriate at the time. Now if she had asked me…"

January 23rd. I feel like I've just been told it's the day I'm going to die.

Suddenly, the paper in my hand feels like it's been lined with lead. My mouth is dry. My head is spinning. My face is hot.

"I have to go."

"Now, wait a minute, son. Don't go off and do anything you'll regret. You can't interfere if this is what she wants."

"What she wants? Fiona doesn't know what she wants."

"You had your shot, August. All you can do now is try to make things right before it's too late."

I shake my head. "It's already too late. We're done. She made that perfectly clear when she chose him over me."

"You can still be there for her. She needs you. You need her."

I ignore him, and turn for the door, leaving him to shout reason at my back. I don't need her. I don't need anyone. And apparently, she doesn't need me. Maybe she never did.

I'M FADING INTO OBLIVION, DRIFTING into a haze of purples and blues and yellows. The smoke tastes like sin in my throat, thick and heavy like 5 a.m. fog. I trade one burn for another and douse the wildfire with gasoline.

I'm in a club full of strangers, flying high above the crowd. There are hands on my thighs, lips on my face, teeth on my ear. I feel it, yet I don't. I'm beyond sensation, beyond bliss, beyond feeling.

I'm nothing. I'm everything.

I've lost count of how many shots we've taken. Sunny and her friends have provided a steady stream of alcohol, courtesy of my credit card. I don't mind. After I left the Colonel's apartment, I knew I needed to get out of my head, get out of my skin. So I called up the one person who wouldn't ask me if I was ok. She wouldn't care if my feelings were hurt or if I wanted to talk. We don't do that, and if we did, I wouldn't remember at this point.

"Here, try this," she whispers in my ear. She pulls back just enough for me to see a small pink pill on her tongue.

"What is it?" I slur.

"Don't worry about it. You'll be fine. My friends and I pop them like Tic Tacs when we party."

I've never done the pill thing. Nicotine and fine scotch were always my drugs of choice. But in the spirit of pissing on the past, I grab the back of her head and snake my tongue into her mouth, drinking in the sweet taste of apple martinis mixed with the bitterness of the mysterious tablet. We stay intertwined like that for what seems like hours, fucking each other with our clothes on. She grips my cock through my jeans and I stroke the skin under her short skirt. Her friends don't notice between taking selfies and dancing to Zedd, and I doubt they'd care even if they did. One of them even alluded to some group love later on.

The song switches to Justin Bieber's "Sorry," causing the girls to squeal with drunken glee.

"Come on, let's dance!" Sunny shrieks over the upbeat melody.

"No, you go ahead," I insist with a wave. I'm all for having fun, but I draw the line at Bieber.

I watch with hazy eyes as the girls grind and touch each other from a couple yards away. They're putting on a show for me, making promises with each wicked sway of hips and ass. This should be enough to stifle the ache, to fill the emptiness. This should be enough to push me into total detachment.

"What are you doing here?" a voice asks me from behind. It's the last voice I want to hear. It's the only voice I want to hear.

With liquid limbs, I turn around to see Fiona, decked out in a tight, black sleeveless dress.

"Obviously, the same damn thing you're doing," I reply without hesitation.

My candor jars her and she shifts on her platform heels. "Oh. It's just…you hate clubs."

"Says who?"

"Says *you*. You've always detested them. Said it was no more than a modern day auction block with an outrageous cover charge."

"Well, I guess you don't know me as well as you think you do," I smirk, reaching over to snag a random glass of champagne from our table. That's when Fiona takes in all the various bottles of bubbly, vodka and tequila.

"Did you drink all this?"

"What does it matter to you?" I shrug. "Where's your fiancé?"

"Home. I'm here with girls from work and some of the ladies from his office."

"Oh. Celebrating the official announcement? Early bachelorette party?"

She fingers her styled curls nervously and her eyes dart around the club like strobe lights. "August, I know I didn't send you an invite, but considering how you feel about Joshua, and how we left things, I didn't think it was…"

"Save it," I say with a wave of my palm. "It's cool. I get it. No need to explain."

The song ends and the girls come bounding back to the couch, a muss of sequins, hair spray and stilettos. Sunny flops onto my lap with a squeak, while her friends take the space at my sides, squeezing in as close as possible.

"Hey, who's your friend?" she asks, looking Fiona up and down with an air of amusement.

"Yeah, August, who's your friend?" the girl at my right chimes in.

I look back at Fi who wears a veil made of blood red rage and pain. Her big, brown eyes stare at me, begging me to snap out of it. Urging me to see past the hurt and humiliation and be the August that she once knew. Unfortunately, that man died the day Hope did.

"Nobody special," I reply to my female companions. "She was just leaving."

Fiona

I hate him.

I hate him, I hate him, I hate him.

I hate that he's so cavalier with his little tramps. I hate that he treats me like I've done something wrong. I hate that he pretends he doesn't care.

I hate that I can't escape him. I hate that I can't shake him.

I hate that I can't hate him.

I walk away feeling deflated on my four-inch heels. I hate these shoes too, even though Joshua thinks they make my calves look great.

"Hey, Fiona! Where have you been?" slurs my coworker, Andrea, as she slings an arm around my shoulder.

"Oh, went to grab another drink," I lie.

"Oooh, good." Andrea looks down at my empty hands and frowns. "Where is it?"

Busted. "Oh, um, I drank it. Thirsty," I reply with a nervous chuckle.

Luckily, Andrea is beyond tipsy and successfully working her way to WGW (white girl wasted) status. She happily shrugs it off and returns to her own little bubble of cheesy man-boys and booze, inconspicuously pointing out some guy a few yards away that just sent her a drink. It's an Appletini. Really? Do we look like college chicks with fake IDs and padded bras over here?

"He's hot, right? Tell me he's hot," she whisper-shouts in my ear, blowing her sour apple-laced hot breath on me.

"Oh, yeah. Definitely." *Not* hot. Seriously, how can your pants be too baggy *and* high-waters at the same time? His ankles look cold and sad.

"You better not just be saying that," she warns playfully. "God, I'm so horny. I haven't had sex in six months, and I just ran out of batteries. He is so coming home with me tonight."

I divert my judgy eyes to the other ladies currently on the dance floor. If Andrea wants to get laid by a guy who thinks an apple martini is impressive and can't even afford a full pair of pants, then who am I to stand in her way?

I fish out my cell for the hundredth time since we arrived to check the time…and to see if Joshua has tried to call. He all but insisted I go out tonight to hang with the girls. Sue, his assistant, had been trying to get together for weeks, but I just hadn't felt up to socializing. Since things fell apart with August, I hadn't felt like doing much of anything.

"Having fun?" Sue asks, wiping sweat from her brow. She's gorgeous—of course. Everyone in Joshua's office is, but I guess that comes with the job. No one wants to take cosmetic advice from someone who looks like Jabba the Hut.

"Oh, yeah. Sure," I answer, trying to slap on a happy face. It isn't working. "Hey, I'm going to go to the ladies room."

"Want me to come with you?"

"Oh, no. I just need a quiet place to call Joshua."

She lifts her brows in amusement. According to her, I'm the only woman Joshua has brought around the office and his employees. "Ok, but you better start having a good time or I may get fired! Hurry back!" Then she's back on the dance floor, hooking some unsuspecting guy's attention, and pulling him along with her.

I sift through the crowd, careful not to crush any toes with my heels. At some point, I give up on saying *Excuse Me*. You can't be polite to someone with their butt cheeks hanging out of their shorts when it's thirty degrees outside.

Once I get to the long hallway that leads to the bathrooms, I find a safe place against the wall and text Joshua. He has an early morning, so I don't call. If he's up, which I doubt, he'll call or text back. My heart sinks after five minutes without a reply. It's not *that* late, but I know he needs his rest.

"Well, well, well," I hear a familiar sneer from down the hallway. "I thought you would've left by now."

With an aggravated sigh, I drop my phone back into my bag, and look up to see August sauntering towards me. "And why's that? Just because you so rudely dismissed me, that doesn't mean I have to leave."

"No, it doesn't. I'm just surprised your loving fiancé hasn't summoned you home by now."

"Whatever, August. I'm done trying to talk to you," I huff, trying to hurriedly brush past him. But before I can escape his rude taunts, he grips my forearm.

"Wait. That was mean. I'm sorry." He sags against the wall and pulls me back towards him. "Don't leave, Fi. I was only joking."

I get a whiff of the alcohol concentrated sweat coming out of his pores and take in his hazy eyes. "You're drunk."

"You're observant."

"You reek. And you're all sweaty," I grimace, pulling my arm from his clammy grasp.

He laughs, tipping his head back and closing his eyes. Even with damp hair and booze breath, the sight and sound of him laughing still completely disarms me. I look down the hall toward the steady stream of patrons rushing for the toilets, just to give my eyes something else to look at.

"What the heck is so funny?"

"You, Fi. You're hilarious. You never minded my sweat before."

I shrug, still averting my eyes. "Well, you never bathed in beer before either. But don't worry. Your little groupies will probably lick it off you later. Just make sure you have them home before their curfews."

"Oh, don't tell me you're jealous."

At that, I spin around to pin him with my best stank face. "Jealous? Jealous of what?" I ask incredulously. "Jealous that I didn't have to use a fake ID to get in here?"

"Hey, now. Sunny and her friends are legal," he insists with a grin.

"Sunny? Oh gosh. Are her friends named Snowflake and Stormy? Will they hit me with the Care Bear Stare if they catch me talking to you?"

August bursts into laughter, and shakes his head, unable to vocalize a decent defense through his chuckles.

"Seriously, August. Watch your back tonight. With their powers combined, they might try to summon Captain Planet. Your apartment is a landfill, and the only thing you recycle is women."

"Ouch, Fi," he snickers. "You wound me."

"Oh, please. That would mean that you actually cared. And we both know that's not the case."

He instantly goes quiet, all signs of mirth wiped clean from his handsome face. Oh, his face. Perfect cheekbones that I've envied since the day we met, almond-shaped brown eyes, a strong chiseled jaw, and by far the most beautiful lips I have ever seen…or kissed. He once told me how he hated his mouth, saying it seemed too sensual, too soft. I almost replied that it was his sexiest attribute, aside from his mind. Instead, I made a tasteless joke involving Steven Tyler and a vacuum cleaner.

Had I'd told him then, maybe we wouldn't be here. Maybe it wouldn't physically pain me just to steal a glance at him. Maybe he wouldn't be drunk and slouched over, looking like he's carrying the weight of the world on his broad shoulders.

"My problem isn't caring, Fi," he says so quietly, I think I'm imagining it. "My problem is caring too much."

I don't know what to say. I don't know if there's anything

left *to* say.

"August, I...," I reach out to touch him, but stop myself. I don't want to hurt him anymore.

He shakes his head before easing it back to the wall. He's panting, and he hasn't cooled down at all. He's still sweating like crazy.

"Hey, are you feeling ok?" I ask, battling the urge to reach over to feel his forehead.

He begins to nod, but then thinks better of it. "I'm fucked up. I shouldn't have taken that pill."

Pill? Holy shhh... "What pill?"

"I don't know. Think it was Molly. Sunny gave it to me. Dammit, I should've eaten or something. I need some water."

I don't resist this time. I rest a hand on his sweat-drenched face, only to find that he's burning up. "August, you need to get out of here. Come on, I'm taking you home."

He shakes his head, but his body is so limp, I'm able to pull him along easily. Now keeping him upright long enough to get out of here, that's the feat.

"What about Sunny and the girls?" he slurs, as I lead him down the hallway.

"They can Uber it. They're probably still dancing." Not to mention, none of them have ventured out to find him.

"And your friends?"

"I'll text them. They're all probably getting lucky tonight anyway."

When we get to the main bar area, August stops me with a slight squeeze of my hand. "I have to close my tab."

"Ok, good. We can get you some water too."

After much effort to keep him coherent enough to pay

his astronomical bill (seriously, how much did he and those girls drink?), I usher him out of the club and into the cold, crisp night air.

"Come on, I'm parked over here."

"Fi, you don't have to do this. I'll catch a cab…"

"Nonsense. You're in no position for that. Come on. It's not much further."

Once I get him safely in my little Honda Accord, I roll down the windows and carefully make my way out onto the slick roads.

"Fi, you'll freeze to death," he groans from the passenger seat.

"N-N-No, I w-w-w-won't-t-t," I reply through chattering teeth. I've got good sense enough to put on my coat, but my legs are still very much exposed. "I'm f-f-f-fine."

Maybe it's the alcohol or the drug in his system that makes him throw all rationality to the cold wind, but without a second thought, he leans over to me, rests his warm cheek on my shoulder and carefully snakes his arm around my waist.

"Better?" he whispers, those full, sumptuous lips much too close, yet not close enough.

Better is the understatement of the year. I'm positively on fire. "Yes. Better."

When we get to his building, the doorman helps me get him out the car and on two legs. In arrogant August style, he tries to put on a manly face and act like he doesn't need help.

"I can't believe you took something, August. What were you thinking?" I gently scold, unlocking his front door.

"I wasn't," he murmurs. "I didn't want to think anymore."

Walking inside his apartment floods me with more emotions than I can name. But I don't have a chance to address them. We head straight to the bathroom where I begin to draw him a cool bath.

"You need to soak for a while until your body temperature comes down," I explain while bending over to check the water. "It might feel cold at first, but you'll adjust."

When I turn around, I nearly run right into August. Naked. August is naked.

"You took your clothes off!" I try to divert my eyes, but it's impossible not to look at him.

"That's what you usually do before having a bath, right?" Despite my gawking, he walks past me to get into the tub.

"Yes, but..." *But it's highly inappropriate for you to be naked in front of a betrothed woman?* Or, *But it's not fair that I can't touch you the way I long to?*

"It's no big deal, Fi," he insists, cupping water in his hands and running it over his face and chest. "It's not like you haven't seen me naked before."

All I can do is nod, then force myself to give him some much needed privacy. Darn.

Remembering my plan, I grab my cell and text Andrea, telling her I was tired and calling it a night. I don't mention August. After I hit send, I scroll to Joshua's name. It's a good idea that I let him know where I am. That's what you do when you're engaged. That's what you do when you're about to pledge to be someone's wife and partner for the rest of your life. You check in. You make good choices. You don't put yourself in situations that would tempt you to do something you may regret.

I power down and stow my cell back in my purse where it will remain, if only for tonight. Then I return to the bathroom, in search of a towel.

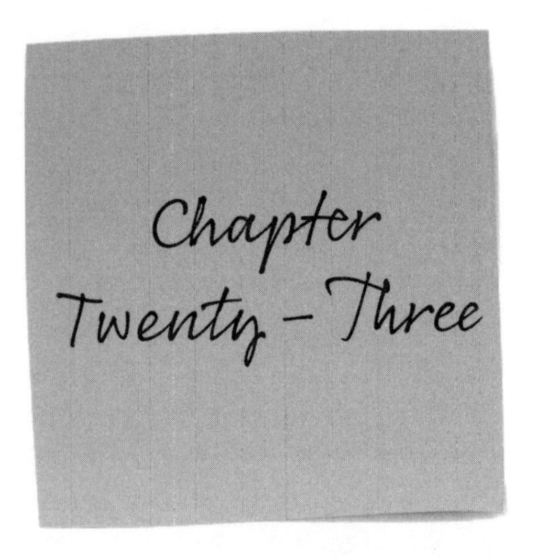

August

I AMBLE THROUGH THE FOG OF forgetting, disoriented and weak. My head feels like lead, my mouth feels like cotton and my body feels…naked. Through the stiffness in my joints, I manage to do a quick assessment and find that I, in fact, have on underwear. So not technically naked, yet not technically clothed either.

With much effort, I peel open the steel doors of my eyelids and peer into the glaring morning sunlight. My retinas are on fire. I bite out a hoarse curse, and roll over, shielding my face from the evil streaming through my window blinds.

"You're awake," a small, raspy voice says from the doorway of my bedroom. My bedroom. I'm home. And damn near naked.

"How did I get here?"

Fiona walks to the side of my bed, and holds out a steaming cup of coffee. She's wearing a strapless, black mini dress that shows off every curve and a good amount of leg. I doubt she just got back from Sunday school. If I wasn't feeling like 50 shades of shit, I'd be able to appreciate the get up.

"I brought you home. Don't you remember?"

"No," I grumble, taking the mug. I hate feeling helpless. I don't want her to see me like this—hungover and, no doubt, looking like I've been the victim of a drive-by stoning. She already thinks I'm pathetic. No need to give her any more ammo.

She sits down on the opposite end of the bed. "You were pretty messed up last night, August. I was really concerned for you. I can't believe you would put yourself in that kind of danger."

If I could roll my eyes I would. "Don't worry about it."

"I am worried about it," she insists. "I'm worried about *you.*"

I frown. "Why?"

"Because you were out of control last night, August. On top of copious amounts of alcohol that even Charlie Sheen would balk at, you took a pill some little tramp gave you, and you didn't even know what it was. I had to get you home and put you in a cool bath. Then I sat up most of the night making sure you didn't have a seizure. Hands down, the stupidest thing you've ever done, and I witnessed your stint with frosted tips. Come on, August. You could've died."

"But I didn't," I shrug. "Why do you care anyway?"

"Because you're my…"

She hesitates. She doesn't know what I am to her. Friend? Lover? Stranger? I'm wondering the same thing.

I shake my head sardonically and sip the black coffee in my cup. I'm grateful for her presence, I'll admit. But I want her here because she wants to be. Not because she pities me or feels guilty. Not because she sees me as some fuck up charity case that can't pull it together.

"I'm fine, Fi," I say, filling the emptiness of silence.

"You were not fine last night, August."

"I said I'm fine." My voice is as hard and unyielding as the two-ton boulder lodged in my skull.

"You're obviously going through something, and I think you should get help. You need to talk to someone. You're not yourself. You're so much better than what you've been displaying lately." She's really trying to put that psychology class from undergrad to good use. Bonus points for the soothing shrink voice.

"How the fuck would you know?" I spit, irritated by her blatant condescension. She reels back as if my words have slapped her across the face.

"Because I know you, August! I know when you're hurting. You're acting out, and it isn't healthy. I'm afraid for you!"

"Worry about your damn self," I grumble, forcing myself out of bed. "Or better yet, worry about your fiancé."

"Why are you acting like this? Why are you purposely trying to hurt my feelings, when all I want to do is help you?"

"No one asked you to be here, Fi. I didn't ask for your help."

"I know that, but I just thought—"

"You just thought what? That it'd make things better? That we could go back to how things were? That all would be forgiven and forgotten?"

"I don't know what I did to you!" she cries, dashing away frustrated tears. "I don't know what I did to make you hate me!"

I snicker darkly. "I don't hate you, Fi. Anger…pain… they're all useless emotions. I don't feel *anything* for you."

That seems to do the trick. That seems to be the blow to her heart she needs to wake the fuck up. To leave here and never come back again. To leave me in my misery and self-destruction so I can get the fuck over her.

I stare down at my cold cup of black coffee until I hear the front door slam. I did it. I finally lost her for good.

With a frustrated growl, I launch the mug in my hand across the room and watch it shatter against the wall, causing shards of ceramic and plastic to fall to the floor in a brown pool of dejection. How can I ever expect Fi to forgive me, when I'll never be able to forgive myself?

From that point on, I'm a robot. I clean up. I eat. I hydrate. I dress. I stare blankly at the story I'd started writing about her.

I delete.

I don't look up until I realize I'm late for Sunday football with the Colonel. I want to flake, but I can't. I can't let the only person I have left down, too.

I hear my cell ring somewhere in the apartment just as I'm brushing my teeth, so I let it go to voicemail. It rings again as I'm trying to find my shoes, and again when I'm trying to find the damn thing.

"8% battery life. Fucking awesome," I grunt when I finally find it. It goes off in my hand. Make that 7%.

I see it's the senior village calling, and with an aggravated huff, I answer. I know I'm late, but damn. Truth be told, I could give two shits about football right now.

"I'm on my way, Colonel," I answer, grabbing my coat and keys before heading towards the door.

"August? August Calloway?"

"Yes?"

"This is Nurse Tabatha, sweetie," she says with a trembling voice. "I…I'm sorry, August. I'm so sorry. The Colonel…he's gone."

Fiona

I FIND HIM CLOAKED IN SADNESS, wrapped tight in pain so thick that it smothers him. He's on the couch. They're talking. He's listening, but he doesn't hear them. They're telling him where they're taking the Colonel's body, and what he should do now. He nods, but it's reflexive. He's too numb to understand. I go to his side once we're alone, but I don't get too close. I don't even think he realizes I'm here. Of course, he didn't call me—the staff did. He was willing to shoulder this alone, like he always has.

"August?" My voice is just above a whisper. He's staring at nothing, unblinking. I don't think he hears me. Maybe he's not ready to.

"We had an argument," he says after several minutes of heavy silence. "He told me to make things right with you. I refused."

I take the space beside him, but I don't touch him. I don't know what to expect. I don't know what he needs me to be.

"I was so…angry. So upset. With him…with you." He shakes his head. "It all seems so trivial. Selfish."

I should say something. I should lend some words of comfort. But what comfort do I have to give him when my own heart is shattered inside my chest? And while my pain must pale in comparison to August's, it still hurts to lose one of the few constants in my life.

"It's not your fault," is all I can offer him.

"Oh, but it is. I should have known." His hands are clasped between his knees and his shoulders are hunched in as if he's trying to lose himself…within himself.

"How could you? He didn't tell anyone. And if he did, it's rare for even young people to survive pancreatic cancer. There's nothing anyone could do for him."

He shakes his head again. "There were signs. He was tired more often. He started cancelling on me. He never cancels… it's me who flaked out on him. And he kept pushing me to patch things up with you, as if he knew the end was near. He didn't want to leave me alone."

"Yeah, I know." The Colonel had asked me to come see him last week. He was worried about August and had hoped we could make up. I tried…I really tried. When I saw him in the club last night, I saw an opportunity to make good on his request. Big mistake.

"He wanted me to go to LA. I didn't want to leave him.

But he already knew he was leaving me."

"LA?"

"Yeah," he nods. "The screen deal. Even after all the Hope shit came out, they still wanted to move forward…and fast." For a fraction of a minute, he turns his head in my direction, but doesn't look at me. "He knew it was a good opportunity for me. A fresh start."

I choke down the words in my throat, but they still echo loudly in my head. *What about me?* The thought of August leaving leaves an empty, sinking feeling in my stomach. But then again, I'm supposed to be moving to the coast with Joshua, but…

"I can't believe he's gone," he whispers. His heart is in his voice—broken and barely beating.

"I know. I can't either."

I swallow my hesitation and wrap an arm around his shoulders. He instantly sags into my touch, releasing a lifetime's worth of sadness. I feel the pain in the marrow of his bones. The devastation is just too much for him to bear—too much for me to bear for him. But I take it. I hold him tight and absorb every ounce of devastation he releases. He needs this. I need this. If I can't do anything else for him, at least I can provide him with just a little bit of comfort.

"He was all I had left."

I rest my cheek against the top of his head and stroke his back. "No, he wasn't."

"I have nothing else. No one else."

"That's not true. You have your parents. They'll be here soon, right?"

"My parents," he snorts. "They think I'm some silly fool

chasing a dream. They only speak to me to ask me when I'm getting a *real* job."

This rare show of vulnerability and honesty is not something I'm used to, and I know it's a passing phase. He's still raw, rightfully so. And I'm still yearning for his approval, dying for him to let me in again. As much as I want to hate him, I can't. I won't.

"Well…you have me."

He stiffens at my side before sitting up to face me. "Don't say things you don't mean, Fi."

"I'm not. It was you who wanted things this way. I never wanted to lose you, Rhys."

He shakes his head, but otherwise doesn't move. We're touching, sharing the same air. Living in a space reserved for lovers. His brown eyes strip me naked and see my insides, painting them with the pretty caress of his soulful gaze. His tongue slides over his bottom lip. I should move, but I can't reject him right now—not when he's hurting. And honestly, I don't want to. I need this too. I need *him* too.

"Fiona? Fiona, where are you?"

The blood drains from my face, and I reflexively jump from my seat and away from August. It doesn't go without notice, but before I can apologize or explain or freak out, Joshua barges into the Colonel's apartment.

"There you are," he says with more drama than necessary before wrapping me in his arms, and placing my head on his chest as if I'm a child. "I'm so sorry, darling. I know he meant a lot to you."

"What the fuck are you doing here?" The words hit my back like daggers—sharp and deadly. I unravel myself from

Joshua's embrace in time to catch August stalk towards us with murder in his eyes.

"Hey, man, I'm not here to cause any problems," Joshua explains, palms up in defense. August isn't hearing any of it. I know that look. I saw it junior year when some jerk tried to corner me at a party and shove his tongue down my throat despite my protests. I saw it two years after that when my mom's loser boyfriend tried to hit on me at Thanksgiving, then lie and say I was the aggressor. I saw it three summers ago when my then-boyfriend gave me an ultimatum—boob job or break up. And I saw it just weeks ago after I told him I had agreed to marry Joshua.

I stand between the two men that mean the most to me—the two men that I love. One is the perfect man in every way. The other is the perfect man for *me.* And with eyes wide and limbs paralyzed in shock, I brace for the very worst.

"You didn't answer my fucking question."

My vision is warped with red. My fists are two tight balls of unspent rage. My body is merely a tightly wound weapon of hatred and jealousy and angst. The Colonel was ours—mine and Fiona's. Not Joshua's. I won't share him too. I won't lose him…

I bite back the anguish still strangling me and take a menacing step toward the blonde, baby-faced asshole and look him dead in the eye. He blanches, yet doesn't back down.

"Listen, August. I'm sorry for your loss, and even though we haven't seen eye to eye in the past, as Fiona's fiancé—"

"Fiancé?" I snort incredulously. "You think I give a *fuck* what you proclaim to be? I don't care if you are her messiah coming to save her soul, you don't belong here. You don't get to be in this apartment. You don't get to pretend to feel sorry for our loss."

"Hey, hey," Fiona says soothingly, a hand on each of our chests. "Let's just calm down and talk about this. It's been an emotional day."

"Yes, listen to Fi, August. She knows what she's talking about."

I nearly choke on my next breath as if I've been punched in the gut. "What did you say?" I inquire, the menacing tone of my voice enough to make Fiona take a step back.

Joshua is visibly startled, yet he soldiers on. "I said, she knows what she's talking about."

"No. What did you call her?" My jaw is clenched so tight that it feels as if it's been wired shut.

Joshua frowns, then looks to Fi for confirmation of my crazy "Uh, Fi. You know, August, if you're having a hard time dealing with—"

There are no words. No thoughts. Just action. I lunge past the barrier of Fiona's petite frame and charge Joshua, tackling him to the ground. I feel wood splinter under us and hear glass shatter close by, but all I can focus on is punching his face. All I can care about is hurting him the way he's hurt me.

Fiona's screaming, begging me to stop. Her cries distract me for just a fraction of a second, but it's enough for Joshua to land a hard punch against the side of my face, knocking me off kilter. Still, I'm punching, kicking, fighting, refusing to give him the upper hand. Refusing to let him take something else from me.

"Stop it! Please, stop it!" Fiona is trying to pull us away from each other, but we've latched on like pit bulls. I taste blood. My body is sore and exhausted, but I don't up. Not on this.

Fiona's shrieks and the commotion grab the attention of nearby attendants who rush in to help. Someone pulls me off of Joshua, giving him the opportunity to donkey kick me in the ribs just before he's disarmed.

"What the hell is your problem?" he shouts, spewing bloody saliva through split, swollen lips.

"You! You're my problem! Your existence is my problem!" I holler, struggling to get out of the tight grasp of what surely is an amateur body builder. "You want my life, my grandfather, my *Fi!* And while she may not see you for the lying, cheating snake you are, my vision is perfectly clear!"

"August! Stop it!" Fiona screams, tears streaming from her eyes.

"*Your* Fi?" Joshua retorts. "If she was yours, she wouldn't be marrying me! She wouldn't be at my apartment and in my bed every night. She wouldn't be agreeing to spend her life with me in a matter of weeks. She wouldn't be moving away and planning to start a family with me. She isn't your Fi, you asshole. She never was! Why do you think you weren't invited to the wedding? Because *she* didn't want you there."

His words hit me harder than his fists ever could. He's right, and it's not fair. He doesn't deserve a life and a marriage and a family with Fi. He hasn't earned it. And that fact just makes me even angrier.

"Let go of me," I demand, jerking out of the attendant's grasp. "I said let go. I'm fine. I'm done."

The man lets me loose but stays close. I wipe blood from my mouth with a single swipe of the back of my hand, and stalk toward the door. I can't look at her. I can't see the confirmation undoubtedly in her eyes.

Maybe I was wrong. Maybe it's *me* who doesn't belong here.

I walk through the main building of the senior center, my clothing ripped, my face cut and swollen, and my heart broken. I ignore the whispers and gasps from Helen and the cougar crew. I ignore the looks of sympathy and sadness from the staff. I even ignore April, who was here to see her grandmother, but had been hoping to lend me support during this time. The only thing I'm remotely aware of is the football game on the television. The Seahawks just won the game. And I feel like I've lost…everything.

Before I reach my bike, I pull out my cell phone, which gratefully, wasn't cracked in the scuffle. The voice on the other end is shocked to hear from me, especially on a Sunday."

"Kerrigan, make it happen."

"Make it… the deal? It's a yes?"

"Yeah. Whatever they want, I'll do it. The sooner, the better."

"You got it, Calloway. You sound a little off. Everything ok?"

"No," I answer truthfully. "It's not. But it doesn't matter anymore."

I hang up before she can ask any more questions. Then I ride away from everything I've ever loved.

I wish there was a time limit of grief.

I wish there was a biological stopwatch that would sound in our heads when it was time to snap out of it. It'd trigger something within us—resolve, strength, courage—and we'd pick ourselves up, dust ourselves off, and get on with living. And even if you hadn't gone through each of the five stages, once your time with grief was up, you were done. You didn't have to feel pain anymore. You didn't have to wake up feeling empty when you realize how alone you truly are. You wouldn't pick up the phone to call or make plans with your lost loved one, because you'd already know. You would be desensitized to the notion that they were gone and never coming back. You wouldn't feel like tearing your heart out of your chest when you realize that the Christmas before was your very last Christmas with them, and hate yourself, because instead of spending the entire day with them, you'd made a date with some chick in a skimpy Mrs. Claus outfit.

I look out the window at the falling snow, and try to remember what it felt like not to grieve. Instead, I think about how the Colonel despised snow. The cold, the hassle driving in it, the way it looked muddy after a few days. He'd complain every time it snowed, and threaten to move to some place sunny. He never did. Then he wouldn't get to gripe about the snow.

Fiona loves the snow. Winter has always been her favorite season, so I'm not surprised that she's having a winter wonderland-themed wedding. She'll make a beautiful bride, all covered in glistening white. She'll be happy. I'll choose to be happy she's happy.

"Want to take a walk outside, Bart?" I ask the slightly less fluffy Calico. I'd bought him one of those embarrassing cat leashes and had put him on a strict diet. No more waffles at three a.m. No more leftover Pad Thai. No more pastrami with extra pickles. The Colonel would like that. He'd be proud of both of us.

Of course, Bartleby hated the idea of a healthier lifestyle, and tries to hurriedly hide behind the couch at the mention of a walk. He's still not in fighting shape, so he can't fit all the way. Still, I give him an A for effort, and let him be.

I'm stalling anyway. The Colonel's passing, the funeral, my parents…all reasonable excuses for not writing. But it's been a month, and I still haven't been able to conjure the words. I'd once lived for the sound of keys clicking, creating Fi's beauty and heartbreak. But all I've felt, all I've known since we broke apart…is heartbreak.

Against my own protests, I sit at my desk, just staring at the monitor of my computer. I touch my fingers to the cold screen. I run them over the worn keys. I sit, and I remember, and I let it all come back to me.

Come back to me.

Please, come back to me.

I take the first step and turn it on. It whistles and whirs to life, greeting me with the familiar flickers of light and color. I point the cursor over the Word icon and click. Blank and barren and white like the freshly fallen snow outside my window.

I don't like it. The Colonel would agree.

She stands over the mess of multi-colored squares, rumpled notebook paper and empty coffee cups with a look of wonder and disbelief in her eyes.

"You've been here all night? Did you even sleep?"

"No," I smile, shaking my head animatedly. "I've got it. I've finally got it. This story…it's big. It's everything I love to read all wrapped up in one. Witty dialogue, smart, complex characters, and real life connections. This is it. I can't believe I'm saying this, but this is it."

"Wow," she gasps. "That's great."

I stand up and hand her a wrinkled stack of papers, covered in black ink and coffee stains. "I know it doesn't seem like much, and maybe it's not, but I want you to read it. Even if you're the only person on earth who does, I want you to read it."

She looks down at the papers in her hands and scans the first page. Within seconds, she's smiling. Minutes, she's laughing. "You wrote this?"

"Yeah. Sometime between midnight and two a.m. I was out at this bar. There were these girls, griping about their "relationships." They'd each been dating these guys that were obviously not as into them as they would like. Staying out late, not calling, middle of the night phone calls. One girl was washing her man's slacks and found a receipt for condoms inside. Condoms that they don't use because she's on the pill. The other girl found an online dating profile her guy had created, so she created a profile too, and has been talking to him while posing as someone else. Insane."

"That is. I can't imagine."

"Yeah, crazy. But you know what's worse? They're staying with them. They'd rather stay in these fucked up relationships than be alone. They'd rather be miserable and suspicious than single. Why is that?"

"I don't know," she shrugs. "Because being single is even more miserable?"

"How?" I frown. "Being a doormat and an idiot is better than having your freedom?"

"No. Better than being lonely."

"Hmph," I snort. "Well, I guess we'll never find out for sure."

"And why's that?"

"Because we have each other," I smile. I take the rumpled papers from her grasp and set them on the coffee table. Then I take her hands in mine, intertwining our fingers. "You'll never

be one of those girls, because you're my *girl. So you'll never be lonely. You'll always have someone in your corner. You'll never know what it feels like to be betrayed. And you'll never, ever have to compete for my affections."*

Her cheeks flush, she grins nervously. "You have girlfriends. Lots of them. What about your affections for them?"

"Who cares?"

"Uh, I care. And I'm pretty sure they care. Don't you think they'll be a bit upset with me for taking up your attention? And honestly, it's kinda hard competing with your army of spray-tanned Barbies."

"Doesn't matter," I affirm, shaking my head.

"It does. To me, it does. I'm not like those other girls." She says it like it's a tragedy.

"No," I say, pressing my lips to her forehead. "Those other girls aren't you."

I sit back and I smile. Not because it's great—it's not. Not because it'll change anyone's life—it won't. But because it's real. It's my heart on paper. And if that isn't the most authentic form of truth, I don't know what is.

Having decided that my grief meter has expired, I venture out in search of inspiration. With Aunties a breeding ground for obsessed fangirls trying to get a peek at Hope, I unfortunately have had to abandon my little slice of literary heaven. So I go to the one place where I was guaranteed stimulation—the Spokane public library.

"Well, isn't this a surprise," Louisa grins like she just won the Powerball jackpot. She twirls her bottle-blonde hair with short-trimmed nails and bats her lashes behind black-framed glasses.

"How have you been, L?"

"Oh, you know. My life is in these stacks. But it's been much more interesting since I learned about your double life. Why didn't you tell me, August?"

"You know how it is," I shrug. "We all have secrets. Some of them are just more interesting than others."

"I'm with you there," she bristles. What she doesn't know is that I'm privy to her secrets. Married. Mother of two. Girl Scout troop leader. Choir member.

Hey, I said I was a writer. Not a saint.

"So what brings you in today? I don't have a break for another hour."

I shake my head, earning a look of disappointment with a tad bit of hurt. "I'm here on business, not pleasure today. I need to read something that hits all the marks—mystery, drama, suspense, comedy…romance."

"Oh?"

"Book research," I assure her.

"So you've been bitten by the romance bug, huh?" she questions amusingly.

"I wouldn't say that. I've been infected for a long time now," I admit. There. I said it. And I feel kinda badass about it.

"Well." Her face sours just a tad, but she comes around the corner and beckons me with a finger. "Follow me. I think I can help you with that."

She leads me to a back room that the general public wouldn't know about, due to the unmarked door. When I step inside, I understand why. Indie and traditional sitting side by side. Erotica, New Adult, Contemporary Romance.

There's even a taboo section, featuring student-teacher, step-brother, and other forbidden romances.

"What is this place?" I ask, as if I've just stepped into Oz.

"There was this lady that would come in every week for months to request books. Stuff that we, a public library, wouldn't usually carry. However, we do accept requests and try to appease our patrons. So, she filled out a request every time she came in. Dozens of them. Her first request was Hope Hughes."

"What?" I turn around to face her, and she smiles back conspiratorially.

"Yes. Said it was her favorite author. When we got those in, she asked for others—stuff we hadn't even heard of. Did you know that people go nuts for sex books involving clergyman?" she asks, visibly horrified.

I bite back a laugh. "No. Really?"

"Oh yes. I was shocked. Anyway, the books were a hit, and other readers began to seek out these titles. The requests kept coming. Soon after, we decided we needed a space for them, but something that would keep the integrity of the library. Many of these are banned books and this is a public library that children frequent, it's not like we could just got around flaunting them."

"I suppose not."

"Right. And while I'm sure you are talented at what you do…"

"It's ok, L," I smirk. "I get it."

"So here they are," she says with a wave of her hand.

"It's a regular Garden of Eden. Sure you don't want to try the forbidden fruit?"

"I'll pass," she chuckles before turning toward the door. I don't try to stop her. This is the most we've ever talked… and it's nice. I see her for who she is, and that person, while perfectly kind and beautiful, is not for me.

"Thanks, Louisa."

She turns and smiles at the doorjamb. "You know, it's strange…"

"What is?"

"That woman," she muses. "She never checked out any of the books. She only requested them. The last time she was in, I asked her if she'd like to take any of them home. She said she had already read them. She just wanted others to discover the *magic* she had."

I nod and look away in hopes of hiding the emotion undoubtedly splayed across my features. I only know of one person that believes in books as much as I do. And she'll always be *my* magic.

IT WAS LIKE ANY OTHER day. Until it wasn't.

I woke up, got my coffee, fed Bart and sat down at my desk. I wrote until hunger was too much to ignore, and then I got back to writing. I got more coffee, dicked around on social media, and wrote some more. Then it came.

-Sorry to bother you. Moving out of my place and need your key. You probably need mine too, right? OK. Hope you're well.

Well.

Fiona hopes I'm well.

Well is so impersonal. It's what you reserve for business associates and people you don't know. For friends—people you've known for an entire decade—you use words like great, awesome, fan-fucking-tastic. You don't wish your best friend well. You wish him the world.

I stow my pettiness and file it under Forgotten. She's moving. I knew it would be soon, but I just hadn't realized that I had less than two weeks. I text her back, not wanting to waste another moment on trivial speculation.

-Sure. Next week good? I'm pretty swamped.

She answers right away, as if she were waiting by the phone. Waiting for me.

-Next week? I was hoping to get it over with asap. I'll be so busy next week...

Next week. Her wedding. She'll be running around like a chicken with her head cut off, but I need the time.

-Sorry. I can mail it if you want...

-No, no. Next week is fine. I can make it work.

I almost smile, but quickly remember myself. Then I get back to writing.

Moving sucks. Big time.

One doesn't realize just how much junk they accumulate until they have to sort through it and organize their life. Luckily, most of my prized possessions are rectangular, so I can fit them easily into boxes. I should have hired a moving company, but I kept hearing the Colonel's voice in my head, telling me not to let stranger's touch my things. "You have two hands…use them," he would say. "That way you know where everything is." I'm inclined to agree; although there's no way I'm hauling all this shit on my own. The studio is paying for the move, and has even set me up with a cushy apartment, fully furnished. So all of my furniture is being donated to an organization supporting our veterans. The Colonel was fortunate. He was a saver, and I took on any expenses he couldn't cover. Many of our vets aren't as lucky, especially in this area.

"You're looking good, Bart," I remark as the feline slinks by, rubbing his side against a cardboard box. He turns and looks at me as if to say, "Yeah, I know." Great. Now he's not just a furry asshole. He's an arrogant, furry asshole. I have a feeling he'll fit in just fine in LA.

The closer I get to moving away from my safe little corner of the earth to the land of dreams and desolation, the more anxious I become. I know this is the right choice. I know that I was only holding myself back out of insecurity and stubbornness. And now that I have nothing keeping me from turning the page of the next chapter of my life, I'm almost excited. Almost.

Hours turn into days. Days blur into a week. I've survived on coffee grounds, unsold dreams and fading memories for far too long. After living my life in the shadows of my secrets, it's time to let go of the past. So here I am, staring down the barrel of my future, afraid and exhilarated, ready to pull the trigger.

I text Fiona, asking her to meet me at our place—our favorite table at our favorite bistro—to exchange keys. I haven't told her about my move to LA, but then again, we haven't spoken since the day the Colonel died. She came to the funeral, but we never spoke. We had run out of words.

She agrees to meet me at our usual time, although she's insanely busy. I don't expect her stay for brunch, but it doesn't really matter. I won't be there anyway. Instead, I watch her walk in from across the street. I watch as the hostess smiles and ushers her to our table. And I watch her check her phone as she waits. And waits. And waits.

Although I know she's moving, the site of her packed-up apartment—littered with cardboard and Styrofoam peanuts—gives me pause. I swallow down the hesitation, and get to work. I'd been imagining this for weeks, long before I had even considered putting my plan into action. I only have one chance—one shot. And after that, I'm done. I won't try anymore. I'll let her live with her decision. And as much as it'll kill me, I'll stay away for good.

After tonight, I'll say goodbye to Rhys and Fi, BFFs. Forever.

Fiona

Unbelievable. Un-freaking-believable.

It's just like August to stand me up. No text, no call. No regard for other people's time or feelings. I check my phone one more time to see if he's responded to any of the dozens of messages I've sent him. Five more minutes, and I'm done with him. For good.

The first of many angry, frustrated tears sting my eyes as I sit in our once-beloved restaurant with a half empty mimosa in my hand. We didn't have to leave things this way. It should have been easier for both of us. I should be celebrating with my best friend. We should be planning parties and dinners. He should be snickering while I try on wedding dresses and rolling his eyes while we choose centerpieces. I should be calling him up during freakouts, and he should be rushing over armed with crispy spring rolls, booze and words of reason.

I shouldn't be angry with him. I shouldn't be missing him. I shouldn't even be thinking about him when I'm set to marry the man of every girl's dreams tomorrow.

I'm waving down the server when I get a call from my building's super. Frantically, he tells me there's a water leak in my unit, and I need to get there ASAP. Great. Just what I need. The cherry on top of this already terrible day. I consider cancelling on the bachelorette festivities tonight, because this will definitely set me back.

I slap down enough cash to cover my mimosas and the tip and rush over to my apartment, praying there isn't any damage. I'm in a fog when I pull up. I'm completely preoccupied when I take the stairs two at a time, so I don't pause when I open my front (unlocked) door and I find no signs of flooding. But what I do find, —what does have me standing there with my mouth open and my eyes as big as the moon—is August. August indescribably handsome and smiling, submerged in a sea of multi-colored Post-Its that seem to cover ever surface of my living room/dining room/kitchen.

"What…? What is all this?" I stammer, slowly stepping inside and closing the door behind me.

"This…this is me," he answers. "Giving you my words. Offering you a piece of my soul and hoping you can read my heart between the lines."

"August, what's going on?" I walk over to the lamp and pluck a pink sticky note from the lampshade. It reads, *The best stories are the ones we live.* I look up to find him gazing at me expectantly, waiting for my reaction. "That's beautiful," is all I can muster. There's another beside it in blue that etched with, *Love without logic.* Purple and pink and orange and green…all boasting a different profound declaration.

I'm sorry.

Forgive me.

Don't leave me.

I pick up another, a yellow one stuck to the couch, and read it aloud. "*Let me be your HEA.* What does that even mean?"

Slowly, he closes the space between us in four feathered breaths and stops right in front of me, close enough to touch. "Fiona, you've searched your whole life for the perfect book boyfriend. Passionate, alluring, aloof, mysterious…you looked for him in every guy you've ever dated, only to be disappointed. They weren't Mr. Darcy. They weren't Heathcliff or Howard Roark. Hell, they weren't even Grey. They never measured up to what you deemed perfection, because those men didn't exist. Therefore, you had given up on your HEA—your happily ever after—and settled for some semblance of true happiness. I know you think Joshua is it, but can you honestly say he's what you imagined when you were curled up on your twin-sized bed dressed in oversized sweats while listening to *"Drops of Jupiter"* on repeat while tears streamed down your face?"

My mouth is dry, but somehow I manage to whisper, "What are you saying, August?"

"I'm saying that I want to be him. I want to be Darcy and Heathcliff and Roark and Blythe and Rochester and Grey and Cullen and all those heroes you've dreamt about every day since the day I met you, glassy eyed and pink cheeked. I want to be your hero, Fi. In fact, I know I could be all of them and more for you—*because* of you. And I want to give you the most epic HEA in history—both real and fictional."

I'm speechless, breathless, as I hold the now rumpled yellow square to my heart. I open my mouth and try to formulate words, but I am shocked into silence. I don't even know what I could say to match his earnest confession.

"You don't have to say anything," he says with an amused grin, reading my stunned expression. "Actually, I don't want you to say anything. Not until you read this."

He picks up a folder from the coffee table that I hadn't noticed until now and places it in my trembling hands. "The most epic love story I've ever written is the one I'm still living. So everything I've ever wanted to say…everything I should've said a long time ago is in these pages. And when you're done, I hope you'll come find me. I hope we'll find each other."

Without another word, August leans forward to kiss my lips. It's soft, sweet and too short. It's exactly enough to keep me planted in my disbelief, wishing he would stay and do it again.

He leaves me to my rainbow-colored apartment and stack of papers tucked inside a folder. On shaky legs, I walk further into the room and sit on the couch, one of the many old pieces of furniture that will be left behind when I officially move out. I like this couch. Many slices of pizza and TV sitcom marathons have been enjoyed on this couch. But it doesn't fit with Joshua's décor. It doesn't fit with his life—I mean, our life.

The folder is an anvil on my lap. I open the cover and come to a white sheet of paper, adorned only with a single quote.

"I wish you to know that you have been the last dream of my soul."

My eyes well with tears as I read it and reread it again. It's from August's favorite book, "A Tale of Two Cities" by Charles Dickens. The Colonel gave him that book when he was just a boy, and he still has that copy—all tattered and faded—stashed on one of his shelves. And the day we met in my dorm room while he studied me as I read, we had been talking Dickens in our British Literature course. He hadn't noticed me then, but I couldn't keep my eyes off him…hadn't kept my eyes off him since the first day of classes. The Brit Lit Nazi asked us to recite our favorite quote from the famed author. August was so confident, so charismatic as he stood up and shared his with us, captivating every eye with the blinding beauty of those words on his lips.

"I wish you to know that you have been the last dream of my soul."

From that day forth, I wondered what it would be like to be the last dream of August Rhys Calloway's soul. I wondered what it would be like to be his everything, like he was *my* everything. I wondered and I hoped and I dreamt that I would be his.

I dash away my tears and take a deep breath, steeling myself before I turn the page, and brace for impact.

Chapter 1

When I met her, I met love for the very first time.

But it was a shy, docile love. A love that didn't want itself to be readily known. It rested in the corners of her mouth when she smiled. It danced on the tip of her fingernails when she turned the pages of her most beloved books. It slept upon the iridescent silk of her eyelids.

I saw love when I first met her. I just didn't know it yet.

The tears begin to fall again and don't stop as I flip through the pages, my smudged mascara leaving ink blots on the white paper. He writes about how we first met, how he looked at me as if I were this beautiful, extraordinary celestial being in his universe. He spins a breathtaking tale of the way we were, and how he secretly wanted us to be. I sit there on my couch, captivated by memories as if I were living them for the very first time. I read and I laugh and I weep and I gasp. He's never written like this before. For as long as I've known and loved him, August has never penned anything so incredibly *real.*

I flip to the very last page of our story, only to find it blank. However, there's a single white envelope. My hands shake violently, but somehow, I manage to open it, and slip out what looks to be a plane ticket.

January 23, 2016
GEG to LAX
Gate 3B, Seat 2B

A ticket to Los Angeles, leaving tomorrow, on what is scheduled to be the most important day of my life—my wedding day.

How could he do this to me? How can he create the biggest cliffhanger in history, and leave me in limbo, torn between a dream and reality?

I sit and stare for what seems like eternity and hold that paper rectangle to my heart, questioning the last hours, days, weeks, months, years we've had together.

Here in my hands lies the continuation to our epic tale. Will it be the greatest romance ever told or a tragedy? Or maybe I'm not seeing this for what it is. Maybe I'm just afraid to let go and accept that this is The End.

August

ONE WEEKEND, FIONA DECIDED SHE wanted to torture me with Twilight. Not just the first movie, chock full of teenage angst and bad acting. Not the second one where Bella gets all emo when Edward bails for no apparent reason, or the third where the cast of Teen Wolf shows up. She wouldn't even let me skip past to the last set of movies when Bella turns into Gollum and gives birth to Hannibal Lector. She made me watch all of them. Every last fucking movie in chronological order.

I should have told her no. I should've made up some excuse about needing to write or give myself an enema. But instead, I watched them. I watched and I laughed and I made inappropriate jokes about glitter penises and dog hair in unconventional places, but I showed up. I showed up because it made her happy. I showed up because I love her.

I showed up.

And now, as I watch the first thirty chapters of my life dissipate from view out of the window of my first class seat(s), I wonder who is showing up for her right now. Friends, family, coworkers. And her groom.

I showed up today, I showed up yesterday, and I showed up every day for ten years, all in hopes that she would do the same. All in a silly plot to win her heart.

That's the way things happen in romance. The hero professes his undying love, the heroine abandons all comfort and common sense to run into his open arms, and they live happily ever after, existing only on their hopes and dreams.

However, reality is not nearly as kind. There are no heroes and heroines, only villains. There are no grand gestures or profound acts of devotion. And there definitely aren't any perfect love scenes completely devoid of awkward afterglows and unattractive messes.

There is no romance in my world. And as I soar farther from my past in Washington and closer to my future in California, there is no Fiona.

Chapter Twenty-Eight

"So give me an update, Kerrigan," I say through my cordless headset as Bart and I stroll along the boardwalk. The former fluffy chubster is looking svelte nowadays, and has even begun to enjoy our walks. We still get a few funny side eyes, but this is LA…everyone's got a little crazy in them.

Kerrigan inhales a lungful of cyanide and blows it into the receiver before answering. Oddly, I'm not even tempted, after adopting a healthier lifestyle as well. Hmph. Los Angeles is rubbing off on me.

"We're still on schedule for the release of Hope's last book late this spring. The publisher has also hinted around a farewell book tour. Are you really sure you want to give up the Hope Hughes brand? You'll still make a killing. Your preorders are through the roof, and that's just for eBooks."

"I'm sure."

"Think about it, August. You can still write whatever you want. You're at a caliber where readers will buy and read whatever you decide to put out. And with the television show coming out..."

"I said I'm sure, Kerrigan. The beauty of being a writer with a pen name is the anonymity. We're able to obtain some sense of privacy and normalcy. I'd like just an inkling of that." I never wanted to be in the limelight. That wasn't part of my dream. But things change...your goals, your aspirations... they change with time and circumstance. I know that better than anyone.

"I hear you. So about the book tour..."

"I can't..." I take a seat on a wooden bench just as the sun begins to set. Bart and I have been coming here for weeks, trying to establish some type of routine. The transition has been interesting, to say the least. It's sunny all the time, warm all the time. Happy and bright and vapid and ostentatious all the fucking time.

"You have to get used to being in the public eye, kid. This is your life now," Kerrigan advises, reading my mind. "You're big time. Start acting like it."

I can just hear the Colonel's voice ringing in my head. *"No one ever achieved greatness by doing what's easy."*

And then there's another voice. A voice I haven't heard for more than two months. *"Don't overthink it."*

I shake my head at nothing and no one, trying to dispel the memory. "Yeah, I know. I'll think about it."

"Seriously, August. Don't let your moment pass you by

because you're—"

"I said, I'll think about it." I look down the boardwalk just in time to see a familiar, smiling face approaching. *Right on time.* "Hey look, Kerrigan, I've gotta go. I'll get back to you, ok?"

"Ok, kid. Sooner than later."

She hangs up without saying goodbye. Goodbyes are overrated anyway.

"Hey there, handsome."

I stand to wrap my arms around Michelle, my DJ friend from my first visit to La La Land. We've been seeing each other casually. Nothing serious. Her hours are crazy, my hours are crazy. We're having fun. The way it should be.

"I swear, if you keep overinflating his ego, he may float away," I reply before kissing her lightly glossed lips.

The model-esque brunette laughs and bends down to scratch Bart behind the ears. He answers with a happy purr. "Aw, not this little guy. Maybe we should get him a set of rollerblades so he really fits in."

"Nope. That's where I draw the line. It's bad enough I've got a cat on a leash."

We stroll hand-in-hand down the walkway to an Italian spot with outdoor seating. Over a bottle of wine, gluten free pasta and seared salmon, we talk about our day, my new developments with the show's script, and her latest gig.

"I got an invite to go over to Dubai for a party. Some prince's birthday, so it's serious dough."

"Oh yeah?" I answer before stabbing a tube of faux pasta. I have to admit, I couldn't stand all the gluten free/fat free/oil free/taste free shit she's had me eat since I arrived. But it's grown on me.

"Yeah. I don't know though."

"What's there not to know? You've been waiting for a big break like this. A prince in Dubai? Can you imagine the press and the exposure for you? Not to mention the payout. Would be big for you."

"I know, I know. And it would let me have more freedom to pick and choose future gigs. Still..." A small frown dimples her forehead.

"What is it?"

"Well...I was wondering what it would mean for us. Doing a job like this would open up a lot of doors for me, meaning I'd have a lot more opportunities out of town working with huge names in the biz. And if I'm going to be focused on my career, things with you and I would suffer."

"Oh." I hadn't even thought about that, honestly.

"Yeah. I mean, I know we've only been dating for a couple months, and we haven't put a label on what we are. But I just want to know—for the future—should I consider you in my decisions?"

I take a beat to choose my words carefully. I could tell her what she wants to hear to ensure she stays in my life in some capacity. That would be the easy way. But if I'm really being honest with myself—something that's still very much a novelty for me—I know I can't *keep* her for my own selfish needs and irrational hang ups. And I also know that I can't promise her something that I'm not capable of giving.

"Go to Dubai. Have fun. Make connections. And if we're meant to be, we'll be. You're young. You have your whole life ahead of you. And I'm not going anywhere any time soon."

"Oh." She casts her emerald green eyes down at her plate.

"I just don't want to make you any promises that I can't keep," I explain.

I wouldn't want you to devote your life to a lie.

We finish our meal in strained silence. I walk her home. She lets me into her home and into her body one last time. Then Bart and I return back to our lavish apartment that suddenly seems cold, despite the balmy temperatures.

This whole truth thing? Totally sucks ass.

Chapter Twenty-Nine

AFTER THE EPICALLY SHITTY SHOWDOWN at Auntie's last year, it's no wonder why I am anti-book signing. But tell that to my publisher, who not only writes my checks, but pretty much owns my ass during release time. With *The Good Girl* being the very last Hope book ever, the big wigs were insisting (i.e. demanding) I give the people what they want. So, I told Kerrigan to make it happen, under one condition: One day, one signing, and then I would retreat back into the serenity of my quasi-isolation.

Women—and even quite a few men—have been lined up around the block at the Barnes and Nobles at The Grove for hours. There are flyers plastered everywhere sporting my headshot (barf), along with graphics of Hope's greatest hits. *The Good Girl* has hit #1 New York Times Bestseller's List for two weeks in a row, the show's development is going great, and there have already been talks of a publishing deal for a new series. Everything I have dreamt about as a struggling writer is coming to fruition faster than I could ever imagine, and while I don't have anyone to share it with, I have my career. I have my cat. And I have my words.

I peek out at the insane crowd of people congregated around a single podium sporting a banner with my name on it. Fuck. This is not good for my anxiety.

"I don't know about this, Kerrigan."

The tiny pit bull doesn't even bat an eye. "You'll do fine. You'll read an excerpt, answer a few questions, sign books and smile for some pictures. Piece of cake."

I pace the floor of the back office, reserved for staff and visiting authors. "Do you see the line out there? It's a fucking mad house! And the press is here. Why is the press here? Do I look like Nicholas fucking Sparks to you?"

"August! Calm down," she says, abandoning her seat and coming to grasp my forearms to still me in place. "You're freaking out, kid. I get it. This is new for you. But you need to own this. At what point are you going to realize that you're not just the pen behind Hope Hughes? You are August Rhys Calloway. And he's pretty goddamn spectacular."

I look down at Kerrigan and nod stiffly. A year ago, I would have jumped at the chance to showcase my work—my words. But things change…people change. Passions, motivations…they all change like the weather.

A year ago, I had people to share this accomplishment with. Now I'm an island, sinking in my memories and regrets. Trying to break through to the surface of letting go.

Someone announces me. There's cheering. Then my Chucks are carrying me to the podium at the center of the room. More cheers. More nerves.

I look over the sea of people, waiting for me to speak. I refuse to make eye contact or actually *see* anyone at all. I take a deep breath. And I give them something I haven't given anyone for a very long. I give them *me.*

"That was incredible. I never imagined you were so funny. Or so handsome."

I look up and smile at the woman standing before me. She slides her hardcover copy of *The Good Girl* to me from her side of the table.

"Thank you, I'm glad you enjoyed it," I reply, flipping to the title page. "To whom am I making this out to?"

"Samantha. Or you can call me Sam. That's what my friends call me. Whatever you want."

"Well, I'll call you Sam if that's cool with you."

"Oh wow, yes, it is," she gushes. "I can't believe I'm meeting you. Your Hope Hughes book, House of Noire, is what got me reading again. Now I'm a proud book whore!"

"Good to hear," I reply, chuckling at her enthusiasm. "I've always been a proud supporter of whores in all capacities."

She's laughs and blushes and gushes some more. I listen and smile and thank her some more.

My next reader is a 70-year old grandmother of six from Texas named Meredith. She traveled all the way to southern California to meet me. *Me*. My mind is officially blown.

Every reader is more inspiring than the next. I had no idea how many people my words—*my words!*—had touched until today. Men, women, old, young, gay, straight. I made an impact on their lives. And I've never felt more proud to call myself a writer than right at this moment.

I did it, Colonel. We *did it. And it's all because of you.*

By my second hour of signing, I've gotten over the nerves and adopted a rhythm. I'm telling jokes, giving hugs, even holding a few babies for pics (at their parents' request, of course). I've received numerous thoughtful gifts that I genuinely plan to treasure, and even a few marriage proposals.

I'm just finishing up with a couple from St. Louis, who claim that my books helped them put the spark back in their twenty-four year marriage.

"So, is there anyone special in your life?" the wife, Sharon, asks.

"Other than my cat, Bartleby, no. Not right now."

"Aw. That's too bad. For someone who writes as wonderfully as you, with so much depth and emotion, I could have sworn you were madly in love in real life."

I smile politely, but inside I'm battling to tamp down the familiar dull ache in my chest. "Well, I thought I was. Once. It didn't work out."

"Oh? I'm sorry to hear that. It'll happen again for you one day. I just know it. There's just too much beauty inside you."

I thank her for her kindness, and the husband quickly ushers her away, whispering for her to *"leave that poor boy alone."*

Then I freeze.

I die.

And I bloom back to life.

All in the span of twenty seconds. The longest twenty seconds in the history of time.

"Would you mind signing my book?" she asks, breaking the spell.

It's happening. It's happening again.

She doesn't hand me the featured title. She doesn't even give me a Hope book. She gives me those pages I offered her in exchange for her heart. Those pages ink-stained with my truth and tears.

"What are you doing here?" The question is almost too obvious, but I don't know what else to say.

"I came to see you."

"Why?"

"You invited me. Remember?"

I want to tell her that that is all in the past, and that plane ticket wasn't just an invitation—it was my heart on a string. But there are people waiting, watching. She must feel their eyes too, because she slides the makeshift book closer to me with the tips of her manicured fingernails.

"So?"

I can hear the whispers, wondering what could be etched on those stark white pages. A secret manuscript? A fanfic story? I bring it closer to me and flip to the first page, revealing a single quote. A quote that held the weight of my feelings for her in just fifteen little words. She had to have known what they meant. She must've known what I was offering her within these pages. Yet, and still, she chose him. I waited and waited, and she chose him. I stared at the phone for weeks, and she chose him. So why now?

"What happened to the Hemsworth?" I ask, unable to

withhold my curiosity any longer.

"You were right. He was cheating." Surprisingly, there's no pain within those big brown eyes. Only clarity, as if she's just seeing the world for the very first time.

"Client?"

"His assistant. Sue."

"Ouch."

"I know. They're currently vacationing in Bora Bora, probably celebrating the divorce," she shrugs, twirling a lock of wavy, shoulder-length brown hair around a finger. "How very cliché, huh?"

She talks about Joshua's affair as if she's bemused by it, the way a person speaks of something that they were half expecting. Maybe she's over him...much like the way I got over her.

I stare at the page before me, uncertain of what to write. *Best wishes? Thanks for the support? Nice knowing you?* What do you say to the person who broke you into pieces yet didn't even know it? I had moved on. I had found the type of happiness that didn't exist between a woman's legs. So many times over the past six months, I'd needed her. I'd see a silly cat trinket in a shop, and want to show it to her. I'd hear an old song on the radio, and want to play it for her. I'd taste something delicious at a new restaurant, and want to share it with her.

She took herself out of the equation. She didn't show up.

It's not fair...it's not fair for her to show up now with her smile and her charm and her scent of lavender. She doesn't have the right.

"Can I just ask you one question?" Fiona pipes up, breaking me from my tortured inner monologue. "Why didn't you publish this? It's phenomenal. It's the most beautiful thing you've ever written. And it's you, Rhys. It's *us*."

I shake my head. Not because I don't believe her, but because I can't stand to hear her words or my name on her breath. "It's just a story, Fi. It's fiction. Besides, I wrote it for you. It's yours." I tack on a shrug to make my nonchalance more believable, but even I can't buy it.

Ten years pass between us. Ten birthdays, ten Christmases, ten Valentine's Days where we got drunk and ate chocolates in front of the television. Thousands of late night phone calls, hundreds of Sunday brunches. More words than I have ink to write them in.

I stare at the girl that was once my whole world, and I'm lost. I'm lost and she is my Home.

"Well, I suppose I better go before I get shanked by one of your fans." Her cheeks blush dusty rose, and she looks down at the stack still sitting before me. "So… would you mind making it out to Fiona, the woman who has been in love with me since the day I criticized her for her love of vampire romance. The woman who saw my heart in every word I ever wrote, and felt the depth of my soul in each of my stories. The woman who hates herself for not believing in me, for not choosing me, when she knew I was her *only* choice all along. The woman that has never stopped loving me, and never will, no matter what hurt and distance and circumstance has done to us. Because she wants to be the one to feed me Jell-O, and get fat when I get fat. She wants to be the one to share ice cream with me in the park.

"Signed, August Rhys Calloway…the other half of her happily ever after."

My pen slips from my fingers, the ballpoint never even grazing the page. We're surrounded by hushed whispers and camera flashes as I climb to my feet and just…look at her. I look at her, and I'm unable to grasp the words to even begin to define the range of emotions coursing inside my chest. So we just stand there, staring, waiting for the other to break.

She breaks.

SHE GRASPS THE WHITE, BOUND pages and cradles it to her chest, coveting the last read line like a sacred jewel. Unable to articulate words or sentences or even hand gestures, she just sits there and *feels*. She feels each letter imprinting on her heart, etching carbon tattoos all over her body. She breathes in each brush stroke, tastes each line and curve like culinary calligraphy. In this moment, she is sustained only by the magic of words. It consumes her, infects her, burrows itself to the very marrow of her bones.

He waits before speaking, giving her time and space to digest each bit of his being. "Well…?" he says after several minutes of heavy silence.

"How…?"

"I know."

"You know." She swallows, eyes closed. Then takes a deep, cleansing breath to conjure her resolve. "Then you know that I need more. *They* need more. Do you know what you've done here? Do you know what I am holding in my hands right now? This is your best work yet! And you've left me dangling over a massive cliff without a safety net. You can't end it here. This can't be it."

He shrugs, and smirks with mirth. "Their story is told. That's all there is."

"Their story is told? How can that be? She comes to the signing, confesses her love and then BOOM. That's it? No glimpse into the future? No white picket fence? No wedding, babies and a dog? What happened to the ex? Hell, what happened to the cat? I hope you like hate mail, because you're going to get a shitload of it."

He makes a noise resembling a mix between a snort and a laugh. "That's the beauty of fiction. Fuck rules and pretty red bows. Besides, isn't it more fun to keep the reader guessing?"

"No!" she nearly shrieks. "It's only fun if there's a sequel. There is a sequel, right?"

He shakes his head. "No. There's nothing left to write. They end up together—that's evident. It's up to the reader to imagine their future. Or they can just relish in the fact that they got their HEA. After all that time, all that pain, they found their way back to each other. They *are* the HEA."

"Yeah, yeah, yeah. I hear you." She looks back down at the manuscript in her hands and runs her fingertips over the top cover. "You've done it, you know. You've really done it. This is going to be huge. It's going make us both a lot of money."

He stands, and with a soft smile on his too full lips, he shakes his head. "It's not about the money. It's about making people fall in love. Even if only for a moment, I want each reader to know what it's like to hold magic in their hearts."

"How noble of you." She had been a literary agent for a very long time. It was *always* about the money. "You know, you didn't have to come all the way here just to watch me read. I could have told you all of this on the phone."

He stops at the doorjamb and shrugs. "I know. I just wanted to see it."

"See what?"

He doesn't answer. He doesn't say goodbye. Just nods and walks away.

On a congested street on the island of Manhattan, he walks alone. The people, the sounds, the smells…it's a sensory overload. He pulls a Moleskine out of his back pocket and jots down some quick notes, wanting to freeze frame the inspiration littered on sidewalks and slicked across the hoods of yellow cabs. There's a story here. He can feel it.

He makes his way to the bistro on the corner, bypassing the hostess station and going straight to the outdoor seating area. He doesn't sit down. He's too wired to sit.

"Ready?" He holds out his hand. A pair of chestnut eyes as bold as the sun glance up at him, abandoning the page of her favorite book. She takes his hand, letting him pull her slight frame into the safety of his body, still humming with the city's electricity. He kisses the top of her head.

"How did it go?"

"Great," he answers, leading her onto the sidewalk.

"And the names...the title. She liked them all?"

"I think so."

She wraps her arms around his waist and squeezes with all passion in her petite frame, causing them to stop in the middle of a busy walkway. Pedestrians filter around them, cursing and throwing annoyed glances. She doesn't care. She'll never let go again.

"I'm so proud of you," she says into the cotton of his shirt. He slides his ink-stained hands up and down her back before tangling them in her chocolate brown hair. She looks up at him and smiles so bright that he's momentarily blinded by her brilliant light. "I love you. I love you, I love you, I love you. This is what you've always wanted."

He shakes his head. "No. *You're* what I've always wanted."

He kisses her deeply—kisses her madly— as if every second with her just isn't enough. As if he's tasting her on his tongue for the very first time.

When he's finally able to conjure the strength to stop, they continue their stroll down to Central Park. It's a warm day, so he buys her an ice cream cone. Like always, she offers him the first lick of vanilla bean. When they come upon a park bench that faces the parade of speed walkers, bicyclists and tourists, they sit and people watch as they share their scoop. A man and a woman pass by, maybe late-twenties, early-thirties. They walk side-by-side, laughing and talking animatedly while discussing a play they've just seen. The woman twirls around, the wind kicking up her tea length skirt, as she reenacts her favorite scene. Her companion watches her intently, admiringly, a soft smile on his lips. Then they both laugh and continue their trek through the park.

The woman makes a simpering sound as she watches the young couple from the park bench, a melting scoop of vanilla at her lips. "Them," she points. "Tell me about them."

He kisses the side of her head and pulls her closer, tighter, into his chest. "He's loved her for longer than he can remember. It started out innocently enough—a harmless crush. But their friendship was more important to him to risk losing it to awkwardness or heartbreak. So he watches her when she dances. He listens to her when she sings. He holds her when she cries. And he smiles at her when she laughs. He gives her the best parts of him, the parts that only come alive when she's around. And in turn, she lets him be who he is, without apology or regrets.

"A few weeks, months, years from now, when his feelings for her become pronounced by time and circumstance, he'll wonder if she could love him too. And while pride and fear will prove to be selfish cohorts, he'll swallow his reluctance and tell her all the things he should have said before. And in turn, she will confess to him that she only danced so he would watch her. She only sang so he would listen. She cried so he would hold her, and she laughed to make him smile."

She looks up at him with tears in her big brown eyes, and asks, "How do you do it? How do you create such beauty and heartbreak?"

He kisses her like she is the very air he breathes, before sliding his lips to her ear. "That's all life is—beauty and heartbreak. I just narrate it… for you."

The End

Like a true procrastinator, I'm scrambling at the last minute to get this in so my formatter can work her magic. So I'll make this short, sweet and to the point. It takes a village to corral all my crazy, and these people have been so patient and supportive throughout this journey.

First and foremost, I want to thank YOU, the reader, for giving me and my book a chance. I want to thank the countless bloggers and book pimps for their shares and support. Without you all, I'd still be writing short stories on a crappy laptop, dreaming of the day someone would actually want to read them.

To my amazing beta team: Mo Sytsma, Lauren Bille, Kristina Lowe, Sunny Borek, Samantha Rudolph, Andrea Kelleher, Sharon Goodman, Michelle Trzecinski and Jennifer Wolfel. Thank you for enduring all my rants and whining, and making sure I did this story justice. My gratitude is immeasurable.

Thank you to Ashley Sparks for creating a fabulous piece of art. You blow my mind with your creativity.

To Hang Le for making cover magic: You are amazing! And always awesome to work with.

Tracey Buckalew, editor and friend, thank you for sticking with me through it all. I'm so fortunate to know you.

Thank you to Kara Hildebrand for your amazing professionalism and enthusiasm.

Stacey Blake, formatting genius, you always rock my socks. Thank you!

Huge thanks to Kristi at Sassy Savvy for being so patient and kind with my baby. And big kisses to Milasy and Lisa at The Rock Stars of Romance for your continued love and support.

Shout Out to Kindle Crack Book Reviews, Black Heart Reviews, True Story Book Blog and Lisa Gandy, the edit queen. You all have been so amazing to me, and I am truly grateful.

Special thanks to all my writer girls in the trenches, my bishes, my sisters in print. I love you.

Much love to my JFJ Girls and my BBFT Bishes! Mwah! You all are the best!

Last but not least, to my family: Thank you for your inspiration, your love, your patience and your support. It's all for you.

Most known for her starring role in a popular sitcom as a child, S.L. Jennings went on to earn her law degree from Harvard at the young age of 16. While studying for the bar exam and recording her debut hit album, she also won the Nobel Prize for her groundbreaking invention of calorie-free wine. When she isn't conquering the seas in her yacht or flying her Gulfstream, she likes to spin elaborate webs of lies and has even documented a few of these said falsehoods.

Some of S.L.'s devious lies:

FEARLESS SERIES

Fear of Falling

Afraid to Fly

SEXUAL EDUCATION SERIES

Taint

Tryst

THE DARK LIGHT SERIES

Dark Light

The Dark Prince

Nikolai (a Dark Light novella)

Light Shadows